copygirl

anna mitchael
and michelle sassa

BERKLEY BOOKS, NEW YORK

BERKLEY

An imprint of Penguin Random House LLC
375 Hudson Street, New York, New York 10014

COPYGIRL

An application to register this book for cataloging has been submitted to the Library of Congress.

PUBLISHING HISTORY
Berkley trade paperback edition / October 2015

ISBN: 978-0-425-28112-3

PRINTED IN THE UNITED STATES OF AMERICA

10 9 8 7 6 5 4 3 2 1

Cover art: photocopy texture © All For You / Shutterstock.
Cover design by Diana Kolsky.
Text design by Tiffany Estreicher.

Penguin
Random
House

For those who think different.

Sometimes you feel like a nut, but be all you can be, because a mind is a terrible thing to waste.

Don't get mad, get glad. When you take a licking, keep on ticking.

Have it your way and never follow.

You've come a long way, baby—keep it good to the last drop.

contents

cat lady   *1*

find it in you   *25*

"hello, std!"   *45*

fake it to make it   *63*

men, money & meat   *93*

valley of the dolls   *121*

being bubbly   *155*

there's no "k" in team   *189*

kiss of death   *217*

roach army   *247*

kolacoo!   *271*

special delivery   *289*

cat lady

It's so hard to think when you have a gun pointed at your head.

"First thing tomorrow, you'd better show me genius," Elliott had warned us earlier. Then he followed up with his very favorite threat: "Remember, I can fill your seats in five minutes."

Come on, Kay, think. *Think*. THINK!

I just need *one* good cat food slogan. It's not like I have to find the cure for cancer or invent some dome that will let us live on Mars.

I type the first thing that comes to my head:

Here, shitty kitty.

And I am pretty darn sure that's not what Elliott has in mind.

Here, shitty kitty is what Johnjoshjay say every morning when they see me coming down the hall of cubicles that comprise our ad agency's creative department. *Here, shitty kitty. Here, shitty kitty.* The boys' club loves to tease me, and this gem is their favorite catcall. (Pardon the pun. Occupational hazard.) It's because I'm the copywriter on Little Kitty, get it? Oh so clever. In retaliation, I refuse to call any of them by their individual name. At least, not in my own head. They deserve one generic identity since they all dress like identical little hipsters: sagging jeans, designer sneakers, ratty but overpriced T-shirts, hats on backward until they come in the door and then drop them next to their computers along with their matching leather satchels.

Those poser suck-ups think they're so great because they get to work on Superfine sneakers and Atlantis—the urban clothing line out of Brooklyn. And I'm stuck penning print ads for "pussy food." Another one of their wink-wink witticisms. But I'm not going to let any of that get me down. After all, Little Kitty is our biggest account. The proverbial cash cow. Our bread and butter. Its big budget keeps the agency lights on, so keeping the client happy keeps my bosses happy. And tonight I plan on coming up with mad genius ideas that wow the Little Kitty execs, so that Ben and I can finally get the recognition we deserve.

Speaking of, where in Manhattan *is* my loyal work partner? I really thought he'd be back from the gym by now with the take-out dinner and brainstorming help he promised. My stomach swoons just thinking about my hunger . . . and, okay, full disclosure . . . thinking about *him*. As much as I want to nail this assignment, I secretly want to nail Ben even more. Cliché, I know. Girl copywriter falls for her hot art director partner. And it's quite possibly career suicide. But we've been a pair—in the work sense—since the second day of advertising school down in Atlanta, and now he's living with me, too. Granted, he sleeps on my couch, not in my bed like I wish. And, granted, the arrangement is temporary, just until he finds a place of his own. But whatever. The point is, he's totally grown on me, which is bound to happen when you spend almost all your waking hours breathing in someone's Axe body spray. Isn't there a name for that? The Axe Effect?

You see, in addition to the cohabitation, Ben and I work side by side *a lot*. That's because we're the lucky new junior team in the creative department of Schmidt Travino Drew & Partners, one of the edgiest advertising agencies in the entire country. We must have beat out like a hundred other fresh-out-of-ad-school copywriters and art directors to score this gig. Just like creative teams at other agencies, we get paid to come up with ideas together, then Ben makes the pictures and I write the words. But unlike other agencies, ours was just named *Advertising Age*'s Agency of the Year so we're "a big fucking deal." Tons of people would kill to steal our jobs, a fact that our creative director Elliott feels he must mention every time he briefs us on an assignment.

Hence, the aforementioned gun pointing at my head.

I know Ben likes me—why else would he have wanted us to take a job together after ad school?—but I'm hoping when he sees the brilliant headlines I come up with to save our asses, he gets so excited that he wants to kiss me full on the mouth. I just need to start writing. Now.

If only I had my own muse, like Olivia Newton John in *Xanadu*, zipping around on her roller skates, feeding that musician guy all those big ideas. "Here, Kay," I can almost hear her saying. "Here are your award-winning headlines. Now put on these skates, hold my hand, and let's roll through this city like we own it."

Sigh. Good muses are so hard to find. Especially when you're starving. My last meal was the little white bag of candied cashews I snuck out for around three this afternoon, a poor substitute for lunch. Looking out the window now, I realize that, unlike me, all the sidewalk food vendors have gone home for the night.

That's a depressing thought . . . but what's not depressing is that here I am. In the middle of New York City! Well, okay, my office is in Chinatown, so technically that's the *bottom* of the city. And I didn't grow up far away, but still, this place is like a whole new world. Millions of people. Infinite possibilities. I like to look at the buildings and wonder who's still in them and who's like me—trying to prove that she deserves a place here.

What's the saying? *If I can make it here, I can make it anywhere.* For me it's more like: If I can make it here, I won't be broke on the next bus back to Jersey. I thought if Ben and I moved to this city together and worked our ad magic, we could take the town by storm. Can I—correction, can *we*—really make a name for ourselves here? And leave all the doubters in the dust? I really hope so. I also really freaking hope Ben gets back soon. Remembering there's a whole world outside these walls is making me feel more alone than I want to be. And after all, we are a creative *team*.

My phone pings with an incoming text, as if some muse has indeed heeded my call. Maybe it's my best friend, Kellie, phoning from halfway 'round the globe with one of her patented pep talks. I could use that right now even more than pad Thai.

Hey Kay, any progress on Little Kitty?

Nope, definitely not Kell texting to say she'll call me in five. It's Suit, the senior account planner, subliminally cracking his whip yet again. Like I don't know I have to present ideas to Elliott tomorrow morning. Like I don't know it's already 8:13

p.m. Why doesn't he just text me a picture of an Uzi aimed at my right cranial lobe?

Paranoid, I peer over my cubicle to make sure Suit isn't lurking somewhere nearby, waiting for me to get 'er done. Nope, no signs of life anywhere on this floor. He's probably out to a fancy-schmance dinner with that uber-beautiful girlfriend of his, the six-foot-tall glamazon who wore head-to-toe leather to the office Christmas party. I bet she's only with Suit because of his height. No way a girl like that is going out wearing flats. I'd dressed all wrong that night, as usual. My silky red top—which seemed retro when I bought it at an Atlanta thrift shop—was so bright that Elliott kept calling me Rudolph. To make matters worse, girls like Suit's gal pal were all over that holiday party—just like they're all over Manhattan—as if put here just to remind the rest of us we don't cut it. Though if Suit was with Leatherette tonight, I doubt something as banal as cat food could divert his attention for so much as a second.

More likely Suit went out with Elliott and his crew for one of their liquid dinners. They're probably at the Hole, the dive bar on the edge of Soho where someone from our agency or another can usually be found. Not that I asked for specifics. I'm just glad to get a few hours of quiet before they file back in here later, buzzed, to play a few rounds of *Call of Duty* on Elliott's Xbox under the guise that they're "working late."

The boys' club had even tried to peer pressure Ben into joining them tonight, though they know full well we're on a deadline. The deadline *Elliott* gave us. I overheard them all by the elevator—our sadistic creative director was being especially loud and obnoxious. Elliott's not used to being turned down when he extends an invitation, so he was riding Ben pretty hard about "which skirt he was going to wear to work out."

Obviously, Elliott is the ringleader of the bunch. They all call him "E"—like he's some hallucinogenic life of their party. And like the drug ecstasy, "E" is known for extreme moods—highs *and* lows. Behind Elliott's back, Ben and I call him E-hole.

His boy network is so notorious they even got their own special mention in the big "Agency of the Year" write-up in *Advertising Age* magazine. The article's exact words were, "The boys' club is alive and well at this downtown denizen of edgy advertising, thanks to Creative Director Elliott Ford and his testosterone-laden band of thinkers."

Testosterone indeed. There aren't many chicks here at Schmidt Travino Drew in general, and technically I'm the only one in the creative department. There's uber-bitch Peyton but she's a producer, which is more like creative support, so that doesn't really count, and then there's Gina, the creative intern who got promoted but everyone still makes her fetch coffee so she counts even less. I'm pretty damn proud of this seat I have, but I know that at an agency like this, there's a long line of people waiting to pull it out from under me. Probably why it's just me here alone in this ridiculous chrome and glass office space while the band of drinkers—I mean thinkers—"works" off-site.

Come on, Ben. Walk off that elevator and come to Kay—show your sexy self. Not that I have anything to show *him* yet, either.

I think I'll go ransack Elliott's office for glossy photography books that might spark an idea. He's got three whole bookcases crammed with them, and on his Lucite coffee table alone are two books full of Japanese anime, a book on street graffiti, as well as volumes devoted to black female nudes, tattoo art, art toys, burlesque dancers, and art inspired by classic 80s videogames. I hate being in this office, no doubt some Pavlovian reaction to constantly being zapped by my boss's sharp criticism, but oh I do love the Eames chairs. I drop myself into one and start flipping through one of the anime books, searching for visual ideas that might help Ben with Little Kitty's ad design. Just a few hours ago, he was sitting in this very chair while we were getting briefed. I smell the seat back and there's his scent, Axe Phoenix . . . mmmmm. I close my eyes and picture Ben's tall, broad frame, tight with muscles . . . his tousled, sandy hair . . . and those eyes of his, both playful *and* brooding. I conjure his hearty laugh—so thickly midwestern, like a warm bear hug that lifts you off your feet. Lord knows I could have used one after our shakedown today in this very office.

Ugh, that was soo embarrassing. Did JoshJohnJay *have* to walk into Elliott's office right when he was telling us that he could find an addict on 8th Street who could do our job better than us? And then those numbskull idiots just go to the video games as if nothing is happening. And instead of actually giving us any creative direction, E-hole just shows all of them the new bug-sized camera he got straight from Tokyo for a small fortune. Or, as he not so humbly put it, "for more than any of you little people make in a month."

As usual, the guys rushed to huddle around E and ogle his latest toy. I swear, there's nothing that man loves more than having the technology that came out a second ago—or even better, hasn't been released to the masses yet.

"It's got a Carl Zeiss lens," Elliott bragged, "so the quality is insane. And it's the smallest camera in the world, so no one will ever notice it." Then he clicked a small button on his computer. "See, I filmed this two minutes ago."

Next thing you know, there I am, in horrifying close-up on Elliott's huge monitor, sweating golf-ball-sized bullets as he berates Ben and me for the last round of Little Kitty ads we'd done. My limp hair, flattened even more by stress. My left cheek indented the way it always is when I'm chewing on it. And I'm squirming like a shoplifter who just got busted wearing ten pairs of Vicky Secret undies under her jeans.

"Looks like Special K is having an allergic reaction," one of the Joshjohnjays quipped. And of course another one chimed in, "Allergic to the big dogs, little kitty?" Then they all burst out laughing . . . at my expense. It was my moment to shoot back some sarcasm and join in their reindeer games, but as usual my tongue was tied tighter than my Converses. Thank God for Ben—the mouthpiece of our team—and his effortless wit. He defused my humiliation with one of his goofy one-liners. "Wow, Kay, I never realized you had such nice pores!" A small victory in an afternoon of feeling like a total loser.

Ben might pal around with those guys every once in a while, but I just know that he would never let the boys' club change him. Ben is too Wisconsin. Too true to his roots. True to me, too . . . I hope. And one day, he'll want to take our partnership to a less professional, more horizontal level. I just know it.

A *click, click* sound snaps me back to reality. Elliott's bug camera! Where is it hidden? I hope it's not on! I scan high and low in Elliott's obscenely big office, feverish with panic. The darned thing could be *anywhere*.

Click, click. I hear it again.

What if Elliott and the boys are watching me right now, falling off their barstools? What if footage of me sniffing his Eames chair floods the morning e-mails? Something hits my foot, and I look down to see a wind-up robot, the source of the clicking noise. Whew! I must have inadvertently knocked it off the table.

I step over the toy, grab a few books, and hightail it out of there pronto. Navigating the row of cubicles back to my own, I notice a wind-up robot on Josh's desk, and then when I pass Jay's, there's another robot just like it. Hmmm. Have they always been carbon copies of each other—or did they become that way when Elliott, Fucking Famous Creative Director, hired them?

To Johnjoshjay, good ole E can do no wrong. I hate to admit it, but there *is* something magnetic about the guy. Luckily I'm impervious to his powers. Or maybe it's that he doesn't ever try to include me in the group with their high-end tequilas or trendy microbrews and whatever fads they "discover" in the pages of *Spin* and *Details*.

And it works for them. All they ever seem to talk about is gaming and indie music, yet they turn out award-winning ads for Superfine and Atlantis. Whenever I've seen them with girls (the few times I actually get to leave the office and have a drink at the Hole) I'm totally intimidated by who they bring around—the kind of women I always see on the street but never in the mirror: beautiful, confident, a few steps *ahead* of the conversation.

Ben can always tell when I'm feeling self-conscious, and when all the guys are hitting on these super-babes, he comes over and talks to me. But Ben has never—not once—made a move on me. I whine about it to Kellie whenever we talk. Maybe

I should give her a quick call now. I know I'm procrastinating, but that's a necessary part of the creative process, right?

Back at my desk, I grab my phone and see there's a message waiting for me: *Hey again. How is the cat writing going?* Geez! That's Suit's third text tonight. No way am I responding. Does he really think I'm so incompetent that I need a babysitter to monitor my progress? I am totally going to ace this assignment. Correction— Ben and I are going to ace this assignment. And when we do, everyone can kiss our little kitties.

I look at the clock. Eight thirty. Ben should really be here by now. WTF? And WTF time is it in Paris? Ever since Kell moved there to study art history, I can't keep track of when she should be awake or asleep. Especially since she's leading the sort of fabulous life we both dreamed of since junior high, completely oblivious to the nine-to-five grind. It's probably pretty late in the City of Light, but at least I can leave a message. We haven't been connecting enough lately, something I'm quick to blame on the time difference and my work schedule, but truthfully, I haven't been trying that hard. It kills me to talk to someone who is always so damn happy when all I want to do is complain.

I speed-dial her mobile and prepare for the beep, but am surprised when she actually picks up. Even more surprising, I hear glasses clinking, and what sounds like a French rock band in the background.

"*Bonjour, mon amie!*" she shouts over the music, into the phone.

"Kell! I didn't think you'd be up! *Where* are you?"

"This supercool *boîte en* Saint-Germain with *mes amis* from *l'université*. Where are you?" She effortlessly mixes French and English in a Parisian accent I could never pull off.

I survey my cube, more a box than a *boîte*, and wince before admitting to her that I am again working late.

"*Mon dieu*, Kay!" Her French accent is so chic. "You make New York sound . . . *très* boring."

"I know . . ." I sigh, putting my feet up on Ben's desk. "It's just that Little Kitty is the client from hell. They want headline after headline after headline. I've only been at Schmidt Travino Drew for four months and I bet I've already written three hundred and fifty lines for them, promising everything from fewer hair balls to ten lives to taste that's 'fur-licking good.' Truthfully, maybe one hundred and twenty-five of these headlines have actually gone to the client. So far, they only bought and ran exactly *one*: '*Kiss your bad fur days good-bye.*'"

"MeeOWW!" Kell teases. "Kiss your bad ad days good-bye."

"I know. Genius, right?"

"Kay, maybe your pussy just needs to get out more, *oui*?"

"Ha-ha. You sound just like Joshjohnjay. At least Ben's still on my team."

"How eez Monsieur Benjamin? *S'il vous plait* tell me he is working on top of you!"

Even though the office is empty, I rise to my feet and make a beeline for the ladies' room. After all, my partner will be back any minute.

"He went to blow off steam at the gym," I tell her once I'm safely tucked into the last stall. "The poor guy ran out of cat food ideas about a month ago. But when he gets back we're going to pull an all-nighter!"

"Ooh la la, Kay, how sexy." Her sarcastic tone suggests disapproval.

"He *is* sexy," I insist. "The way he looks at me when I'm sharing my ideas with him. And that mischievous laugh of his . . . Kell, when is he going to finally wake up and kiss me?"

"FaceTime," she demands, and after I tap the icon, I can see the beautiful, glamorous face of my oldest friend staring at me accusingly from the screen of my phone. I can also see that she's in the bathroom now, too, so we can have some privacy.

Kellie drops the Franglais affectation to scold me. "No makeup? Kaykay, is that really the way to woo him? And let me guess. Baggy button-down? Not what a French woman would wear to an all-nighter."

I look at myself in the mirror for the first time all week—limp, wheat-colored hair, pasty skin, ratty flannel shirt, and day-old jeans—and concede her point.

"I know. I know. But with these crazy deadlines, I'm lucky I have any clothes that *look* clean."

"Purse. Now," she orders, and I dart back to my cubicle as she launches into one of the speeches I so love her for, even when they're more like bitch slaps. "Stop waiting for shit to happen and start making it happen, Kay. Ben already likes and respects you. He's just waiting for you to give him a sign. *Tonight*, you are going to get your sexy on, a little eyeliner, some blush, perfume, and for the love of all that is good and inspired by *Vogue*, take down that ponytail and brush that mess."

Safely back in the bathroom, I follow her instructions.

"Now unbutton your shirt. One more—and push those boobs up to the high heavens. It's not called a push-*down* bra, for God's sake."

"You *know* I don't have any boobs." I try to effectively repackage what I've got.

"Kaykay," she sighs. "Sexy is an attitude. You should see some of the ugly cows here in Paris who get hot men just by knowing how to flirt."

"I'm more of an ugly giraffe." I survey my boyishly stick-thin frame and the Adam's apple bulging from my neck. I have to admit, though, my minor modifications have helped. A little. Maybe this could work.

"He's bringing beer back, too, right?"

I nod.

"You're going to actually drink one, maybe two. Screw worrying about ads and give your life a little attention. I want you to sit close, laugh at everything he says, touch his hand once in a while, and when the moment is right, I want you to bat your hazel eyes at him and lean in for a kiss."

My eyes stretch to saucers.

"It's time, Kay," she insists. "The two of you have been working together *for years*."

She makes it sound so easy. But then again, she's always been the Laverne to my Shirley. I have doubts. I may not get to the kiss, but at the very least, I will flirt. Or listen attentively and not say anything stupid.

I hear footsteps in the hall outside and whisper. "Ohmigod! Kell. He's back."

"Go get him, *mon petit chou*. Send me a ShoutOut later with the details, *bisou bisou*." She starts French-kissing her phone.

I tap end as I see an extreme close-up of her tongue, pierced with a silver barbell. Is that new? No time to find out now. I grab my bag and walk as calmly as I can back to my cube, cooing, "You better have brought spring rolls, Ben Wilder. And maybe some of your big ideas, too . . ."

I look up eagerly, offering Ben what I hope is a playful smile. Only it's not Ben. Standing in my cubicle is Suit. Damn! Ignoring his text messages obviously was not the right thing to do.

Suit. Suit. *Suit*, who none of us actually call by his real name. Seems that everyone around here gets an alias or alter ego. Which makes sense when you consider that advertising has got to be the fakest industry on the planet. But hey, kids, it's fun! You can wear flip-flops to work! Just don't expect to be liked for being yourself!

Usually I try to avoid Suit like the plague. Not because he is a strategic planner, a group notorious for siding with the clients. And not because he's so stuffy and polished in his crisp Robert Graham sports shirts, a blatant contrast to all of us laid-back creative types in our sneakers and jeans. No, I steer clear of Suit because he's always popping up when I think I'm alone, always sticking his head in my cube to check up on my writing. It's so passive-aggressive. *Just ask* when I'll be done, I feel like telling him, instead of acting like you care "how things are going."

And the guy notices everything—if anyone can figure out that I'm stalled, it's him.

"Bit of writer's block?" he says now as he lingers by the entry to my cubicle, nodding to my tote bag as I settle back into my seat. Is he insinuating that I'd left the office for a while? Passive-aggressive stalker!

"Just a bathroom break. I know we're on a deadline, but that's allowed, isn't it? Or do I have to pee in a bottle at my desk?" I don't struggle for words around him like I do around my other coworkers. Probably because he infuriates me like my older, holier-than-thou brothers used to, and I'm used to fighting back with *them* verbally. Plus, I'm not trying to impress him.

"Sorry. I just thought I caught a whiff of the perfume counter at Saks. It's going well, then?" Suit walks over to my computer screen. And that's when I realize I never closed my last Microsoft Word page.

"Here, shitty kitty," he reads aloud. That's all I ever did get around to typing. "Kay, as amazing as this little stroke of genius is, I don't think I'll be able to present it to the client. I do hope this is not the best of your work?"

"Oh, that?" I fudge. "It's a joke for Ben. He's coming back so we can mock up your lines. I've got pages and pages of winners."

Ugh. *Winners* is ad speak for the very best lines you've got. I hate it when I fall back on the clichés people throw around the office.

"Good to hear." Suit smiles, no doubt relieved. If Ben and I fail, he's the one who will have to tap-dance for the client.

"Can I see what you have?" he asks in a friendly tone, but deep down I know he's just being passively pushy.

Suit's job is to develop the winning strategy for clients and make sure we creatives stick to it. Because cat food is so competitive and the differences between the products are small, he has done a lot of work with the Little Kitty execs to figure out how to make them stand out. All those meetings have made him the agency's strongest link to the client, and that also makes him a favorite of Schmidt and Travino. Everyone else really likes him for other reasons that I'm not aware of. I've never spoken to him about anything except cat food. But I guess I can see why clients might find him charming. Ben said the guy's from somewhere down south. Alabama or Georgia or Louisiana or whatever. When you grow up on the East Coast, all those states kind of blend together.

"Where are you from?" I blurt out suddenly, anxious to avoid what he just asked me at all costs.

Suit's eyebrows wrinkle up, then he smiles, thrown by the randomness of my question.

Kay, if this is how you play coy, you'll never manage to seduce Ben tonight.

"New Orleans," he's saying. "It's a little town in Louisiana; maybe you've heard of it."

Duh, I know New Orleans. And of course I know Louisiana. Kind of looks like a boot. Or a flag. They had the horrible hurricane; it's all coming back.

Don't ask about the hurricane, Kay. You're cooler than that.

"Mardi Gras!" I offer.

Um, better. Sort of.

"Yes, in New Orleans we celebrate Mardi Gras." Now he is practically laughing at me out loud.

From nowhere, I remember him laughing at the Christmas party. I'd been surprised that someone so straight looking actually had a sense of humor. Suit would probably get along swimmingly with my brothers, the Wondertwins. Brett and Brian are both successful financial analysts, a fact that only fuels our mother's belief that nothing *I* do is good enough. Thanks to Attila the Mum, I have no idea how to take a compliment, let alone believe one.

You were born bald, a scrawny little chicken. I used to scotch tape bows to your head so the nurses would know you were a girl, Mom loves to tell me in that I'm-just-kidding-but-I'm-not way of hers.

One bassinet over, there was a plump, pretty baby girl with big blue eyes and golden ringlets of hair. I told your father to switch name bracelets so we could take her home instead.

She always follows this dig with deep belly laughter and the occasional snort. It's hard to be heard when you live with someone who's in love with the sound of her own voice. That's why I turned to writing. For as long as I can remember, it's been my go-to medium for getting out the words I would warble if I tried to say them out loud.

You wanna be a writer? *Why not just become a homeless person instead?* Mom would say encouragingly .

But no matter what she thinks about my craft not paying the bills, I'd rather do this than work in boring old finance. Sure, she brags about the Wondertwins to anyone who will listen. But really, who cares if both my brothers own—not rent— apartments in Tribeca. Buy! Sell! Numbers. Yawn.

"So . . ." Suit is staring at me. Did I miss something he said?

"Yes?"

"I asked if you were going to join the party since you're done here. I don't think I've ever seen you wear lipstick."

Shoot. I did miss something. Daydreaming. Another one of my fatal flaws.

"No party for me. Not tonight." I was actually hoping for a party but I'll be damned if I'm going to give the slightest indication of that to Suit. Kellie is the only one who needs to know that. Some secrets are best kept in the ladies' room.

"Well, suit yourself," he says.

I look up to see if he could possibly be joking. But there is no irony in his eyes. In fact his eyes are unreadable. If I had to guess whether the guy was in a good mood or a bad mood, I might as well flip a coin. Nothing like looking at Ben; one second of eye contact and I know exactly what he is thinking.

Ah, Ben. Maybe Kellie's plan could work . . . We'll eat dinner, brainstorm a little, drink a couple beers. What did she say? That I should lean into his nose? No, duh, *lean in close.* Okay, I'll lean in close all night and then we'll go to the apartment to watch TV. This is when I usually fall asleep but maybe if I bat my eyelashes it will keep me awake *and* I'll look flirty, as a bonus.

"Ahem."

I snap back to reality, hoping to see that Ben has arrived. No such luck, still just Suit. If he weren't so relentless, I'd feel bad for the guy. It's not his fault he has to make sure us creatives actually deliver the stellar work he's promised to the client. Nor is it his fault when we'd much rather be fucking off than actually writing copy.

"Sorry," I say. "I'm just really focused on this assignment, not much for conversation tonight, I guess."

"Well, then we'll talk again in the morning. I'm sure we'll be the only ones *here*, judging from what's happening on Shout-Out." Then he turns to leave. Finally. His footsteps are so damn loud on the concrete, I am relieved when they get farther and farther away.

I turn to the computer, delete *Here, shitty kitty* and instead write *Meow.* I don't have the foggiest clue where this thought could be going. Yet.

Maybe I'll surf ShoutOut. Wait. What did Suit just say . . . ? What's on there? I guess I'll wait for Ben to check that out. It's our thing to take breaks for the videos and make fun of people together.

And he'll be here soon.

Any minute now.

Man, it would be awesome if there were just one cashew left in that little white baggie. Just a snack while I wait for Ben.

Since he is probably just about to show up.

And I don't want to be ravenous when he gets here. The point is to impress him, and I'm pretty sure Kellie would say that sucking down an oyster pail of noodles in five seconds flat is not an aphrodisiac for anyone involved.

Surely the white bag is around here somewhere, probably just stuffed behind the back of my laptop . . . no, not there. Maybe it fell on the floor? Rats, not there, either.

Ah! Must. Focus.

Okay, I'll just check my phone once more *to make sure* Ben hasn't called or texted to explain where he is.

Nope. Nothing. Just the same old, same old picture of me and Kellie that's been the background on my phone forever. It would be amazing if tonight went well. Then I could change my phone's wallpaper to a picture of Ben and me. And then he could come home with me for Easter and hang with my family and maybe for our summer vacation we could go to Europe or something . . .

I might be getting ahead of myself since it's only February.

But I do have my phone in my hand . . . and I could use just another couple seconds of procrastination . . . plus Suit's comment did pique my curiosity . . . so I tap the ShoutOut app on my screen. To this day I have never posted to ShoutOut—a social media network where people upload videos of themselves talking or doing stuff—but Ben and I check on what's happening there all the time. Once or twice he has suggested we do a video for the Schmidt Travino Drew channel, our agency's network, but I shut that down immediately—speaking on camera is not an activity in which the chronically shy excel.

As soon as the app opens, there are eight new videos to watch. I roll my eyes because one is from my mother. My brothers decided to set up a family network, probably so they could figure out the technology well enough to talk about it like experts—which is how they talk about everything. Why they taught it to our mother is totally beyond me.

Then there are two other videos from the network I'm on with my ad school class. Blah blah boring.

The next five are posted by E-hole. All in the last two hours.

What the hell could be happening at the Hole on a Tuesday night that's so interesting it needs to be filmed?

I choose the last video and immediately I see what's so interesting about their Tuesday night. For starters, they aren't at the Hole. Not unless the usual bartender Louie turned into Louise, lost thirty pounds *and* his shirt, and then spent about two grand at Agent Provocateur.

Those scumbags are at a strip club! While I'm at the office! And, ewwww. What exactly *is* that dancer doing on Elliott's pant leg?

Of course he has his new bug camera rolling, and from what

I can tell, it's perched on top of E-hole's glass: The footage has the distinct point of view of a straw.

Joshjohnjay come into view, one by one. What a surprise! All with the same dopey looks of drunken glee plastered across their faces.

And there's Peyton, wearing knee-high black cat boots. Jesus, who invited her?

On second thought, they all probably invited her.

Peyton, Peyton, Peyton.

That bitch. I still am not over the first time I met her, when she stepped around me without even introducing herself so she could shake Ben's hand. I tried complaining about it to Kellie but that went nowhere. Leave it to Kell to ask if there was anything I didn't like about "this Peyton girl" besides the fact that she was eyeballing the guy I was eyeballing.

Her question completely offended me (I do more than eyeball the guy, we are friends and partners *and* roommates), and so I promptly explained to Kellie that Peyton gives off the distinct vibe of being a girl who a) has a daddy-sponsored personal shopper at Barneys, and b) is from Oregon.

I happen to be aware that not only does Kellie detest spoiled rich girls, she also has a thing against Oregon that dates back to a really horrible family camping trip there in 1999 when it rained the whole time and Kellie's brother puked in her lap on the plane. These are the bits of information only a best friend would know, and know how to exploit. As planned, she promptly joined me in hating Peyton.

Just wait until she finds out that Peyton is at a strip club with the boys. This is worse—*way worse*—than putting shoes you couldn't pick out yourself on Daddy's charge card because you also can't afford to pay for them yourself.

Oh good, the camera is pulling out and wait . . . wait . . . wait a minute. That blue sleeve looks really familiar. I need Elliott to move the glass to the left a little . . . okay, yes, that way, Elliott . . . move it that way. There, perfe—

Ohmigod. Not perfect at all. That blue sleeve is familiar because it's connected to the face I spend almost every waking minute of my life about six feet away from.

How can this be happening?

Why wouldn't he have called to tell me?

Ben is at the strip club?

Holy shit, I need air. But more than that, I need to see what's going to happen next on the video.

Ben looks like he might be wasted. He's doing that thing where he throws back his head to laugh, and that's not really Ben. Ben is more of a low chuckler; he bows his head when he is going to laugh really, really hard. But his head is thrown back and now . . . wait . . . ohmigod, *that whore*. Why is Peyton walking up to Ben? Why is Peyton straddling Ben with her slutty boots? What is that in her hand—a shot glass? Why is she tipping that shot glass up to Ben's mouth?

I peel my eyes off the screen and frantically look around because I need to ask someone: *Why is Peyton tipping her mouth to Ben's mouth?*

I snap my head back so I don't miss a thing and . . . they are kissing.

Kissing in front of everybody in the creative department.

Except for me because . . . I'm still at work? Writing lines for cat food?

I know I should wait and see what happens next, maybe even click through another video. Who knows if they've been kissing all night. Maybe they've been kissing all month and I had my head buried too far in my stupid fantasies to see what was happening.

Stupid, stupid, *stupid* to think Ben would ever go for me over some girl like Peyton.

Flannel versus fabulous.

A girl who lives on paper versus someone who lives in the moment.

The list could go on and on. I would have been too nervous and worried and fearful—of what, I don't know—even to set foot in that place. But not a girl like her.

I swivel around so I can see out the window behind my chair. Usually I don't sit this way because it opens me up to a view of Joshjohnjay, but now it doesn't matter. It's starting to snow outside and I should be thankful that it's a beautiful night in the city, that I'm in a warm office, that I have a paycheck and an apartment, and that list could go on, too.

But I am not thankful, not for anything. The only thing I want is the one thing I don't have: Ben.

Oh shit. The tears are coming. I can feel the dull ache underneath my ears and that's the indicator that I have about four seconds to get out of here or else waterworks are going to erupt and *I will not cry* in this office. Even when it's empty—this is a no-cry zone. It's bad enough I have to menstruate here once a month.

I leave my computer with one word—*Meow*—still on the

screen. I don't have time to pack it up. Instead I just grab my bag and run for the elevator. In the lobby I can hear the low-level ambient tunes that play around the clock. I'm pretty sure I recognize Coldplay chords. If Ben were here he would make a joke about how we only have a couple years left until our music is elevator music.

But.

Ben.

Isn't.

Here.

I'm jamming my finger on the down button, and the second the doors open I can hear footsteps coming down the hall from the other side of the building. It's probably Suit heading home for the night, and there's no way I can let him in the elevator with me. My four seconds are up and the faucet is about to blow.

I don't even have a Kleenex. My mother would be so appalled.

I jump into the elevator then reach for the close-door button and start pounding, pounding, pounding on it to *work, dammit!*

Finally the doors shut, probably just as Suit was showing up in the lobby, but I didn't bother to look because I couldn't have seen anything, anyway. The water that has been filling my eyes is now overflowing onto my cheeks and my chin—there's too much evidence of heartbreak, I can't wipe away the tears fast enough, and so I give up trying.

I lean against the wall of the elevator as it starts to move, and I close my eyes.

The last thing I want to see is the chrome reflection of a silly, silly girl who makes a living off words but refuses to see the writing on the wall.

find it in you

Surely there are worse places in the world to suffer major heartbreak than in the middle of a snowstorm in the middle of Chinatown. I could be at my parents' house. That would be bad. But at least I'd be warm, and in the bed I grew up in, which doesn't actually sound all that terrible.

The Hole, on the other hand, sounds like a depressing place for the lovelorn . . . though at least they serve beer.

Maybe the middle of Chinatown *is* the absolute worst place to be, snow or not. Any other time, I'd catch snowflakes on my tongue, but my face is already soaked in sadness. Before I turn into a lyric from a Death Cab for Cutie song, I should get the hell out of here.

The agency is behind me, for tonight at least. Any second now Suit will probably be barreling through the front door. I bet he'd think it was amusing to see me in meltdown mode. Every person in that place has a sick, twisted sense of humor. Makes me think I should have taken a job at one of the agencies that wasn't quite so *agency*. An agency that's sweeter than Schmidt Travino Drew.

Where everybody does detergent ads and the hottest conversation point is if moms prefer apple scents or floral scents to linger on their laundry. I've heard Midtown is full of places like that.

Sounds like a mental massage compared to my every day.

In the few months I've worked here, I've learned that Chinatown gets way empty at night—too empty for a girl who grew up in the suburbs to feel safe walking the streets alone. My favorite tchotchke store is shuttered up now. Just two days ago Ben and I had stopped in on our lunch break and I showed him the turquoise castle I've had my eye on since the first time I passed by. Eighty bucks seems like a lot for a piece that probably costs a dollar to make in China. But it's got a moat and a tower where you can really imagine a princess hanging out. I showed Ben the intricacies of the design and he picked it up and turned it over in his hands—for a split second I thought maybe he would buy it for me; wouldn't that have been sweet? Instead he said, "You have a great eye, Kay. You could be an art director and a writer."

Which I had also taken as sweet. Why? Because I told myself that's the ultimate compliment from an ad guy. And because, obviously, I am clueless.

I'm moving as fast as my sneakers will go, which isn't too fast with all the ice on the sidewalks. But I get past the shop; I cruise past the closed meat markets. The poor little pigs are probably still hanging in the windows, dangling from spindly legs tied with twine, but with the lights off you don't have to see any of those gory details.

I know I'm hungry because *pig* makes me think *bacon*, which makes my stomach cry out for attention.

The street level is dark but on the higher floors of the buildings there are lights on. I can imagine families sitting around with bowls of rice—who am I kidding, probably boxes of pizza—watching *So You Think You Can Dance*: the American dream. Not that I'm one to judge dreams, since in the last hour every one of mine has proven futile, infantile, and ridiculous.

Geez, Kay, stop it.

It's hard to be a writer during moments of despair. The English language has far too many words that describe failure.

Maybe food will help. There's a restaurant nearby that everyone has been talking about—a noodle shop purposely buried back here to keep tourists away. I decide to find it. Hopefully there's a bar where I can sit alone, cuddled up in my jacket. Warm, slippery carbs will solve my most immediate problem: starvation. After that I can start to deal with the fact that the one man I have ever loved in my life was just sucking face with a coworker on ShoutOut. While at a strip club. On a Tuesday night.

Is this the sort of thing a person goes to counseling for? Or is it more of a Jerry Springer scenario? I'm just twenty-four. Came from a decent family. Got straight As in school. And while my apartment *is* smaller than a trailer home, I live above a wine bar, so that classes me up a bit. I'm not a scene from Jerry Springer, not yet, anyway.

Instead of turning on Canal I go straight and then take a right on a side street.

I overheard Elliott talking this place up to his boys the other day. "Noodles are the new thing," he declared. "People from all over the island are going to this place. You have to hit it before everyone finds out about it and it gets ruined."

Really more of a lecture than a recommendation. Elliott's little black book of tips on how to be cool. Rule 1: When the masses arrive, what was good is instantly gone. Rule 2: People who are part of the masses have no place at Schmidt Travino Drew & Partners.

Good news for me because I most definitely am completely, totally alone tonight.

Up ahead I see the glow of a restaurant open for business. There's one black town car lingering at the top of the block, and a cab stopped in front. For some reason I freeze when the taxi doors open, as if of all the restaurants in the whole city, one of the ten people I know is going to be getting out. But my brain is not functioning at 100 percent. Everything that used to make sense—Ben, work, what the hell I'm doing in New York City—it's all gone up in smoke. That I might happen to bump into someone seems totally rational.

Three girls and one guy spill onto the sidewalk. They are all laughing in that loud way that says they've already been drinking. I definitely don't know them, but I know their type. The girls are all dressed in knee-high boots with skinny jeans. Two have buns wrapped up on top of their heads, and the other has a braid that goes all the way down her damn back. In other words: stylish. The guy is paying the cabbie from a fat wad of bills he pulled out from his pocket. I can see pink cuffs barely peeking from underneath the sleeves of his designer suit.

I stop walking and tuck into the shadows of the building. I want to let their party of fun—I mean, four—get in the restaurant before I roll up.

What would Kell say if she could see me now? I should update her but I know she's going to want details. And that could take a while. I need to wallow just a little bit longer . . .

Okay, the party group is in so now's my time.

I throw my shoulders back and try to stand up straight, like my mother would tell me to do if she were here.

I haven't taken a look at myself since I was in the ladies' room at the office earlier, but at least then I put on lipstick; that's more than I do on a normal night. And it's so damn cold I can get away with leaving my jacket on. This will hide the stylish clothes I'm not wearing. One of these days, when I'm not holed up in the office, I really am going to learn to dress like a New Yorker.

I fling open the door with my head raised much higher than I feel like it should be. And immediately, before I've even taken a step inside, I know I've made a huge mistake. This is supposed to be a noodle shop in Chinatown—I'm totally sure that's how Elliott described it. But this place is a swishy freaking nightclub. There's a jazz band in the back and the lights over the restaurant tables are a cool blue. I can't even start to check out how "jazzy" all the people probably look before the host cuts me off at the pass.

"Can I help you, Miss?" He looks right through me.

Is there anything worse than being called *Miss*? Single and young wrapped into one patronizing package. *Ma'am* might be worse, but at least with that you get some Southern hospitality.

I tell myself to speak slowly, not to let my voice crack. Just because this place is five hundred times fancier than the joint I was expecting is no reason to back out. I'm a woman . . . no, an *independent* woman. I'm an independent woman who makes my own money, and I can hold my own in a blue jazz club noodle shop hot spot.

"Table for one?" I know my voice does not have that independent woman ring to it. Mental note to work on that in the privacy of my own home.

Oh no, my home, which I sort of share with Ben. *Stop, Kay. Focus.*

The host wears an earpiece and is carrying a clipboard to give the illusion of super importance.

He looks down at the clipboard, but I have the distinct impression he is not actually reading anything.

"Our tables are all filled up tonight, Miss."

I want to reply, *Well, Mister* . . . but instead mutter, "Is there a bar where I can sit?"

He looks at me. "We serve drinks at our tables, Miss. No bar."

The group of four that just got seated are settling into their chairs and opening menus. My eyes fix on the guy. Now that his jacket is off, I see he is built like Ben. Lanky. But strong.

Focus.

I divert my attention and immediately spot an empty table for two.

"Is that an empty table there?"

"Oh, Miss, that table is reserved."

Now I notice there are empty tables all over the place.

"Well what about that table?" I point behind the guy. "Or that one?"

"They're all reserved, Miss. For people with reservations."

He says *reservations* like my mom says *education*. I know the tone, and I know that it means the same thing to both of them: *You do not register without one.*

It's not like me to argue, but I can't imagine that all three of the empty two-tops are going to fill up. And all I want is a bowl of noodles.

"Look. I'll be out of here in a heartbeat. I just want to order and eat, and then your table will be free for your reservation."

This time the guy doesn't even bother to look at his fucking clipboard. "We just don't have space for you, Miss." And then he walks away.

I am pissed but all that anger is fighting hard with shame. The girl with the blond braid throws her head back, laughing like the waiter is the most hilarious person on the planet. He's balancing four perfectly poured martinis on his tray. Perfectly poured for their perfect little table. Perfectly sure there's no space for you, Miss.

I reach into my purse and pull out my sunglasses because I can feel tears coming again. In a second I'm out the door and on the street, and this time I don't bother with walking carefully, I just start running.

I don't know where I'm going, but I can't get there fast enough. There's a vague ringing coming from my pocket. Maybe it's Ben! Not that I want to talk to him, but could it hurt to peek at the screen?

I fish my phone out of my pocket without slowing down. I am a master multitasker. Nope. Not Ben. It's Kell. Probably getting my telepathic call for a lifeline. I take it.

"Hey," I say, out of breath.

"Oh *mon dieu*, why does it sound like you've been working out?" Kell greets me. Then she half shrieks/half whispers, "Are you in bed with him?"

I start running faster. Canal Street is up ahead.

"No, Kell. I'm most definitely not in bed with anyone!"

"*Qu'est-ce qui se passe?*"

"I can't explain now, I'm running."

Silence from Kellie. Then, "Like, on a treadmill?"

"Of course not."

"Are you running away from someone?"

"Sort of, I guess, I don't know, Kellie, okay? Tonight has been the worst ever, and Ben is in love with this slut from the agency, and they're together at a strip club—he's probably getting a lap dance or something right now—and I just got turned away from a noodle shop, and if I don't eat something soon I'm gonna die!"

"FaceTime!" Kellie demands. But I just remembered the McDonald's on Canal.

"Not now, Kellie."

"Yes!" she insists.

"No!"

"Yes!"

I hold my phone out in front of my face to scream "No" as loud as I can, when I either skid on a patch of ice or maybe my feet just give out—this is more running than I have done since my freaking presidential fitness test in junior high—because the next thing I know, my legs are no longer under me.

For a split second I'm in the air. I think, *Falling, help, I'm falling, who will catch me?*

I get my answer from a thick slab of ice. *Gotcha, girl.*

In the gutter. I'm faceup in the cold, slushy gutter. My legs are splayed—one foot pointing to the Williamsburg Bridge and the other to Hell's Kitchen. My neck feels like it was snapped by a nutcracker. My phone lands next to me, and I know without looking at it that the screen is shattered. I am shattered.

A pair of high-heeled boots walks toward me. To help me up, I assume. But their owner, yet another six-foot glamazon in a motorcycle jacket and updo, just steps around me. The last thing I hear before I give in to sobs is Kellie screaming into the phone, "Kay? Are you there? Kay! Answer me! *Are you dead?*"

The phone still works. Not the miracle I was wishing for, but it's something.

McDonald's gets a bum rap. The eat-organic crowd hates it. And the pro-animal people. And the people worried about their kids turning into Pillsbury Dough boys and girls.

But right now at this moment I love McDonald's so freaking much I could cry. And probably would if I had any tears left.

The cashier didn't look twice at my muddy clothes or my pink face, and she definitely didn't tell me there wasn't space enough for me in their hamburger establishment.

"Come one, come all." That should be their tagline. Or maybe "Let them eat cake, we'll serve comfort."

Is writing taglines in the middle of a nervous breakdown a sign that I've been working too much? Am I turning into the guy who checks his BlackBerry in the middle of his own wedding reception?

Not that I should judge someone checking his BlackBerry at a wedding reception—at least he found someone who would marry him.

They call my number and I go to pick up my hamburger. It's a one-patty wonder with ketchup only—no onions—the way I've been ordering since I was short enough to trail after my brothers through the PlayPlace. Do kids who grow up in the city know most McDonalds actually have a jungle gym? My heart seizes with love for my suburban upbringing. I miss the bubble of it all.

Leaving the counter, I start to walk to the table I had scouted out while I was waiting, but rats, it's been taken. By a man who looks to be homeless and has a small McDonald's cup in front of him that might date back to the nineties. I guess if you want a place to sit, you've got to have a cup.

Instead I take the closest seat I can find, wedged between two tables whose occupants are also dining solo. Careful not to make eye contact, I unwrap the burger and it is a sight to behold. *Oh, Kay; oh, Kay, you finally did something right.* I do a two-handed grab and bring it to eye level.

You are Peyton and the burger is your Ben.

You are going to devour this burger.

Your tagline should be "Burger eater today, man-eater tomorrow."

Dear God, I am working too much.

I'm mid-bite when I hear a voice to my right. "Dear, aren't you going to smile and say hello?"

Surely this voice is not talking to me. I couldn't possibly know anyone *here.* But as I chew through bun and cow, I hear the same voice, louder. "I said, dear, aren't you going to smile and say hello?"

Freeze. A little voice inside me suggests that this person is talking to me. I turn my head left—an Asian guy reading a newspaper with his hand so far in a french fry container I can only see his wrist. I turn right and there she is, the speaker. She's looking at me expectantly, as though I need to answer her.

I rack my brain. My grandparents all have passed away (God bless their souls) and the only other old people I know are my parents. And they aren't old, old, like blue-hair old, like this lady old.

"I'm sorry?" I say.

"You young kids," she clucks. "Turning sentences into questions. *I'm sorry* is not a question. *I'm sorry* is a statement. *Excuse me, I didn't hear what you said* is a more specific and appropriate statement. And if you insist on raising your voice at the end of your sentence as though it were a question, *Were you speaking to me?* would work."

"Do I know you?" I ask.

"That's better." The woman raises her hand up to pat the tight gray curls on top of her head. I lower my burger and scan her person for clues of who she is.

Then I have it. Elliott, that bastard, he's doing a hidden camera on me. I half stand up in my bucket seat and look around for the bug.

"Going somewhere?" The woman eyes me with fascination.

"No, just looking for someone—er—something."

There's no sign of a bug. Or an overgrown E-hole wearing Gucci. I guess my Elliott guess was wrong.

"I don't mean to interrupt your dinner, but it distresses me that people no longer smile and say hi to each other the way they used to."

This stops me short. This is something *I* usually say. In fact, I have said almost that exact thing to Ben time and time again. It bugs me that people don't say hi to each other when there are only two people in an enclosed area. Like an elevator. Or waiting on a curb for a cab. Especially in New York—it just feels like people are trying to be assholes. And that can't be how people really are, can it?

Did I do that to this woman?

"I'm sorry, I'm having a bad day." I force a smile. "How are you?" I add by way of greeting. My mother might have slapped fifty shades of insecurities on me, but she did teach me to respect my elders.

"I saw you come in and you looked lost," the old woman confesses.

I scan her table for signs of who she is. What she is. There's no shopping cart with a coffeemaker or a pillow stuffed inside. And she looks really well put together. Her purse is nondescript but her dress could be made of a fine material I can't identify. Out of place in McDonald's. Hell, out of place below Central Park.

"I remember being your age, just starting out in this city. It's easy to lose hope when you don't know your way. The best thing about getting older is that I finally know who I am, and that brings me peace."

"Of course," I say. Because there's nothing else to say. I don't know whether it's bad or good to get old. What I can confirm with 100 percent certainty is that being twenty-four is confusing with an order of suckiness, supersized.

"The worst part," she says, "is that no one sees you anymore."

I feel awful suddenly. That was exactly what I had done to the woman, not even bothered to look at her. It wasn't personal, though. I'm young and no one looks at me and I don't take it personally.

Or do I?

She is standing up to go and now I feel like I need to say something.

"Do you need help?" She's already doing the side shuffle out of her table. I notice she has no food, no trash.

She gives me the littlest smile, the corners of her mouth just barely ticked up to her gold clip-on earrings. "No, dear, you enjoy your dinner."

Then she starts to walk away, opening the door to the outside world, the world that looks right past her. For a second I just sit there, picking at my burger. I look over at the Asian guy next to me to see if he has been following this weird exchange, but his hand has obviously been soldered to the inside of the fry container. A surgical procedure might be required for removal.

Then I remember the fall I took on my way here. I *cannot* let that happen to this little old lady. I stand up with my purse wrapped around my body, do my own side shuffle out of the tables, and then walk fast out the door. She is standing there, under the golden arched awning, looking out at the snow piling up on the icy sidewalk.

"It's slippery," I warn her. "That's why my clothes are soaked."

I take her by the arm, offering to help her navigate the treacherous pavement. She's reluctant, proud, but I don't give her a choice. She motions to a parked town car waiting by the curb. I walk her there and a driver emerges, opening the back door.

She gets in, and right before the driver shuts the door, she looks up at me. "Whatever it is you're looking for, you won't find it here." She gestures toward Canal Street, to the activity all around us.

"You've got to find it in you."

Huh. Talk about taking unsolicited advice to the next level.

And like that, the car is gone. It's as if she disappeared into thin air.

Slowly I walk back into the McDonald's. But I don't feel the same affection for it as I did before. In fact I don't feel much at all. No anger at Ben. No embarrassment about being shut out of the noodle shop or about having fallen in the gutter. I can't even muster up enough emotion to scream out when I see the homeless guy standing over my table, eating my burger. Letting him have this small victory is the least I can do to make up for a world that doesn't see him, either. And at least he can upgrade his cup.

Obviously I am not meant to get dinner tonight. Or anything I want.

For about a millisecond I think about not going home. Obvious reasons for this hesitation. One, what if Ben is there. Two, what if Ben isn't there.

But after wandering down Canal Street in the cold, I quickly decide there is no other option. Usually the walk up to the West Village only takes fifteen minutes, but tonight it takes twenty-five. If I fall again, I might not stand back up.

I need my pajamas and my bed and a dark room, in that order. There's a playlist lurking on my iPod from my senior year in high school that has all kinds of deep, dark emo music—maybe once I am curled in my cocoon that is what I will listen to. What was it the little old lady said? *Whatever it is you're looking for, you've got to find it in you.*

At the top of the six flights of stairs it takes to get to my apartment, I pause to catch my breath. ("Think of the money you'll save on a gym membership!" the real estate broker had practically sung.) I look haggard enough without laboring to get air into my lungs—in case Ben is there, I don't want to walk in the door wheezing, too. I make my best stab at composure and put my keys in the double locks, then push, then let out a deep sigh of relief: The coast, as they say, is clear.

Jesus, it's good to be home.

Well, is this really a home? It's more of a closet furnished by IKEA, but at least I'm alone, off the streets. Out of nowhere, I start imagining the home that the old woman from Mickey D's went back to . . . a retirement community? Nah, there was nothing dependent about her. Maybe my guess about her dress was right, and she is currently kicking back with a G&T somewhere on the Upper West Side. That's definitely the nicest possible ending to the fairy tale.

I go straight into my room and strip off my wet, sloppy clothes. Damned if the laundry basket isn't overflowing again. I wish I were better about laundry, but I'm not. I always act like I am going to do it on Saturday, then Saturday comes and I end up working all day and the dirty clothes never get cleaned . . . until I bite the bullet and drop them off at the dry cleaner's, shelling out fifteen bucks for eight quarters' worth of water and soap.

Somebody somewhere is putting money into a savings account. But not me. I can't even maximize my investment in a McDonald's hamburger.

All night I thought if I could just get home my life would feel better, but now I am here, lying in my cotton panties and non-matching fake-silk bra, on my bed, and I'm still so numb.

Have I lost my way like the old woman suggested? One thing she said *is* true. I am totally hopeless. There's no room for me in a world filled with Peytons and Bens and Little Kitties and Elliotts and Suits and apartments so small you can only throw a dinner party if you have one friend.

I turn the lights off and my iPod on, but not even Paramore is making the ennui bubble up into any sort of feeling.

That old woman is just still on my mind.

There's a light scratch on my window. It's louder than the music in my ears. I sit up straight. Sleep is useless. Even in the dark. I have to get out of my own head, get that old woman out of my head—she's like a cryptic fortune-teller that read my cards but is unable to tell me how to play the hand I was dealt.

You've got to find it in you.

There is the shoebox.

No, not the shoebox, my head says.

Yes, the shoebox, my little voice of intuition fights back.

No, yes, no, yes.

Jesus, it's exhausting being me.

I take the upper hand and give the middle finger to all further thought, crawling across my bed so I can reach into my closet and get the shoebox from the back.

One benefit of living in a miniature place is that you can do everything in your room from the comfort of your bed.

Wait. Is this me sounding optimistic? Guess deciding to do *something* is a step in the right direction.

Kellie is the only other person on the planet who knows about the shoebox. It carries no stilettos, oh no. This box has a higher calling, or at least I used to think it did. I stare at the top for a while and then open it up. Inside, I see all the familiar materials . . . and I see me and Kell. Kell and me. Cruising down the road together, same as we ever were.

We're in high school, young, maybe freshmen, but I picture myself without bangs and that was definitely a sophomore year mistake, so maybe my mind is playing tricks on me.

We're in her dad's car. Was it a Granada? Or a Crown Victoria? I don't think her dad ever knew we "borrowed" it. All I remember is that the car was so old it still had a tape deck. Kell and I would blast the one cassette from my mom's collection that we actually liked: Pat Benatar. Get Nervous. *We were cruising by the lake in our town just to see if we could spot my brothers' cars parked where all the older kids stop to drink beer, and sure enough, they were there. We wouldn't show our faces, no way. We just wanted to see what the cool kids were up to.*

Kell says, "I don't know if America is for me." And I kind of think she's joking, because, you know, who says that? America is for everyone, right? Is it a choice? This is where we are born and there are people who, like, swim across oceans to try to be a part of it.

I ask, "What does that even mean?"

She says, "It means I don't know if I am happy here. And I just think about France all the time."

And then she tells me about this movie she watched in French 101 about these nuns who live in a cluster—or a cloister, or maybe a clustered cloister—and how they spent all their time making these dolls . . . and that they all had such peace of mind.

This movie has convinced Kellie that the only way she'll get peace of mind is if she lives in the shadow of the effing Eiffel Tower making art. Though the nun thing is definitely not for her.

My mother has a saying that I decide to repeat to Kellie at this moment. In retrospect, most things my mom says usually piss people off. "You know what they say, Kells. No matter how far you run, wherever you go, you're still there."

This is where my memory stops, probably because after I told her that, Kellie made me get out of the car and walk home.

But it was like a month later, or two. My French teacher showed us the film Kellie was talking about. And all these nuns really were making wax dolls from nothing—with basic supplies and their own two hands. I was way into candle making at that age, but this was some next-level wax-sculpting skill. Of course theirs were figurines of people like Jesus and Mary—folks who could save your soul. But they looked so cool that I was inspired. So that night I got out a slab of beeswax left over from the candles I'd made my family that Christmas and formed my first doll mold out of clay. As I poured the melted wax into the hardened mold, I pictured how I would paint and dress her—a tiny wax replica of me, only better. Much better. Maybe she could be my guardian angel.

This act of sculpting and shaping was so soothing, it took me far away from everything that stressed me out. And it relaxed me in a totally different way than writing; when I was working with my dolls, I didn't need to search for the perfect words—everything was just pictures and feelings.

I haven't opened this box since I left for ad school in Atlanta. There was something about being around all those people who really considered themselves artists . . . This isn't art, it's just a hobby. It's just the way I lose myself.

I think about the old woman's gray ringlets. Her green tunic dress. The delicate wrinkles on top of the clear complexion.

The way her voice almost cracked when she said no one saw her anymore.

I hear the crack of the ice when I slapped down in the middle of Chinatown, in the middle of a heartbreak.

I don't have enough words to explain sadness. Or find happiness. Inside I am a blank page. And so I think it's time to get back to making dolls. Time to reshape my world with my own two hands.

"hello, std!"

Sunlight shoots through my bedroom window like a laser beam, simultaneously waking and blinding me. Must have forgotten to wear my sleep mask. Guess I'll never find out what happened between me and Rick Springfield at my senior prom on the moon. Which sucks, because we were just grinding on a zero gravity dance floor, and he was telling me that I was way cuter than Jessie's girl.

I reach for my phone and see that it's almost nine a.m., which is late for me. Why do I feel so tired? I peel myself off my Shabby Chic for Target duvet, a housewarming gift from my mom that I lied about liking. I'd had my eye on a Calvin Klein comforter I saw at Macy's. Not that she cared enough to ask.

Time to wake Ben, and get this dog and pony show rolling. I walk eight feet forward, transitioning from my coffin-sized bedroom to my bathroom-sized living room—don't even ask about the kitchen—calling out, "Hey, Wilder, you whipping us up an omelet?" Which is funny, because it's not like we have eggs, or much else in the way of adult groceries.

I look up and see Ben's Packers blanket still folded and draped neatly over the back of the couch, a telltale sign that he hasn't slept on it.

What? He never came home last night?

And that's when it all comes back to me like a flash flood carried in by a tsunami. The boys' club. Elliott's bug camera. Ben, wasted, throwing his head back in laughter. And Peyton, with her slutty black boots wrapped around his pelvis, leaning in for a kiss. My kiss.

That motherfucker slept at motherfucking Peyton's?

The thought blasts through me like the M-80s my brothers and their derelict friends lit and threw into all the sewers on our street one summer day, erupting in a series of amplified explosions. I pick up one of Ben's Converse Jack Purcells and hurl it at the apartment's lone prewar brick wall, a remnant from when apartments like mine were big but got divided up into servant's quarters. The sneaker makes a satisfying *thwack* on the bricks, so I pick up its mate and throw that, too. Next, I chuck one of his Chuck Taylors, then the other. Then, I grab both of his overpriced John Varvatos and launch them as hard as I can. *Thwack! Thwack!*

Having exhausted Ben's entire Converse collection, I move on to his ironic trucker hats. "Employee of the Month" *thumps* against the bricks. "My Other Hat Is a Chapeau." *Thump!* "Born to Fish" and "Cheesehead." *Thumpity! Thump!*

It's not as satisfying as the shoes, so I throw Ben's prized book of Charles Bukowski poems. It knocks over a rack of CDs, scattering classic rock discs and shattered plastic jewel cases everywhere. I let out a primal scream and burst back into last night's tears, collapsing on the couch. I'm shaking uncontrollably, so I wrap myself in Ben's blanket and cover my face with his pillow, breathing in his scent, a mix of Speed Stick, Axe aftershave, and Carmex. Peyton is probably *tasting* his lip balm right now. I feel like I've been punched in the stomach.

Something under my head starts buzzing. It's my phone, which I must have dropped on the couch in my hissy fit. Must be Kell! Wait till I tell her what that whorebitch did to me. I glance at the shattered screen—I forgot about that, too—and scan the on-screen notifications. I have a new ShoutOut. From Ben.

I open the video, and there he is, bloodshot and disheveled, but still sexy. He's talking to the camera. Talking to *me*.

"Hey, Kaykay. Crazy night last night. Crashed at the guys' apartme—"

He's interrupted by a guy in the background yelling, "*Wisconsin, you're a wild man!*" Was that Josh? John? Jay? No sign of Peyton . . .

Ben looks off camera. "Shut up, bro. I'm filming . . . Kay, do me a favor and bring one of my ball caps and a T-shirt to the office? I don't have time to stop home. Thanks."

And like that, the video is over. No mention of lap dances or Peyton's tongue. Not even an apology for standing me up on Little Kitty . . .

Oh. My. God. Little Kitty. I haven't written a single line.

We're supposed to show ideas to Elliott today! *Merde!* I spring into action, picking up all of Ben's sneakers and arranging them neatly by the door. I hang up all his hats except for "Employee of the Month," make up the couch he never slept on, and grab his My Chemical Romance T-shirt, the one he looks so hot in—charcoal gray, soft cotton, fitted to his shoulders—stuffing it and the good-luck-charm hat into my ratty old tote that doubles as a briefcase. No time to worry about the heap of mangled CDs.

It takes me exactly six minutes to pull together my "look," starting with a black oversized hoodie sweater. I have five more just like it, in shades from onyx to ebony to charcoal, with one in heather gray just to lighten things up. I retrieve yesterday's skinny jeans from the top of my laundry pile and examine them for any glaring stains. Nope. All good. I zip up my black Converse high-tops, spray some dry shampoo on my long, limp hair, wrap an elastic hairband around my wrist, and I'm off like a prom dress.

I'm not worried about being late. It's well understood in the creative department that you don't need to be in before ten. I could even push it to ten thirty without anyone looking for me. Elliott, our group creative director, likes to start his days at eleven, which he justifies because he always stays at the office so late. Usually, he's playing Xbox with the boys' club till midnight. But, who asked me?

I *am* worried about getting those headlines written. Actually terrified. If I drop the ball, Elliott will stick my self-confidence in the shredder, or worse. Little Kitty has this whole new direction they want to go in. If we can't get it right, they're threatening to leave, and you can guess who'll be out the first revolving door with them. The creative team Ben and I were hired to replace had only been at Schmidt Travino Drew for three months when they failed to come up with a campaign that was on strategy. Or more accurately, they failed to use the tagline Elliott had so generously "gift wrapped" for them. E-hole took one look at the work they had done, then told them it was time to go celebrate at the Hole. After three shots of Gran Patrón Platinum, he fired them *and* stuck them with the $270 bill.

I board the D train near Washington Square, navigating a sea of Mohawked punk rockers, tattooed artists, and Goth NYU students. It's not your typical commute for sure, a fact my parents have noted on more than one visit as I put them on an uptown train back to Penn Station.

"There's not one person here wearing a suit or carrying a briefcase, Kay," my mom said last time, eyeing up the artsy, not-ready-for-Wall-Street crowd. "How are you going to meet a nice, professional man, living in a neighborhood like this?"

As if I'd ever want some dull banker or stockbroker, or anybody who wears a tie. I only want deep, funny Ben . . . but now Peyton does, too, the whorebitch, so I'm going to end up all alone, fulfilling my mom's biggest prophecy. Usually, Ben and I make the trip to work together and he always gives me the empty seat. Sometimes if there isn't one, he'll announce, "Pregnant lady coming through," to guilt some young punk into surrendering his. But this is NYC, so that doesn't always work. Then, like today, I'm forced to stand.

Right now I'm sandwiched in between a strung-out junkie and a Spanish nanny pushing a towheaded kid in the latest Bugaboo. As the subway car starts and jolts, the nanny struggles to keep the stroller steady, unaware that she keeps rolling one of its large back wheels over my toes. The junkie is sweating profusely and mumbling something to me about the end of days. "Dark Angel," he whispers, "I can show you the way to redemption." Great. This is the type of guy I *can* get. Memo to self, Kay: *shower more.* Maybe *that's* the way to redemption.

Trying to ignore him, I fix my gaze straight ahead and pretend to study the subway map. Next to it is an ad for Jonathan Zizmor, the balding skin doctor whose rainbow-striped billboards bear the promise, "Be Acne Free with Dr. Z!" It's one of Ben's favorites. We love making fun of all the bad ads we always see on the train. And I love the way Ben leans down over me, one muscular arm hanging on to the handrail above, whispering in faux German, "Dokkter Z vill take ze zits and squeesh zem to zittle bits!"

It's the same bad accent he uses to imitate Peter Schmidt, our agency's head strategic planner and most erratic of the head honchos. Known behind his back as the crazy German, Schmidt is a short, skinny white dude who sings along to gangsta rap in his thick Bavarian dialect, unable to pronounce his *w*'s or the *th* sound. The whole effect is unintentionally comical, but not as funny as Ben's reenactment of it. "Vats za dilly yo, dogg? Fo shizzle mein nizzle!"

Cracks me up every time, and even now, in my misery, I laugh to myself. The junkie mistakes this for conversation and starts laughing, too. Thank God it's my stop, Grand Street. Chinatown. Though only a five-minute subway ride from my apartment, it's a far cry from the West Village, or, really, anywhere else.

I make my way up the subway stairs and enter an alternate universe where all the signs—even the ads—are written in Chinese symbols. Last night's snow has already melted, and the sidewalks are paved with eager street vendors peddling counterfeit handbags and watches in front of stores that dangle duck carcasses next to red paper lanterns. Arrows point up stairways that lead to second-floor offices offering acupuncture and Tui Na massages. It's the last place you'd expect to find one of the hottest ad agencies in town, and the partners and Elliott like it that way. Most of the city's advertising "boutiques"—shoptalk for agencies supposedly driven by creativity, not money—can be found nearby in Soho, and our biggest rival, famed British agency Blood Pudding, just opened its U.S. doors in Tribeca.

So of course, Schmidt Travino Drew & Partners had to one-up them all, to prove that we're not just edgy, *we're on* the *edge.*

"Chinatown is totally the next Williamsburg," Elliott explained to us in that feverish way of his. "In a couple of years, all the art galleries, hot restaurants, and cool clothing stores will relocate here."

Then I guess you'll have to move to Jersey, I wanted to say, pleased with myself for my sassy wit. But before I could give word to my thoughts, Ben beat me to the punch, affirming to Elliott that 190 Grand was indeed the best possible locale for the best agency in the world, and that coincidentally, I, Kay, was a sucker for Asian food. It was our second interview so we were still selling ourselves. Ben's been our charming spokesperson ever since.

At least the dining options around here *are* awesome. Dumplings and lo mein just steps away. But it's a good thing there is a bagel cart on our block, too. I can't do Chinese for breakfast, not that I even know what that would consist of.

I stop at that bagel cart now, beyond famished, and my stomach insists on the bacon, egg, and cheese. The Asian vendor asks, "You no wan one fo yo boyfren?" accustomed to seeing me here every morning with Ben. *My boyfriend? I wish.* I blink hard, handing him my money without looking at him, and walk away without saying a word. *No more crying in front of strangers, Kay. No more crying on the street.*

For the next half block, I give myself the pep talk Kellie would have if she were here and not in class an ocean away, five hours ahead, or maybe six. If ever I needed my best friend, it was now. She'd tell me it was only one kiss. *For God's sake, Kay, he crashed with the guys. Couldn't have been that hot for her if he didn't go home with her. And it's not like he even knows you're into him.*

I approach the front door to our office and take a deep breath, willing myself to put on my game face. My phone rings and I see it's my mom. An actual live voice from her is a rarity these days, so I answer it though I'd rather not, ducking into an alley to avoid potential coworkers.

"Oh good, Kay, you're there," she exhales, already mid-thought. "You never responded to my ShoutOut, text, or e-mail, and I was worried maybe you got abducted by one of the weirdos who hang out in your neighborhood. Do you know how many starving artists turn out to be serial killers?"

I start to say, "Mom, I'm fine," but she's already moved on to her agenda.

"Your father and I are coming into the city Friday night to take you kids out to dinner. Brett just got a promotion so we're celebrating! He's bringing that Simone girl—isn't she stunning?—and, of course Brian is bringing Naomi, those two are inseparable. Wedding bells any day now! Of course you can bring someone, too, if you're dating anyone. I hope you've found someone nice, though how you'll meet anyone in that crack den they call the West Village is beyond me . . . How are you doing?"

Promotion? Wedding bells? I'm going to lose it right here and now.

"I've been better . . ." I admit, my voice quavering, but now she's talking to someone in the background, probably her assistant Polly.

"Kay, my ten o'clock is here, have to fly. Great talking to you and I'll see you Friday! Polly will text you the details. Kiss kiss."

Okay. No sympathy from *her*. Mom's a one-woman dynamo, a high school dropout who went back to get her GED and college degree in record time as soon as I was out of diapers. Now she's a high-powered accountant on a trajectory to take over her slice of the world. There's no way she'd let some stupid boy derail her success. Or forgive me for doing the same. I have to get it together. Now.

Attitude adjusted, somewhat, I head back toward the office but am stopped by two guys wearing suits. One is tall, trim, well tailored, the other portly and red-faced in an ill-fitting three piece that's probably off the Men's Wearhouse rack. Executives. A rare sight on this block. They must be clients.

"Excuse me, Miss," Tailored Guy says with a slight Southern drawl. "We're trying to find 190 Grand? All the numbers seem to be in Chinese."

I wish Ben were here to witness this. Spotting confused clients is another one of our little joys. You see, there is no name on our office door, no number, no sign to clue you in to your whereabouts. Your only hint? The door is painted bright green. Elliott's idea, I was told, after much wine one night at French restaurant the Little Door in Los Angeles. He'd "done dinner" there with famed director Ridley Scott—you know, *Gladiator*, *Thelma & Louise*, *Blade Runner*, that guy—and the posh hideaway inspired him to conceal our agency's entry, too. If it hadn't been for the story about "Ridley," no way would he have copped to copying.

Our account people always tell the clients to look for the green door right between the noodle and tea shops. As if we work at some super-exclusive nightclub. Except the block is *littered* with noodle and tea shops, so if you're not in the know, you're shit out of luck. One time Ben and I were coming back from one of our midday Starbucks run/concepting sessions. (I know. Starbucks in Chinatown! There is a God. And he's quite possibly Asian.) As we approached the green door, we saw three frustrated executive types being accosted by a little Asian man trying to sell them "massage with happy ending." We didn't stop. Just kept walking right into our lobby, cracking up in hysterics.

A half hour later, those same men were seated in our conference room. Turns out, they were the Little Kitty clients, there to brief us on our first painful assignment. Karma has a wicked sense of humor.

The two high-powered men standing on the street now look positively impotent. I actually feel kind of bad for them.

"Schmidt Travino Drew?" I ask knowingly.

They nod and I tell them to follow me.

"Interesting neighborhood," Tailored Guy remarks as I hold the green door open for them. "Not at all like our Chinatown in Atlanta."

"Chinatown Mall?!" I blurt. "Best dim sum ever!"

"You know it?" He's surprised.

"I went to ad school there. I mean, not there, but in Atlanta, Portfolio Center, in Buckhead."

"So you're a creative?" he asks with interest.

"Yes, I'm a writer, well, actually a copywriter, but that makes us sound like patent attorneys or something, doesn't it? My uncle still can't understand how I got this job without going to law school. I tried to tell him that the word 'copy' is just advertising speak for the words used in magazine ads or TV commercials, and that I write those words, but he was all like, 'So, you copy other people's words? Like a legal transcriber?'"

Oh, Kay, you're rambling again.

Tailored Guy is staring at me, amused, as if he's listening to a precocious child. I have that effect on people.

"How long have you worked here?" he asks, but before I can answer, we're interrupted by Fred Travino, agency chairman and CEO, who I now realize has been standing in reception, witnessing this whole exchange with morbid curiosity. It's so unlike me not to sense his commanding presence.

"Richard! Tony!" he bellows, moving past me to shake their hands. "Glad to see you found us okay!"

"Your copywriter was nice enough to show us the way." Richard, the tailored one, gives me a friendly salute.

Travino acknowledges me with a smirk and a barely raised eyebrow, then leads the men back through the frosted glass doors to the executive offices, for whatever wheelings and dealings I can only imagine. Though he can be dismissive and gruff, everyone respects Fred Travino. Partly because he knows his shit when it comes to starting up creative boutiques—he's done it a few times over and made millions—and partly because he claims to have worked for the mob when he was growing up in Boston. There's this rumor that he once killed a guy, which he will shrug off but doesn't deny.

He's a hard man to watch, mostly because he only comes into the office for meetings with important clients and otherwise likes to work from his collection of penthouses and yachts, but when I am around him I listen to every word out of his mouth. He may be more indimidating than a Hell's Angel, but he's also smart as hell. And even though I only admit it to myself once in a blue moon—when I'm feeling really, really confident . . . or drunk—I wouldn't mind having his office someday.

Fueled by that thought and anxious to get going on Little Kitty, I make a beeline for the elevator, relieved not to see Veronique, the office receptionist. She's impossible to miss: always a bright red, blue, or green muumuu with a matching headscarf. She makes them herself from fabric her sister ships her from Trinidad. I swear she hates me. Always gives me the evil eye when I move through the lobby, like she knows I don't belong here and it's just a matter of time. She's probably fetching a catered three-course breakfast for Travino's big powwow. Must be an important meeting for her to leave the phones—and her sewing—unattended. She answers every call, "Hello, STD!" which Ben and I think is a riot. The partners, not so much. But whenever one of them starts to reprimand her for it, she stabs her sewing needle into this voodoo doll pincushion on her desk and gives them a bug-eyed look that sends them packing. I'd kill for one-tenth of her confidence.

Things seem quiet on my floor as I step off the elevator and head toward the creative cubicles. But then I hear Gina Bouffa, our department's intern—more accurately, I hear her designer boots click-clacking down the cold, hard floor. "Hey, Kay! Morning!" Her New York accent is as thick as her Chanel No. 5.

I brace for conversation, but something distracts her. "E! Hey! Love your shirt! Is that Jil Sander spring collection?"

I drop my breakfast down on my desk and catch sight of the

egg grease slowly seeping through the thin white paper bag. My stomach growls. The last person I want to see is Elliott, who heads my way right this second. He looks impressively alert considering how many empty shot glasses I saw in front of his seat last night. He pauses at my cube, peers into the baggie that is my only hope for joy that morning, and reads the sticker slapped on its contents. I twist my lips into what hopefully passes for a smile.

"Hi, Elliott."

"*Bacon?* Special K, don't you know that stuff will turn you into a porker? That why you're rockin' the whole baggy hoodie look, covering up the junior fifteen?"

E-hole. Like he has to remind me I'm only a junior copywriter. And that's not even a real thing, like the freshman fifteen was for some girls in college. I am so not in the mood today for the teasing he sells as uber-cool hipster wit.

"I haven't had a bagel . . ." He looks at the ceiling and pretends to think, but I know his games. The man never really thinks, he instructs others to think for him and then regurgitates. "You know, I think the last time I had a bagel was back when flannel shirts were in style."

I look down. I am 99.9 percent sure that I did not grab a flannel shirt this morning, but I got dressed so quickly and there were all those tears. When I confirm I am wearing wool—a *far* cry from flannel—I want more than anything to tell him, no, to scream at him, that I've eaten over two thousand bagels in that time, and still can't gain weight, but I know in his twisted brain he would take that as bragging. Instead, my speech delay rears its nasty head. I've got everything clever to say but by the time I work up the nerve to actually say it, of course, nothing comes out.

I must have winced ever so slightly, because Elliott is eyeing me up and down like a predator sensing wounded prey. Damn. I never want him to see me sweat but today I just do not have the energy for the pretense.

Now he turns on his trademark flip-it-and-reverse-it, and retreats with a post-jab compliment that's supposed to make it all okay.

"You know I'm just messing with you." He flashes his white-washed smile. "Everybody knows you're my favorite writer. By the way, how are those Little Kitty lines coming? I want you and Ben in my office at noon. And that shit had better rock . . . or heads are gonna roll."

I mean, seriously. Who talks like that? The man eats nothing but granola and kale (except when he's trying to prove his epicurean superiority at whatever restaurant Zagat just gave five stars to) and still he has the stomach to spew this b.s.

I swear he has a personality disorder, like Schizophrenic Napoleon Syndrome or something. But part of me doesn't hate him, probably because he hired me. Me. Of all people. Here, at Schmidt Travino Drew. Everyone here is so goddamn *talented*.

I still remember the interview. It was one-on-one. He'd seen my portfolio, sent by a recruiter, and liked it enough to actually meet me. He introduced himself without standing. "I'm Elliott but the guys call me E."

I willed strength to my hand as I shook his, mumbling, "I'm Kay."

"That's cool. Like short for Kayla? Or Kayte? Or Karina?"

"Nope. It's just Kay."

"Right. Even cooler," he said.

Elliott loved my writing. I'm the one who got Ben in the

door here. Not that you'd know it. Ben's so lovable and always does one hell of a job selling our work. I'm happy he's doing well. Though it would be nice if occasionally he realized why.

My egg bagelwich is starting to cool, yet I have to turn on my MacBook and find genius. And still no sign of Ben. Not that I want to see him. No, I definitely don't want to see him. But I do need him to work.

And where the hell do Johnjayjosh live? In Connecticut?

I need caffeine. And a miracle. I spring over to the coffee machine, resolving to focus on the daunting task at hand when— *bam!* I walk headfirst into the queen slut herself. Peyton. Also amazingly pulled together, of course. She's sporting a designer outfit, snakeskin boots, and that glossy black hair that makes it seem like she has a live-in stylist. What the what? How can these people party all Tuesday night and look so fresh-faced come Wednesday morning? This behavior can only be performed by professionals. Yet another reminder of what an amateur I am.

Peyton gives me her signature hair flip. "Hey. How's it goin'?"

I murmur hello, knocking over the rack of K-Cups. She doesn't have any hickies, at least none I can see.

"Hear about the big pitch?" she continues.

I nod like an idiot, trying to act like I know, but, as usual, I have no idea what she's talking about. Sometimes it seems like Peyton's main purpose in life is to make people like me acutely aware that there is some private club to which we don't belong.

It takes all my focus not to spill the milk or my packet of sugar as I fix my coffee, but I doubt Peyton notices the weird vibes I'm sending her way. Now that I think about it, I doubt she's ever noticed me at all.

I race to think up a snide remark that will change that. Should I mention the video, ask if Ben gave her any dollar bills? Before I settle on anything, Bouffa click-clacks over and starts chatting Peyton up about her Marc Jacobs sweater. I take the opportunity to escape without saying a word and make it back to the safety of my desk.

Time to examine my notes for Little Kitty. It's not good. Not good at all. I start tapping my keyboard:

Feed Your Kitty the Furry Best.

Mmm Mmm! Feline Good!

Thank You Purr Dinner!

Enough with the puns, Kay. You can do better.

But this new strategy is all wrong. Little Kitty can brag about their "big taste" all they want, but unless we get cat owners to pour themselves a bowl and start chowing, why the heck would they believe it? I don't even believe it. I've smelled the stuff, and it reminds me of one of Elliott's nasty kale health shakes. *Bleck.*

A thought pops in my head, and suddenly I'm excited. I start typing like mad. It's a totally different direction, sure, but at least it's honest. And, if I craft it right, it will have an emotional benefit those cat owners will eat up. Though probably not literally. Because, still, nasty.

I'm going to turn this day around, save our butts, and be the superwoman Ben needs but doesn't know he wants! Yes! We won't be the junior team for long. Next stop, associate creative directors, then look out, Elliott. I'm coming for *your* job! When it's all over, Ben's going to want to kiss *me* full on the lips.

I reach for my bagel and start devouring it with one hand, typing with the other. I love it when I'm in this flow state, when the words spring from my fingertips like rays of sunshine from God above. Wait till Elliott hears my idea. Kell is always telling me to make things happen. I'm totally going to present this and wow the hell out of him and Travino. No more hiding behind Ben's effervescence.

"*Here, Shitty Kitty! Here, Shitty Kitty.*"

Shit. What's with the interruption?

I look up from my screen and see Jayjoshjohn collapsing into their cubes, looking far worse than their fearless leader. Still, they have the energy to tease me. Bringing up the rear is Ben. He dumps his gym bag on the shared table that divides our desks and mutters, "Heykay."

"You look like something the cat dragged in," I start. "And speaking of, thanks for leaving me hanging on Little Kitty."

"Ughhh . . . pussy food," Ben groans, sounding just like one of *them.*

He slowly reaches for the hat and T-shirt I brought him and eyes my half-eaten breakfast sandwich.

"Wanna bite?" I push it toward him. A peace offering.

Smelling the eggs, he moans, "I think I'm gonna hurl." Then he's up, running for the bathroom.

My desk is too far away to hear his actual retching, but I do hear Peyton shriek, "Ewwww!"

If I could find one silver lining in this messed-up morning, that would be it.

fake it to make it

Elliott is reading us the riot act. "I gave you *three* days to work on this. That's, like, an eternity. Coppola could've shot the *The Godfather* in less time."

Ben and I are slumped in his two Eames chairs, normally more comfortable than they are at this moment. It's just past noon, and we've been called in here for our "Showcase Showdown" on Little Kitty. Clearly, we won't be winning any cash prizes or a new car. We'll be lucky to score a one-way ticket back to ad school.

We're doing our best to talk up what little work we have. "Fake it to make it and act as if," Kell always says. Probably how she morphed overnight into a Frenchwoman.

Ben tries to rally with some semblance of his usual razzle-dazzle. He starts in on his amazing ideas for the layout: beauty shots of cats in high-contrast black and white. But Elliott's bullshit meter is finely tuned, and without actual visuals to see, he's not buying our smoke and mirrors. He asks if that's all we've got, and I read my punny headlines, which only makes the whole thing worse.

In ad school they teach you that internal creative reviews are checkpoints, when you align with your creative director about the direction you're going. But Elliott's idea of aligning is making sure you are heading in *his* direction. I should go back to ad school and teach a class in reading people's minds; that's what you need to get ahead at Schmidt Travino Drew. If mind reading fails, ass kissing is the second-best option.

I'm starting to sweat and feel nauseous, even though the last thing that can happen is for me to get sick, too. The whole office knows about Ben's exorcist episode in the men's room that morning. If they didn't hear him actually heaving, then for sure they heard Bouffa retelling how "*ew gross*" it was five hundred times in the breakroom. I don't know how that girl has so much time to hang out in there. God knows she's not actually eating or preparing food; all I've ever seen her leave with is a Diet Coke. That and anything designed by Marc Jacobs are her two favorite accessories.

For a split second, I actually think about sharing my new direction with Elliott, hoping I can save this train wreck. But before I can work up the nerve, Elliott launches into his scary, "I'm so disappointed in you" routine. It's the same tone my mom has used on me hundreds of times before, and it's so awful it always shuts me down.

"There are tons of fresh-faced ad school kids who would kill for what I can teach you," Elliott warns. "If you can't hack the work hard/play hard attitude needed to make it here at STD, I'll find a team that can." Then he turns his venom squarely on Ben. "What kind of little girl can't take a couple tequila shots and still pull his shit together enough to get some kitty chow ads done?"

Halfway through his soliloquy the door opens. I look up and it's more bad news. Suit is standing there, wearing his non-client-day uniform: perfectly fitting slim dress pants and a pressed button-down in an eye-catching print that's just edgy enough to suggest, *I may be a Suit, but I'm NOT an accountant.*

"How's the work?" he asks. Maybe Elliott actually likes him, because he doesn't even freak that Suit cut him off mid-tirade.

"What work?" Elliott levels his gaze on Ben until Ben starts squirming and shoots it over to me quickly. I'm already squirming, and can't look him in the eyes.

"I talked to the client. Instead of reviewing work in a meeting tomorrow, I'm going to take him to a relaxing lunch. So you guys have an extra twenty-four hours," Suit tells us.

Is he serious? It's the best news we could possibly get. I look up from my lap to make sure he's not joking and see Suit staring right at me. All my joy falls away. Suit knows how late I stayed last night. Surely he can put two and two together and realize me working late plus Elliott thinking our work sucks means I don't have what it takes.

"Looks like it's your lucky day. Now get out of my sight and go figure out how to reskin this cat." Elliott looks down at his phone, scrolling through texts like we're already gone. "I want you back in my office tomorrow morning with work that will make this client do cartwheels."

"Even though the client is seventy," Suit says with a totally straight face.

I can't help myself, I laugh out my nose loud enough that it breaks through Ben's hangover and he gives me a look that says, *Shut up, we're almost out of hot water.*

"Do I have to tell you twice to get out of my sight?" Elliott demands.

He doesn't. Ben and I practically run out of his office. Suit will probably tell Elliott how I put in long hours coming up with the crappy work we just showed him, but it won't matter. Ben and I have twenty-four hours to come up with new Little Kitty lines and I'm going to get 'er done. All I need now are cashews, some help from Ben, and possibly the emotional boost of seeing Peyton fall off her four-inch heels onto her face in the middle of the office. Ben collapses into the chairs in our cube. I skip taking a seat and lean up against the wall. I'm actually feeling okay until Ben throws his head back and closes his eyes like he could fall asleep right then and there.

"I'm surprised that's the best you had," he finally says. "Usually you've got a hundred lines that are doable, but that pig was hard for me to lipstick. Didn't you stay here and work last night?"

I lean forward to get a better look. Is this really Ben? The same Ben I've always known? It can't be. That Ben knows a team is made up of two people. Not one person pulling the weight while the other person does an oral exploration of Ms. Manhattan herself.

"Are you serious?" It's the only thing I can think to say that's short, to the point, and won't show my voice cracking in tandem with my heart *for the second time in two days*. Who is this guy kidding? Am I kidding myself to expect something more from him?

Ben must realize he's over the line, or maybe he does hear something in my voice, because he opens his eyes to look at me.

"I didn't mean to hurt your feelings. I just, well, I know you hate getting reamed by Elliott more than anyone."

This is true, but it doesn't really make me feel better.

But then Ben closes his eyes again and groans. "Jesus, I wish I'd never gone out."

And this does make me feel better. Could Ben be regretting all of it? Not just the tequila, but Peyton, too?

I hold my breath, hoping Ben will keep talking. Which after a few seconds, he does.

"I'm definitely not ever doing that again."

Hope! There is hope! And if there's hope for me and Ben, then there's hope for Little Kitty.

I practically leap into my seat and then I roll the chair up to Ben's side.

"Here's our plan . . ." I begin. I can feel some color coming back into my cheeks. With a little effort maybe we can re-create the old working sessions we had in Atlanta. Just me and Ben and food and our brains and talking into the wee hours of the night.

"Let's tell everyone we're going to the store to look at cat food and do competitive research. And that after that we're going to work at a coffee shop." I speak in a low voice, so only he hears. "If we're going to knock this Little Kitty thing out of the park, we need to get out of here."

Ben usually likes to stick around the office to work because he thinks face time is important. Not the FaceTime on cell phones. The old-fashioned kind, where people see your face and believe you are a hard worker. I, on the other hand, think people will care a lot more about seeing this Little Kitty work done than seeing Ben's still-greenish face around the office today.

I want to create something that will blow people's minds. And surely I did enough staring at a blank page, listening to the dank old heater last night. Not to mention that if I happen to run into Peyton again, I might use what's left of my creative energy thinking of ways to wring her bony neck.

"C'mon, c'mon," I whisper to Ben. Freedom is so close. All I want to do is get him out of this building so it can be just us again. Maybe he can explain away everything that I saw on ShoutOut, even though really he wouldn't have to—if I could just feel our friendship again, the way it lights me on fire, I would know there was still a chance.

Ben takes a long look at me and I do my best not to melt under those emerald orbs. It's easy to ignore the slight smell of puke lingering in our shared cubicle with a deep gaze like that.

Finally he speaks. "Okay." Or maybe he says, "Oh, Kay." It's a downfall of my name; I can never tell those two comments apart. But it doesn't matter because he's already throwing a notebook and some pens in his cross-body bag, so I know we are on the move.

I pack up quicker than I ever have before and don't even give him a minute to rethink his answer—I'm heading for the reception area in the blink of an eye.

The last thing I hear as Ben follows me onto the elevator is Veronique answering the phone, "Hello, STD?"

We manage to hold in our laughter until the doors close, and then we both explode. I know it's not quite as funny as it feels, but all my stress from last night and this morning has to go somewhere. I laugh all the way down to the ground floor and when the doors open again, I have to wipe tears out of my eyes.

"I'm glad we're doing this." Ben's load seems lighter as we walk out the front door of the agency, all of Manhattan in front of us.

I don't even have to search for the perfect response, which means things really are getting back to normal. "Tell me about it," I say.

In the end Ben does tell me about it. About last night, at least. I guess it was a stupid dare by stupid Elliott for Peyton to give him a shot and then a deep-throated kiss. He doesn't even remember it . . . or much of anything else, for that matter. Jayjohnjosh had to fill in the blanks, with a little help from ShoutOut, of course.

A little voice inside me asks, *Is this how it feels to ask a man why he keeps getting random text messages at three in the morning and have him say—"whatchu talking about, babe?"*

But I shake off that worry and decide to take Kell's advice. All day I just *act as if* things with me and Ben are exactly as they should be. I put Peyton out of my mind. I offer him hand sanitizer from my purse, just in case the germs from any of those dollar bills he stuffed in strippers' skirts are still lingering there.

And in return I am rewarded with the following bits of perfection:

1. When we are walking by the Victoria's Secret window in Soho, he sees me look at the mannequins and comments, "You've totally got the body for that stuff, Kay."

2. When I offer him the chance to go home and take a shower, he says he'd rather cruise around town with me first, that this is the most fun he's had in weeks.

3. On the subway heading to Central Park he looks at a little girl standing on the train and then looks at me and smiles. I just know Ben would be such an awesome dad.

4. When we step out of the train at 57th Street, I admit to him that lately I've been wondering, just a little, what might have happened if we'd taken a job at a smaller shop, in a smaller city . . . one of the Minneapolis agencies, maybe. He says, "I think about that, too, Kay, but we're here and we're in this together." I think I might *fly* to Sheep Meadow, Central Park's largest lawn, I feel so light and fluffy and happy.

5. Last, but certainly not least, when we are finally at our destination—the only two souls on this huge, snow-covered field—I suggest we start talking about Little Kitty, and he shakes his head. "Let's leave work out of this for just a little longer. It's nice not feeling like those people are crawling on our backs." Then, with the skyscrapers all around us, we make snow angels! I send Kell a text that says, *Full recovery, life is good—never been better—don't ever worry about me again. XO.*

When we decide it's time to head home because all the Suits are getting out of their offices and we know the city is gearing up for rush hour, Ben offers to carry my laptop bag for me. I tell him "no thanks" because I don't want to seem needy—I know he likes strong women. When we are back on the train heading to my apartment, I do want to take his hand in mine, but *that* would be too forward. For once I don't notice all the perfect people bundled up around us. I'm not worried about being the girl who's left out, because it seems I will always belong when Ben is by my side. Now all we have to do is hole ourselves up back at my place and get our mad advertising skills on, which I am pretty certain I could do with my eyes closed now that I'm feeling so good. Of course this is when I notice Ben actually does have his eyes closed on the train . . . Uh-oh, hope he gets his catnap in now because we definitely have a long night ahead of us.

"We've been robbed!" Ben yells after opening the apartment door. He's motioning toward the mess of CDs all over the floor that I never did pick up. His CDs. Oops. Need to cover my tracks.

"I did that," I quickly tell him. "A mouse ran by and I freaked out and threw a book at it, but missed."

Perfectly plausible, right? I hate to lie—though the book part *is true*—but I'd rather die than admit what truly went down. Maybe someday when we're a for-real couple and can laugh about how we got there. But not now. I'm trying to forget last night happened.

"Sorry I didn't clean it up," I continue. "But I woke up late and was all stressed about presenting to Elliott."

A look of guilt comes over his face. And then, the mother lode.

"No, *I'm* sorry. I should have never bailed on you last night, but I swear I didn't plan to. It's just that F.-hole started ragging on me about not coming out with the boys for drinks, and he was doing his Jedi mind tricks, acting like he was really offended. And I just can't afford to be on Elliott's 'out' list, you know? I'm not like you, Kay. You're so naturally talented, and everyone expects you to knock it out of the park every time. But me, I'm just your obedient wrist, making pretty pictures from your words using Photoshop. Totally expendable. If I'm not careful, I'll end up back in Wisconsin, bartending and living with my parents, another failure. I figured if I went along with Elliott's crew, it would help me get on his good side . . . you know . . . so he'd want to keep me around."

I drop down on the couch, blown away. Ben always seems so self-assured. I didn't realize he, too, has been struggling to belong. Now I feel guilty. Obviously, I wasn't even considering *his* feelings last night.

"Ben Wilder, you are not expendable!" I'm looking straight at him, willing him to feel what I feel. "You have amazing designs and such original ideas. Any agency would be psyched to have you, even if we weren't partners."

He gives me one of his gooey smiles and says, "I'm glad we are," punching me in the shoulder. It's sort of, kind of, almost a Hallmark moment, maybe the third one today. Then he hands me a stack of takeout menus and tells me to pick out whatever I want—he's buying—and he picks up all the scattered CDs and cases for me, cleaning up every last bit of broken plastic.

After Ben orders our dinner, he's says he's going to grab a quick shower so we can start working. The thought of him, all freshly scrubbed, sitting next to me on the couch all night, gives me a little thrill.

I'm brought back to reality by Ben's phone, which he waves in front of me.

"We have a new ShoutOut from Elliott at the office. The title is 'Pussy Genius.'"

I roll my eyes and Ben gives me a knowing look. Whatever Elliott wants, it can't be good. But we can't ignore him. Ben plays the video and there's E-hole in his video rocker, flanked by Johnjoshjay, in the middle of a round of *Call of Duty*. This irony is not lost on me.

"Yo, I got it," he's saying into the camera. "The winning line: 'This kitty don't cuddle.' Client's gonna love it, right, guys?" John and Josh sit there frozen, then Elliott repeats the line again: 'This kitty don't cuddle.' Now they nod and Jay tells E it's great. "Special K," he continues, "write some rad body copy about how the coolest cats go crazy for Little Kitty. Wildman, I want you to art direct the hell out of it. Like that skateboarding book I showed you the other day. Maybe a graffiti font and a cool posterized effect. This is gonna save your asses. You're welcome."

Video over. Game over. Just what in hell cool cats have to do with Little Kitty's strategy of great-tasting cat food is beyond me. And, um, don't people want cats that DO cuddle? Isn't that the whole point of a pet? Oh well. Elliott's marching orders are pretty clear, so now all Ben and I have to do is take his idea and blow it out into a campaign. Not much real thinking involved, but it does mean we won't have to work into the night searching for greatness. Maybe Ben and I can even rent a movie . . . He's so eager to make amends, I bet he'll let me pick out a rom com, instead of one of those old Bruce Lee flicks he favors.

He's finally in the shower now, probably a cold one since he's all boiled up about what just went down with our deluded creative director. His phone pings again, signaling another Shout-Out, so I grab it, assuming Elliott's got more wisdom to impart. I click play immediately, and immediately see I was wrong.

It's Peyton.

OMFG, why is she videoing him?

"Hey, Wildman." She's in the breakroom. Is that Bouffa behind her? "Just wanted so see how you're feeling, you poor thing. Last night was so fun, wasn't it? Just wish you weren't in such a bad way. ShoutMe later, Kay?!"

I'm so startled she just said my name, or I thought she did, that I accidentally delete the video.

Fuck. Because I'm not sneaky like that. Like some manipulative chick in a Lifetime movie. And double fuck, because, why is she checking up on him if last night was just some stupid dare? And, in front of Bouffa? Peyton is so brazen, not even trying to hide the fact that she's after him. Must be marking her territory, letting us other agency girls know he's off-limits.

I'm glad I never confided my feelings for Ben to Bouffa, because I have no idea where her loyalty lies. While Peyton's made it pretty clear she has no use for girlfriends, that hasn't stopped Bouffa from shadowing her, trying to infiltrate her designer world. In all fairness, Bouffa has been very nice to me, too, which is more than I can say for some of the other creatives. It's probably because I'm the only other female copywriter, and we girls should stick together if we want to take on the boys' club. Also, I think there's a part of her that looks up to me—just a little—because I launched my career the legitimate way, *by earning it.*

Gina Bouffa started out at STD as an intern—her wealthy dad once worked with Travino (likely in some mafioso capacity), and that's how she got in the door. No portfolio, no ad school, and not much of a real clue about advertising, from what I've seen. But she does dress the part, from her tongue ring and tattooed wrist bracelet down to her edgy outfits from

Barneys. A month ago, she was moved up to junior copywriter in an effort to "chick up the place" for clients, but we all forget and still treat her like an intern. Kudos to her for not really caring. I guess coming from money is its own brand of confidence.

I pick up my phone to text her. Maybe if I say Ben is feeling much better and that *we've gone home together* to work, she'll mention it to Peyton. That's definitely what I'd do if I were the manipulative Lifetime movie type. Then maybe Peyton would back off. But who am I kidding? Peyton doesn't think I'm a threat.

Ben emerges from the shower, hair tousled and glistening, and immediately cracks open a beer. "Need a little hair of the dog if I'm gonna make Elliott's shit shine." He grins. I put my phone down before sinking to yet another low. It pings at exactly the same time as Ben's, reminding me of what I just stooped to seconds before. As he reaches for it, I cringe, but he tells me Travino just sent an urgent ShoutOut to the entire office. Now what? Ben hits play and there is Travino in his cavernous, practically empty corner office, smirking like he just swallowed a canary.

"Team! I have news. Please be in the main conference room at nine a.m. tomorrow morning for an emergency staff meeting. And, Elliott, that means you, too. Nine a.m. Sharp."

Now what?

I have not been in the office this early since the first week I worked here. Veronique has actually ordered in carafes of coffee and a platter of bagels and fruit, which Ben is unabashedly raiding, though no one else dares. I scan the conference room, but there is not a client in sight, so the spread must really be for us lackeys. Is it someone's birthday? Maybe Travino is going to announce he just sold the agency to a European holding company for mad cash, and now we can kiss our dreams of doing great work good-bye. I guess floral-scented laundry detergent really could be in my future.

Suit comes over and offers me a cup of coffee, then asks how I'm doing.

I see right through his good-cop act. "Don't you really mean, *How is Little Kitty doing?*"

He makes a cat hissing sound and puts on a wounded face. "I was just trying to be nice."

He's wearing an actual suit and tie over one of his natty button-downs, and it reminds me that he is taking the Little Kitty execs to lunch today. Taking one for the team. Now I feel bad. He did help us out in a big way yesterday.

"Thanks for buying us time with the client. That was really nice of you."

He leans in close, lowering his voice. "I saw you leaving the agency looking rather upset the other night, and I guessed maybe things weren't going to turn out as well as you'd hoped."

I'm blindsided by his admission, and my cheeks are turning redder than Bouffa's MAC lipstick—which, by the way, is seriously bright for an early morning agency meeting.

He saw me? Crying on the street? Does he think I was crying about Little Kitty, or does he know I was crying over Ben?

He must have seen the lip lock on ShoutOut, too, since he was the one who told me about it. My brain is in full-on panic mode as he awaits some sort of response, the way normal humans communicate, back and forth in a timely manner. But before I can speak, a flurry of laughter erupts into the room. It's Peyton and Elliott flanked by Johnjoshjay. They're all carrying cups of Starbucks, acting like they just left some better party to stop by this lame one. Veronique gives them her evil eye, eliciting Elliott to flash her his award-winning smile.

"Office coffee! Thanks, Veronique. If I'd known, I would have waited!" I know he's laughing inside, but he doesn't dare do that out loud, not to her. To further appease her, he helps himself to a bagel—which, according to him, would be his first one since flannel shirts were in style. Then his boys do the same.

Peyton smiles without an ounce of apparent irony, either. "Hey, Veronique, love the new muumuu. I just saw one like that at Bergdorf's, but it was, like, a bikini cover-up." Then she takes exactly one grape.

Veronique nods her head, muttering something in her Trinidadian accent that sounds to me like "skinny white girls." As if on cue, Bouffa comes bouncing over. "Hey, Peyt! Veronique! Any idea what this powwow's all about?!"

Peyton and Veronique exchange a look that says they both know, but they're not talking. How weird. Did our agency producer and our receptionist just share a moment? Couldn't be. No way would Peyton deign to commune with the help.

By now, Ben has come over to give me a sesame bagel fixed just the way I like it, thick smear of cream cheese with a tomato topper, and any further delvings into what Suit may or may not know can thankfully be tabled. Schmidt arrives at 9:12, a reminder that promptness isn't necessary if you're a major shareholder, greeting Elliott and the boys with fist bumps and his usual, low-talking "Vat's up, dogg?" He's wearing ridiculously baggy William Rast jeans, a flat-bill ball cap that reads "Compton"—even though we all know he's from Munich—and a bright white T-shirt with holes in it.

"Two hundge," Ben whispers, pricing Schmidt's tee, another fun office pastime.

"Nah-uh," I shoot back. "Three hundred. Holes so perfectly imperfect do not come cheap."

Suit settles the debate: "$428. John Varvatos. Saw it in the window of the store on Spring Street. It also comes in black and gray."

Of course Suit shops in Soho. Probably with Leatherette Girl. I bet he holds her Prada purse while they pop into boutiques so she can try on the latest fashions.

There's no sign of Travino, but Schmidt walks to the head of the conference table to get things under way. "Holla! I know many of you peeps are wondering vat's za dilly yo, *und* so I'm going to let Travino tell you."

Our IT guy fiddles with a speaker on the table, and suddenly Travino appears, larger than life, on the conference room's huge video screen. He's on his yacht. Sitting out on deck having breakfast. His personal chef is setting out silverware.

Ben nudges me. "Someday, Kay. Whatever it takes."

Travino's voice booms through the conference room and we all sit up a little straighter. This is in pointed contrast to the palpable awkwardness that's evident whenever Schmidt walks into a room and suddenly everyone is eager to study their shoes.

"Greetings, friends!" Travino radiates the American dream— self-made millions, eternal optimism, and servants. I want whatever he's having—and it looks like a Bloody Mary with a side of poached eggs.

"Today is the dawn of a new day for everyone at Schmidt Travino Drew. We've already proven we have what it takes to do the kind of memorable, controversial work that makes people stop and listen. As Agency of the Year, we are the shop to watch, and to beat. Now it is time to really put ourselves on the map and show the world we are not just some flash in the pan, another edgy boutique that's hot today and gone tomorrow. We are in it for the long haul, and as a measure of what true contenders we are, we have made it to the short list for the pitch every agency would kill to win: Kola, the number-two-selling soft drink on earth!"

Everyone cheers and applauds. Kola is the big leagues. Celebrities, Super Bowl ads, and sexy TV shoots. The stuff I dreamt of in ad school.

Travino motions for quiet so he can continue. "Glad to hear you are as excited as I am. We are competing against two formidable foes, Blood Pudding and GGD Meadham, but we are better, smarter, and hungrier. Kola is a multimillion-dollar account. For us, such a high-profile win would mean huge growth, job security, and respect. Other brands will want to abandon their agencies to come work with the geniuses who rebrand Kola. We have two months to dig deep, band together, and create work that will knock the soft drink giant's carbonated socks off. Everyone here will play a part. You're the best of the best, and we can win this."

Travino goes on. "It won't be easy. The hours will be long and the fight will be bloody, but on the day of the pitch, we will prevail."

Then he looks right at the camera with a dead-serious expression. "We'd better prevail."

I know it's impossible, because he's on a video screen, but I feel like Travino is staring right at me.

Suddenly, from the back of the room, someone declares in a voice full of bravado, "There's no 'I' in team, *team!*"

Instantly we all swivel to see who would dare mock the big man, and I should have guessed—it's Todd, graphic designer extraordinaire. He may not belong to the boys' club, but he's the one guy who's been the consistent at every agency Travino has built (and then sold for big bucks).

Of course none of us is as established—or indispensable—as Todd, so we can't laugh. But that doesn't bother the guy a bit. He just cruises to the fruit tray, and as he pops a pineapple cube in his mouth, he gives his audience a big smile.

I wonder how many pitches he's done in his life. A hundred? A thousand? To him a new pitch is probably as newsworthy as . . . well . . . another junior copywriter like me getting hired. Biggest news of my life, but to him, a dime a dozen. The guy amazes me.

Schmidt ignores the outburst, mumbling under his breath in German—this seems to be his standard reaction to Todd—and wraps the meeting. Through his butchered hip-hop speak I piece together that for the next week or two he, Suit, and the rest of the account planners will be working on a strategy for Kola, then "vill be a briefing at ze creatives. Zen Achtung Bee-yatch!" Which we've all come to learn means: *Then it will be "go time."*

When Schmidt gets done speaking, the whole room is silent. I hold my breath. Large group silences are so awkward.

But of course, Elliott shines. "We're gonna kick ass!" he shouts, with real eye-of-the-tiger gusto.

And then every person in the room loses their too-cool-for-school attitude and starts to cheer. For a moment, we all get to be excited just for the sheer possibility of greatness to come.

Next to me, Ben is clapping. Joshjohnjay lets out a growl. Bouffa lifts up her Diet Coke can to salute the moment, and Schmidt reaches across the oak board-room table. "Shorty, zat is kaput." He takes it from her and drops it in the trash.

Everyone laughs and Bouffa looks confused for a split second, but then turns on her Upper West Side smile and joins in on the laughter. "Uh, thanks!" she says. Now we all laugh louder.

I'm giggling so hard I barely even notice when Peyton and I make eye contact. If I weren't so sure she and I were secret enemies, I would think she just gave me an extra-large grin.

"Time to get back to work!" Veronique hoists herself out of her chair. "Those phones aren't going to answer themselves."

No one argues with Veronique. No one *ever* argues with her. Who knows if she really has her thumbs in some crazy island religion, but the rumors are enough to keep even the big dogs on her good side. Maybe I should add a voodoo doll or some other spooky talisman on *my* desk. I could make one out of wax.

Just thinking about the doll takes me back to cloud nine. Yesterday was hands down the best day I've had since I moved to New York. Partly because of the day spent with Ben, but partly because for the first time in years, I got to work on one of my dolls again. I thought it might take me a while to get back in the swing of things. But once I got done perfecting our Little Kitty work, I had my supplies dumped out of the shoebox and all over the floor. Within minutes I was pouring melted beeswax into the same mold I always used in the old days, and I was having so much damn fun I totally forgot my slight irritation that Ben had passed out before he got to help much with the real work.

I decided to do a Manhattan version of me. Which is sort of like every other version of me, except more tired and slightly stressed. Tonight, if there's time, I'll finish the painting details. Fingers crossed there will be time.

Elliott's voice snaps me out of my reverie. "You two, in my office in five."

I look up and see he is pointing at me and Ben.

"Ooh," Suit teases from the other side of the room. He has been sitting on a windowsill but jumps down. "Sounds like somebody's getting called into the principal's office."

I definitely feel like we're getting called to the principal's office, but it would be great if Suit didn't feel he needed to point that out to everyone else in the agency. As all the people slowly filter out of the room, Todd turns back around to smirk at us, humming a funeral hymn.

"We've got your cat problems solved, man," Ben tells Suit. He raises his hands in a cool, relaxed gesture. The opposite of how I feel, but that's why he's the spokesperson for our team. And, of course, Ben hasn't even seen the work I thought up to go with Elliott's stupid tagline. I guess I'll be presenting it to both him and Elliott in five minutes.

I push back my chair to stand up and hustle to my desk so I can print out the lines I wrote. On my way out, I brush by Peyton. She's leaning in the doorway of the office, like she's waiting to talk to someone . . . probably Ben.

"I meant to tell you," she says as I pass by. I look around thinking she must be talking to someone else, but it's definitely me that she's got her green eyes fixed on. "I really like what you've been doing with your hair lately."

Is this some sort of mean-girl-trick/compliment? Last time I checked, my hair was doing the same thing it always does, hanging in stringy, kinky waves around my face.

"Um . . . thanks?"

"Relaxed waves are so cool, I wish my hair would do that." Then she kind of shakes her head, like she wishes the Japanese straightening treatment she just paid five hundred bucks for hadn't made her hair so, well, *straight*.

I'm totally flummoxed by this random communication and so I just zip back to my desk. Ben shows up a minute later and asks if we're ready for Elliott.

"Um, yeah, *we're* ready," I say. I click print.

But my annoyance melts away when I look up and see his wide green eyes looking at me. It's not his fault he was so tired last night. And I can't help but remember what he confessed yesterday— that he worries he isn't as talented as the rest of us. My job is to make sure he and I make it to the top. This Little Kitty work should help to get us there. But the next step, the big step, will be conquering the Kola assignment—I will come up with the idea that wins that pitch and gives Ben and me all the recognition we deserve.

"You ready?" I dip my head in the direction of Elliott's office.

"I go where you go," Ben says. And my heart melts into one big pool of creamy cashew goodness—that's what I want him to say. For, like, forever.

He snatches my page of lines off the printer and walks toward Elliott's office. As we pass the breakroom, I notice the building maintenance guy is wheeling away the office Coke machine. I guess Schmidt wasn't kidding. Elliott motions us into the chairs and before either one of us can speak, he orders, "Don't speak."

We obey.

"After what you made me sit through yesterday, I don't want any of your snow blowing. I'll look at the work and decide what I think of it."

Ben hands over the page and we take a seat.

It's so quiet in that room you could hear a mouse squeak. Though if Elliott had mice in his office, they would probably be so fashionable they wouldn't dare squeak—they'd just sit around pouting prettily in their designer furs.

A good two minutes tick by. They feel like ten.

Then Elliott leans back in his chair—he knows he has our full attention. He probably knows we're scared.

"Well, you two . . ." he begins. And then leaves us hanging on the cliff for another minute before he announces . . .

"Have finally proven why I hired you. This is decent work." Then he leans forward, punches an extension into his phone, and hits speaker. It rings once, then twice, then Suit picks up.

"Y-ello."

It must be the Southern charm that lets him get away with such blatant uncoolness.

"They did it," Elliott says.

"Told you they would," Suit replies, not missing a beat.

Suit told Elliott we would nail the assignment? Am I hearing things?

"Of course, they did it with my tagline. I told you that was the missing piece we needed." Elliott would take credit for the Bible if it weren't so out of date.

"That's why you're the boss." I think there is a touch of laughter in Suit's voice. I *must* be hearing things. "Be down there in a few minutes to go through it with you." And then he hangs up.

When he puts down the phone, Elliott actually smiles at us. His favor has my head spinning—not to mention Suit's faith in us. Where did that come from?

"If I were you I wouldn't stick around long enough to give me reason to doubt you again," Elliott says. He's texting as he talks.

This time, Ben and I don't need to be told twice. We're up and out of his office in a flash.

But Ben doesn't head back to our seats; he passes up the entry to our cube. "Let's see what everybody is up to."

Everybody probably means Joshjohnjay, and normally I would rather stay at my desk than mingle, but I'm already up, and Ben asked, and it would take a lot to knock me off the cloud of approval I'm currently sitting on.

When we get to the small man-cave the three stooges have constructed around their desks, I immediately remember why I never visit them. On the massive Mac computer screen is a huge piece of bird poop that has birthday candles in it. I'm so grossed out I speak without thinking.

"*What* is that?"

"Hello to you, too," one of them responds. It's Josh, I think—today they are all wearing varying shades of washed-out Levi's, tiny holes scuffed in the right knee.

I can barely bring myself to ask, "Are those candles in a piece of—of—*poop*?"

"Bird shit," the three of them say, almost in unison.

"You know about the Crap Corp, right?" Ben asks. I shake my head no.

"They"—Ben points to Joshjohnjay, a little too admirably for my tastes—"scour the city and decorate pieces of pigeon poop they find on the sidewalk."

"Then they photograph it?" Now I'm even more grossed out. Ben shakes his head.

One of the Joshjohnjays speaks again. "Birthday candles are kind of cliché. Usually we do cooler shit, like spray paint shapes around the piles. And one time we draped these huge bird droppings in a nest of human hair; that was rad."

I almost ask where they get real human hair to make poop wigs, but then I realize I don't care.

"What do you do with the pictures?" I ask.

"Crap Corp has a website," one of them says. "Want to see?"

I tell them I do, even though I'm not totally sure. But in a few seconds the website is up on the big screen and they're scrolling through. Sure enough, there's a picture of a human hair nest around a pile of pigeon poop.

Then pigeon poop on a cab windshield, with a tiny LEGO man holding a squeegee propped next to it.

I'm about to say something like, "Wow, cool," so I can get out of there, when I see an oddly captivating shot of a park bench covered in bird crap, decorated with brightly colored paint splatters. It looks like a Jackson Pollock painting.

"The site gets five thousand unique visitors," one of the Josh-johnjays adds.

"A month?" I find this statistic sort of impressive. Little Kitty barely gets that. And Little Kitty is, like, a for-real company.

"Naw," Ben replies. And now I know there is admiration in his tone. "They get five thousand unique visitors a week."

I'm about to voice shock and awe when Todd walks past us en route to his office. He's the only one of us without a creative director title who's not stuck in a four-by-four cubicle. Clearly, seniority has its perks. I can only hope to work here half as long as him, but I doubt I'll survive without thick skin like his. Todd pauses, lowers his nerd-chic glasses down his nose, and peers over them to look at the "artwork" on screen. "Keep up the good work, boys." He winks before ducking into his office. "Elliott always said you hipsters could make shit shine."

I laugh out loud at this, unable to stop myself, but Joshjohn-jay don't even notice because Bouffa and Peyton have suddenly popped up over the cubicle partition.

"Hey, guys." Peyton nods. I assume she's talking just to the boys, but then she freaking smiles at me again. I mumble hi back.

"I just scored permission to run a tab at the Hole this after-noon for some 'preemptive team-building.' Only people work-ing on the pitch can go, which includes all of us."

"Can't," Joshjohnjay says, "we're working on Crap Corp today."

"Oh please," Peyton scoffs. "Like you're going to choose pigeon poop over free beer, even if poop beautification is the only way you ever pick up girls."

Geez, I guess everybody knows about Crap Corp except me . . . and about how successful it is. This just makes me want to dominate Kola even more. Ben and I are way smarter than people who decorate poop.

"Yeah, okay, we'll come," a different Joshjohnjay tells her. The other two look at him, but then shrug their shoulders. He must be the Mini-E of the three. "Might as well play nice with you all now, before things get ugly when we nail the winning idea for the Kola pitch."

"Not so fast," Ben says. "Kay and I are in the hunt, too."

"Hunt all you want," Joshjohnjay sneers. "I heard lately all you've been firing is blanks."

He stands up and high-fives his two counterparts.

Peyton rolls her eyes and flips her hair. "I thought there was no 'I' in 'team.' Lose the egos and let's get to the bar."

Two points for Peyton. And Ben did say the kiss was only a dare. Maybe I've underestimated her and she's not so bad after all.

"Seriously, guys," Bouffa finally speaks. "Let's get to the Hole; I seriously need a rum and Diet Coke."

"Thought Schmitty told you to stay off the that stuff while we're pitching Kola," Joshjohnjay says. "You can't be caught drinking the competition."

"Yeah," Peyton laughs. "If you get busted, they'll make you an intern again lickety-split."

Bouffa's eyes get big. I can tell she's weighing the risk. Finally she whispers, though it's really closer to a whimper, "Do you really think they'd do that?"

"Okay, enough of this standing around. Let's get going," Peyton says.

I see that I'm about to get stuck with these jokers for the rest of the day and I don't want my good mood spoiled so quickly. "I think I actually need to hang back. We've got Little Kitty work going on."

One of the Joshjohnjays teases, "The pussy is calling." But I don't see which one it is, so I can't properly assign the dirty look I throw in their general direction.

"Yeah, we're going to have to hang back," Ben agrees. And this is such awesome news. I hadn't gotten far enough to guess whether he would go to the Hole without me. I hoped he wouldn't, but Ben likes beer as much as the next guy. Maybe he's turning over a new leaf.

Another Joshjohnjay swivels in his seat. "And the pussy answers the call." He gives us a smug frat-boy smile.

Instead of getting pissed, I just shine my full-wattage smile in their direction. At that moment I make a personal vow to leave their arrogant asses in the dust with our Kola idea.

"You kids have fun," I say, as Ben and I turn and walk back to our seats. "ShoutOut if anything interesting happens." Which I'm sure it won't. If Ben's with me, then I have everything I'm interested in within the walls of our cubicle.

Clearly Peyton can't let the mention of an outrageous Shout-Out just hang in the air like that—a girl like her has to pounce. An hour after everyone leaves, Ben checks his phone and announces there is a video update from the Hole.

"Who's on it?" I ask. But I'm not sure I want to know.

Elliott is cruising by our cube and hears the conversation. "Name the one person in the agency wild enough to dance on a table in a dive bar before the sun is down."

I can't tell if he means "wild" like wild-good or wild-bad, but I don't have time to think about it because I know that description is dead-on for Peyton.

I grab Ben's phone from his hand.

"Hey, get your own phone," he says.

"Uh, mine's cracked," I say. Duh. He knows this, we've covered it. And obviously I haven't blamed the crack on him because he doesn't need to know about the little breakdown I suffered at the hands of his strip club visit, but deep down I know it's his fault. Now that Peyton is up to her usual tricks, I am mad about that night all over again.

I hit play on the latest ShoutOut video and sure enough, there's Peyton, shimmying on a *freaking* table at the freaking Hole while the freaking sun is still up.

"Is she joking?" The question is out before I can stop it. Ben takes it as an invitation to lean over my back.

"No, she's serious. I mean, that's Peyton—always into a good time, right?"

Ben sounds like he wishes he were there, having a good time right with her.

"Sounds like you'd rather hang at the Hole than stick around here," I spew before I can help myself. *Damn, Kay, you sound like a jealous wife.*

"Aw, Kay, don't be so sensitive. You know I want to get Little Kitty right. I'll stick here as long as it takes."

Peyton has started talking on the video, asking why the rest of us losers aren't there yet. I turn it off before Ben gets any bright ideas. If he's sticking here as long as it takes, then I'm sticking here. I'm going to get more than Little Kitty right—I'm going to figure out a way to make things with Ben right. I'm going to make it so he doesn't even notice Peyton, because I, Kay, queen of the advertising world, will be all he can see.

men, money & meat

Empty. My closet is practically empty and I am officially freaking out. My parents will be here soon and if I'm not ready to go when they ring the buzzer, Mom will park herself on my sofa and start pressing Ben for the "inside scoop" on my life. *Is Kay eating enough?* she will ask him. *Is she cleaning behind her ears? When's the last time she had an orgasm, and was she alone?* Okay, so maybe I'm exaggerating, but that woman does more prying than a fireman with a crowbar, so you never know. She claims I don't tell her anything, but the truth is, I try. She just never waits around long enough for my answers.

Stupid laundry basket. The majority of my mediocre options for tonight are somewhere here in this overflow, waiting, hoping for the miracle that will get them washed. *I know.* I meant to do a load last night in anticipation of tonight's family dinner, even got quarters on the way to work, but I've been floating so high since the Kola pitch announcement that I completely forgot. When I am a big famous creative director, I will have my interns do the fluff-and-fold run for me.

I slam the closet door over and over, dropping f-bombs like I'm going to war. Which, in a weird way, I am. Though with better food. Ben is on the other side of the paper-thin wall, watching TV, and can't help hearing me.

"Everything all right?" he calls out. "Your momma's gonna Purell your mouth out, you know."

Advertising creatives. We can't help speaking in brand names and catchphrases. It's a side effect of the job.

"Just a wardrobe malfunction!" I yell back, hoping to divert him with memories of Janet Jackson and her nip slip.

He knows better, knows what an evening like this can do to me, but there's no need to pull him into my personal psycho-drama right now. He'll hear enough later, when I get home and recount the details of an evening spent overshadowed by Attila the Mum and my brothers' uber-model girlfriends. At least it gives me a reason to lean on his meaty shoulder.

I survey my wardrobe to see what's still clean. There's the mustard silk blouse I wore to the office holiday party. Not quite right, but less wrong than one of my fallback hoodies. Wait—didn't I wear that to New Year's brunch with the fam and the girlfriends the last time I saw them all? Oh yeah. Mom remarked that that shade of yellow made my skin look pale, although she conceded it was nice that I was actually wearing *color*. I'm used to her so-called compliments, so this doesn't deter me from the blouse. But thinking about Brian's girlfriend, Naomi, does. In the three years he's been dating her, I don't think she's ever worn the same lipstick twice, forget about clothing.

Next option? A plaid button-down shirt. I have a few—they were my go-to choice for nights out in ad school. Dressier than a hoodie, but just as comfortable. Only one is clean. It's gray and red, so at least I won't be criticized for wearing something monochromatic. I put it on and consider leaving it unbuttoned with a cute tank top underneath, the way Kellie always tells me to style it. *If you've got it, flaunt it,* she'd say, urging me to show my shape. But the only shape I see is pencil-like, so I button up for safety. I'm relieved to see my black skinny jeans on a hanger in the back, because they are the dressiest pants I own. I pull them on and want to add my Converse high-tops, but that's just asking for eye rolling.

My only alternative is the pair of red silk Chinese slippers Kell made us each buy from a street vendor near my office right before she left for France. Three bucks a pair! "Let's get 'em, Kaykay," she'd said. "We can dress like Harajuku girls," Kell had begged, preying on my love for all things Gwen Stefani. I'd rejected the slippers on sight as being too girly, too dainty, too flashy for someone like me—plus, like I told her, Harajuku girls were *Japanese*, not Chinese—but she made the street vendor bag them anyway, and they've been at the bottom of my closet ever since. I slip them on now and think maybe *I can* pull this off. I'll say "slippers chinoise" are the latest trend from Paris—Kell wears them—and act like I know something they don't.

Me knowing something they don't. Ha. I wish. But I'm still in fake-it-to-make-it mode, and after the success of our bogus Little Kitty work this week, I'm in a good mood. Mostly. *This kitty don't cuddle? This copywriter don't get it!* But the client fell all over the work we created using Elliott's tagline, calling it "prolific" and "fresh," (insert vomit noise here) and Ben and I went from zeroes to heroes in their eyes—and the agency's. Word is, we're the team to beat on the Kola pitch. Not that I plan on letting *anyone* do that. Wait until I tell my family, I thought. I could even get to make Super Bowl ads. They would die!

I check my look in the mirror. Passable, although I wish there was something I could do with my hair. Then the Chinese slippers inspire me. I twist my mane into a messy knot, the way I always see the girls on the street wearing it, and secure the do with a pair of unused chopsticks I'd been saving for just this opportunity. It looks cool. I feel cool. Almost.

Right on time, the door intercom rings and I'm glad Ben is sitting close enough to buzz my parents in. I have sixty seconds left to put on mascara, lip gloss, and my metaphorical bulletproof vest. I make my entrance into the living room, anxious to get Ben's stamp of approval. But he's watching his favorite Bruce Lee movie, *Enter the Dragon*, so he addresses me without glancing up. "Have fun, Kaykay. Bring us home leftovers."

I'm about to ask him point-blank how I look (why do men need so much direction?) but there is a light thump on the door—not exactly a knock—as if someone just kicked it. I open it and there is my dad, huffing and puffing, holding a large cardboard box that he obviously just lugged up six flights. *This* gets Ben's attention.

"Mr. Carlson, let me get that for you." Ben grabs the box and puts it down in the middle of the living room.

"Bobo!" My dad calls me by his pet name for me, giving me a great big hug. "You look beautiful, so grown-up!"

Ben nods and gives me a thumbs-up. My smile widens. I could stay here forever with my two favorite men. But someone is missing.

"Pop, where's Mom?"

"With the car. We're double-parked. She insisted we drop off these boxes."

"Plural? There's more than one? What's in them, anyway?" I'm in a panic, motioning to the box that's taking up one-quarter of my living room.

"Oh, your mother was cleaning out the attic and found a bunch of your old stuff. She thought you'd want it. There are two more boxes downstairs."

"How thoughtful." My words drip with sarcasm. "We'll just get rid of the couch and sit on those instead."

"I *told her* you didn't have room, but you know your mother and her projects," Dad sighs. Then he mimics her. "*Get it done, Gene! Whatever it takes!*"

I join in. "*A place for everything, Kay, and everything in its place. These coats aren't going to hang themselves!*"

Ben laughs at our little improv, and I suddenly feel self-conscious. Talking in funny voices is a thing my dad and I do together, but not usually in front of an audience. Dad does the best impressions, from De Niro to Gollum from *The Hobbit*, and he can quote entire scenes of Monty Python in character. He could have easily been a stand-up comic, if he were more outgoing. And if Mom didn't insist he take the bar exam instead. Now he uses his talents to entertain juries. He swears that being a prosecutor is just like being in showbiz, but with even more drama.

Ben, sweet midwestern boy that he is, insists on getting the other boxes, so the three of us walk down to the street together. Mom is sitting in the passenger seat of their Saab, barking orders into her cell phone, but she pauses to greet me by looking down at my shoes, homing in like a heat-seeking missile.

"Flats in February, Kay? Won't you be cold?"

Then she notices Ben, and smiles warmly. "Oh, hi, Ben. I didn't know you were still sleeping on my daughter's couch."

He waves. "Hi, Mrs. C. Yup, still here for now, but I think I found a place."

What?

This is news to me, but before I can question him, Mom's on to the next thing, barking at my dad.

"Gene, we really need to get going if we're going to find a parking garage in this neighborhood."

Mom resumes her phone call and we leave Ben on the curb, struggling to lift my boxes of God-knows-what. Dad drives the car toward dinner, which is only a few blocks, but light-years away.

I am in a Strip House. The one on 12th Street. It's a trendy restaurant chain (if you can call four locations a chain) that peddles overpriced steak to the Manhattan Haves who crave a scene with their protein. The walls are papered in bordello red, and covered with black-and-white boudoir pics of starlets and pin-ups from days gone by. The vibe is much like I imagine it must have been at the go-go bar the boys' club dragged Ben to on Tuesday night: men, money, and meat commingling in the dark.

Brian, my oldest brother by two minutes, chose this place because it's a favorite of his clients, and when your parents are footing the bill, you might as well take them somewhere you normally only frequent on an expense account. Sure, Bri could pay for ten dinners like this with the crazy salary he makes as a financial analyst, but guys he works with get fired every day, so he'll pinch a penny if he can do it without looking cheap. I don't even think I could afford the tip.

I scan the place and see that Brett, aka "twin Baby B," is at the bar, sampling some wine selected by his newish girlfriend, Simone. Simone works somewhere in Tribeca as a *sommelier*, which Brett once explained means she "oversees wine procurement and service for a fine restaurant." When we all met her for the first time, at brunch on New Year's Day, Mom had remarked, "So, I hear you're a waitress."

Brett got defensive, which was the first clue I had that Simone might be more than another one of his Barbie dolls. His explanation of her employment elicited the proper *oohs* and *aahs* from Mom, who, for some reason, we kids all live to impress. Apparently, Simone had studied her trade for something like three years, in Italy, which she uses as proof of her I'm-not-a-waitress status. Brett works as a finance advisor, managing the investments of millionaires—correction: billionaires, hence the promotion we're celebrating—so the difference between studying in Italy and studying in Iowa is pretty huge to him.

Brian and Naomi are at the bar, too, drinking martinis while the table gets set up. I personally enjoy that they aren't bullied into the sommelier bottle.

I'm pretty sure Naomi doesn't get bullied into a thing. She's an analyst at the same bank where Brian works, and makes even more money than he does. I only know this because she got so drunk at the surprise thirtieth he threw for her (at Soho House, naturally) that she confided in me in the ladies' room. She also admitted that she wasn't sure if it was her skills or her looks that sent her shooting through the glass ceiling at work, and frankly, she really didn't care.

I'd probably admire her if I weren't so damn intimidated by her.

I debate whether I should head straight to the bathroom to avoid contact with my sibs and their ladies before my parents come inside the restaurant. There's no telling how long Mom will give the garage attendant lessons on how to park her car, and Dad's stuck waiting for her. I couldn't stand out there another second—my feet were freezing in my Chinese slippers. Mom doesn't need to know that, though. She gloats enough as it is without me admitting she was right.

Decision made, I head toward the ladies' room, when I hear Mom make an entrance. People all the way in Harlem can probably hear her, too.

"Oh, Brian! Brett!" She waves for their attention as if they're across a park—*Earth to Momzilla, this is a steakhouse, not a county fair.*

But of course the Wondertwins can't be shamed—that would be so pedestrian, so normal, so unexceptional—and so they rise to the challenge of making a scene by calling out their return greetings, one even louder than the other. For them, even saying hello is a pissing contest.

Each of their dates perks up as well. Naomi instantly turns from the bar with a well-manicured hand wrapped around her martini glass and Simone-the-sommelier manages to rise from her chair without flashing her underwear to the entire restaurant: quite a feat considering the swatch of fabric she is trying to pull off as a skirt. I have bras that are bigger. And I'm, like, an A cup.

I reevaluate the situation and decide it would be better to

greet everyone right now and get it over with instead of continuing on to the bathroom. It's bad enough I'm alone. I don't need to call further attention to that fact by making a solo entrance once they're all seated. My dad's right side looks like a good place to linger, and so I go and attach myself to his elbow. Luckily they're all done with the shouting and on to kissing cheeks, but I stay far enough away to render my participation in this awkward ritual impossible. Cheek kissing is another skill I plan to perfect one day, but right now the last thing I need or want is an accidental lip lock with one of my brothers' girlfriends because I turn my head the wrong way.

"What's up, K-Nine?" Brett asks.

"Where's Benny-boy?" Brian says at almost the same time. They do that a lot, the speaking-at-the-same-time thing. Luckily Mom is usually around to interject, before anyone has to choose which question to answer first.

"I kept telling her to bring him," she says now, taking the opportunity to pounce. "Of course, when we just saw Ben at Kay's apartment, I thought to invite him myself, but he was hardly dressed for the occasion."

I force a smile, but mentally note to give Brian a wrapped-up piece of charcoal next Christmas.

"Must be the fashion at the agencies, the casual look?" Mom smiles brightly.

I smile brightly back. There we are, a family of lightbulbs. But inside, my filament is flickering. I wonder about the possibility of actually transforming myself into my father's elbow joint. It would be so nice to be a real elbow instead of just feeling like one all the freaking time.

Luckily the hostess saves us from ourselves and takes us to a table that has been set especially for us.

"Thanks for the special treatment, Corinne," Simone croons as we arrive at a prime location in the center of the restaurant.

My dad leans over and whispers in my ear, "Nobody puts baby in the corner."

"Patrick Swayze, duh," I answer. Obviously I shadowed the right person tonight.

After we are all arranged around the table—the happy couples together and me wedged between my parents—I find that I have actually chosen the worst chair. I'm in the hot seat.

In point-two seconds, Brett starts in with questions about the agency and how work is going. Have I written any TV commercials yet? Will I ever get to travel to LA on a film shoot? How long until I can be managing partner at the agency? That sort of thing.

I wonder about matching pieces of charcoal—perhaps I could get them both monogrammed with Bs.

"Do you work with Travino a lot?" Brett is asking. "Man, I would love to get my hands on that guy's assets."

At this, Simone giggles, and I barely repress an eye roll. The good news is that I actually have something positive to say about my job. I start to tell them, slowly but surely, about how work has been going really well lately.

Naomi leans forward and acts as though she is interested. This buoys me onward.

I tell them that I finally nailed work for one of the top-roster clients and that last—but certainly not least—the agency has been selected to compete in a pitch for the Kola business.

"Travino actually briefed us just the other day," I add. This is a slight embellishment—by "us," I technically mean the whole agency—but the family doesn't need to know that. "I think Ben and I have a shot at having the big idea."

"Well, that's great news, honey," my dad starts. But then Brian cuts him off with the old fork-on-a-glass routine.

"Sorry, guys, I just can't wait any longer. And since Kay is talking about big ideas, it's the perfect time for me to tell you about my latest, biggest idea."

All eyes at the table shift away from me and I can't help being bummed. I feel like a dog who just offered his belly for rubbing but has to settle for a few pats on the head. I've been hearing about Brian's genius since I was in the womb, so I keep my ears on him, but turn my eyes to the menu. No single-patty hamburger options available, but the rib eye should do.

"We're here to celebrate Brett's big promotion, of course."

Brett's big promotion. Brian's big idea, la-la-la, lame.

"But Naomi and I have news of our own."

On my right, my mother takes in such a sharp breath that the whole atmosphere shifts. There is definitely less oxygen at the table than there was a minute before.

"I had the big idea to pop the question and we're engaged!"

Brett, who obviously already knew, and Simone, who has dreams of being next in line for a Wondertwins proposal, both break into applause.

My mother reaches over me to hug my father and whispers into his ear, which is directly in front of my face, "Thank God, I thought he was going to say she was pregnant."

"Well, you know what they say," my father whispers back. "Expect the worst and you'll never be disappointed."

Truer words have never been spoken. Even though they weren't spoken to me, I take them to heart. I'd come to dinner expecting awkward conversation and got news that one of my brothers had taken yet another step on the ladder I am barely holding on to, and that on top of that, there's a high probability I will be wearing pastel taffeta in front of hundreds of people sometime before the close of the year.

Can a girl get a drink around here or what? I think to myself.

But before there can be alcohol, we all have to stand and do the congratulations shuffle. There is no dodging the cheek kisses this time. Both of the Wondertwins insist on doing a Kay sandwich, which still feels the same way it did when they devised the move back when I was twelve. This is the only bright side I've found yet for having zero boobs.

Simone starts screaming about wanting to see the ring, and my mother definitely isn't going to get left off that train.

"Let's see if my boy knows how to pick out a diamond!"

Naomi looks slightly embarrassed, which surprises me. "I told Brian I didn't want too much flash, but he couldn't resist."

"We'll have to show you the blinding lights next time, Mom; it's getting resized right now," Brian tells her. "I was so focused on cut, color, clarity . . . you know, the four Cs, that I forgot to check Naomi's ring size."

I'm about to ask Bri what the fourth C is, but then I understand Naomi's embarrassment. She wanted the finger-flaunt moment and couldn't have it. What a waste of a perfectly impeccable manicure. Now that I know she is going to be my sister, I feel kind of bad for her. Especially since she'll be inheriting my mother.

"People are starting to stare; I think it's time to sit down," I say now to defuse Mom.

But she's in rare form. "Oh, Kay, don't worry. Your time will come, too, someday."

As if I'm jealous of Naomi and Brian for getting engaged. Please. Mom doesn't know half my worries. I'm not even aiming for marriage—just a first kiss from Ben would be nice.

My dad finally corrals us all back to our chairs, and then Naomi sends her phone around the table so everyone can gawk at the Tiffany's brick she'll soon be sporting. Simone looks just a little longer than is appropriate, and Mom raises her eagle eye in Brett's direction. Maybe if Simone manages to shave another centimeter off the skirt, my other brother will make an honest woman out of her, too. The Wondertwins can have a double wedding, and I can be a double disappointment.

"Cheers to the happy couple," my father proposes. And everyone raises a glass. The waiters have been avoiding our table because of the commotion and shifting bodies, so I still haven't been able to order the liquor I need. Earlier, I thought a vodka cranberry would do the trick, but now I'm seriously leaning toward scotch.

Not that I've ever had scotch. But it's what my dad has been drinking to unwind after a hard day for as long as I can remember. And this definitely qualifies as a hard day.

"And to Brett," Mom chimes in, "for his fabulous promotion!"

Maybe someday I'll get mentioned in a family toast, but not tonight. I'm forced to suck up the moment with wine. It goes down so smooth when I chug it—nice choice, Simone—that I pour myself some more.

For the rest of the meal I take my dad's advice and simply expect the worst. And it works. I'm not disappointed. Not when my steak arrives and is the size of a quarter. Not when Naomi confirms my fears about pastel taffeta with her pledge that "the bridesmaid dress will so totally be rewearable for another occasion."

A statement like that is the kiss of death for a bridesmaid: I'll look hideous, for sure.

No, it's not until after the meal has finally wrapped and I'm more than a little buzzed that disappointment rears its ugly head.

After my mother has said for the fiftieth time that Naomi will be such a beautiful bride. (And added: "And what beautiful babies!")

After my brothers have devised a plan for them and their girlfriends to stay for champagne. (They invite me, but I decline.)

After I think I am going to get out of here and am just starting to let myself hope that the night can end decently. If I can get my woozy self home and up the eighteen hundred stairs to my apartment, Ben will be waiting. We can pop popcorn and the two of us will sit on my couch and watch TV. During commercial breaks I can entertain him with stories of Simone, tripping over herself to nab a ring of her own. And, maybe, just maybe, we'll laugh so hard that we kiss.

And this is where I go wrong—looking on the bright side—because as soon as I stand up from the table, wobbly even though I'm wearing flats, the absolute worst thing that can happen does, in fact, occur. I look up to see Suit heading my way.

Is the wine playing tricks on me? Am I at the office? I look around and see a photo of Marilyn Monroe straddling a stallion. Nope. Still the Strip House. How did he find me here? Did Little Kitty crash? Is he here to summon me back to work?

But Suit isn't alone. He's with his perfect girl. Or, because maybe she's Southern, too, his perfect *gal*. Leatherette. She's dressed very steakhouse chic—a simple black sheath with patent pumps that give her another four inches and make me feel like a shrinking violet in my flat, unflattering slippers. What is she, like six foot two? She'd be better matched with Dikembe Mutombo. But Suit doesn't look at all fazed to be shorter than she is. I don't think I've *ever* seen him look fazed.

I turn to see if my dad's elbow is available for a hiding place— at the very least, if it can stand in for a walking stick—but he is helping my mother up. The other couples are all standing, too, locked in conversations with each other. This is the definition of being a seventh wheel—totally unnecessary for the truck to keep rolling and nowhere to position yourself for low visibility, always just dangling somewhere under the wheelbase, unattached.

I put on the best smile I can muster and that's when I realize that Suit hasn't even seen me yet. From behind me I hear Naomi squeal, "What are you doing here?"

And then the girl Suit is trailing through the restaurant says, "We're here to celebrate—of course."

The diners around us look up, probably because it's so rare to see two women that beautiful in one small, square space. They rush to each other and hug, and my fuzzy brain still hasn't quite caught up with what's going on, but so far I have the following evidence to work with:

Suit and his girlfriend are friends with Naomi.

This might mean Suit is friends with my brother.

Thank God I didn't embellish my work stories too much. I'm sure Suit would love exposing me as a fraud to my family.

When the girls finally finish their hugs, Naomi starts introducing the girlfriend to Simone—she's named Cheyenne. (Really?!) And then Suit reaches the group and shakes Brian's hand.

"Glad you guys could join us," Brian says.

"We wanted to wish you congratulations in person, my friend," Suit answers.

Now that it's obvious Suit isn't here for a work-related reason or to drag me back to the office, I wonder if there's any way for me to make it out of the restaurant without being seen. Maybe I can "lose" an earring and crawl toward the door? In my current state of buzzification, this seems like a good idea, so I bend down below the table as if I've dropped something.

Just then, good old Brian says, "We're here with my parents and my sister, Kay . . . Kay, *what* are you doing down there?"

He's getting coal for the next five Christmases. Busted, I immediately stand up, and bump my head on the table. This knocks the chopsticks clear out of my hair, causing my updo to unravel in front of everyone, and I'm standing there looking stupid and feeling stupider.

"Just looking for my chopsticks," is all I can think to say. I hold them up as proof. "Found 'em!"

Suit is staring at me, confused. Everyone else is staring, too.

"Kay?" he says.

"They serve sushi here?" his girlfriend says.

"You know each other?" Brian says.

"You know each other?" Brett repeats just a half second later.

I don't answer, because we do know each other. I can hear Suit's voice in the conference room just the other morning. *You looked rather upset.* Jesus, if he told my brothers about that I would be so embarrassed. Even more embarrassed than I am at the moment, with my hair all wonky, and Suit zoomed in on me.

"Kay and I work at Schmidt Travino Drew together," Suit explains.

"Aw, man!" Brian slaps his own forehead. "I didn't realize that was your agency, I thought you were at another shop—it's hard to keep them all straight!"

"What a funny coincidence!" Naomi remarks. She's still arm in arm with Suit's girlfriend. "We all went to Tulane together!"

I had forgotten that Naomi went to school in New Orleans. That would explain why she's so nice to me: Southern hospitality. I had chalked it up to pity for the little sister.

"This guy here used to take us to the *best* underground music clubs," Naomi tells us, turning to Suit. "Remember the time we were all on Frenchman? You got onstage with that punk band and played the guitar."

Suit knows the underground music scene? He *plays guitar*? I feel like I'm in the twilight zone.

"Well, dear." My mother speaks to me as if I'm five years old. "Why don't you stay and have a drink now that your work friend is here." She's ready to leave; there are people to call with Brian and Naomi's news. Neighbors to brag to. The Plaza to be reserved for the ceremony. I can only imagine the to-do lists unfurling in her brain.

"Oh God no!" I blurt. And this outburst is like breaking a wineglass in the middle of the restaurant, because everyone stops and looks at me. "I mean, I think, well, *they* all should celebrate together and, yes, I'd love to have a drink, but I've already had several, and I've got to do some work this weekend, tonight actually, so I really need to get home. And do work. But thanks, anyway."

Suit cocks his head to one side and I see that sly smile creeping up. Why does it always seem like this guy has my number?

"Kay's been a real star at the agency lately," he tells everyone, to my surprise. "I sold some of her writing this week to one of our biggest clients."

I start to blush.

"Yeah." Brian nods. "She was telling us tonight how she's going to win Kola for you guys and get some Super Bowl ads under her belt."

Holy Mother of God, I can't believe he just said that. *The shame.* Now my face is redder than my stupid Chinese slippers. Why did I open my mouth about the freaking Super Bowl ads? Oh right, I wanted my family to be proud of me. Well, time for Suit to tell them there's no way in hell that's true so they can go back to believing I'm just barely scraping by.

Instead, he says, "I wouldn't be surprised if that's exactly what happens."

"Chop, chop!" my mother interjects, not even registering Suit's compliment. "Time to let them get their party started and for us to get on the road."

I mumble something lame about seeing Suit on Monday and then a "Congrats" in the direction of Brian and Naomi, and follow my parents to the door. Inside, I am dying. Suit didn't tell the group how dumb my Kola fantasy was, but now he knows all about it . . . Bet he'll have a good laugh over it later with the boys' club.

When we get out of the restaurant, the wind is whipping. I huddle into my jacket and can feel the cold on the tops of my feet. All I want to do is pull my phone out of my purse and call Ben to make sure he is home. I need to get back and tell him everything that happened so I can get it off my chest, then wake up tomorrow energized again—ready to go—more Goodyear Blimp flying high and less of this balloon-with-a-slow-leak feeling I'm currently rocking.

At the parking garage, as my mother gives the attendant her ticket along with explicit instructions on how to pull the car up to the curb, I tell my dad that I'm just going to walk home.

He looks like he's about to pull a movie quote out of his back pocket, but then he must see the helium leaking out of my heart because he stops short. "You okay, Kay?"

I want to tell Dad that I'm not okay. That every time I start to feel like I might be okay, something happens that makes me sure I have no idea what okay even looks like. I want to tell him I don't belong in this city. That the buildings are too tall, the people are too determined, the pace is too relentless. That no one notices me here—not just strangers, but people who matter, like Ben.

If we were at home and I could sit at the foot of his recliner and tell him about my life, maybe I would. But we are far from the comfort of his study. Those tall buildings are looming in the distance and the weather is too cold and life is moving too fast for anyone to slow down and spell out what matters.

"I'm fine, Dad," I lie. "Thanks for asking. I just want to walk."

Then in a few minutes they are in their car and driving off. I stand on the street next to the parking garage and watch their sedan head back to the suburbs, my mother's head shaking and rattling in the front seat. I imagine she's already started recounting every small detail of the dinner for Dad, even though he was there to see those details for himself.

I pull my phone out of my jacket pocket. Ugh, the cracked screen. Gotta fix that soon. As soon as it wakes up it announces ShoutOut notifications, one new text, and zero missed calls.

The text is from Kell. *Can u chat today? I landed that internship working at the Louvre! Can you believe it?*

I write back: *Superb Kell! Just celebrated Brett's promotion . . . and, Brian & Naomi are engaged.*

Before I send it I change the period to an exclamation point. *Engaged!* Seems more sisterly than *engaged.* And as a sister I am excited, I think. It's just that engagements and promotions and such are what I expect for the Wondertwins, so it's not like general success is some kind of news in my book.

I find the number for Ben and call him. His ShoutOut said everyone from work was going out, but that it would be later, and when I was done with dinner we could figure out what we were going to do.

That *we* had felt really good when he said it, but now it was far away. Hours ago, actually. I try to squeeze a little more comfort out of the memory but the well is dry.

"Hello?" Ben answers.

"Ben?" I can barely hear him for all the background noise.

"Where are you?"

"At the Hole. Come meet us. Everyone's here."

From the sounds of it, *everyone* is half of lower Manhattan, two tambourine players, and some kind of donkey whinnying in the background.

"Are there animals there? It sounds like something's dying."

"Some guys from Blood Pudding are trying to play acoustic. They suck! It's awesome! You've got to see it for yourself to believe it—those guys think they are so cool."

I don't actually need to see it to believe it. I can imagine the scene. All the Schmidt Travino Drew creatives huddled up in one section of the bar. The Blood Pudding people in the opposite section, cheering on the impromptu band.

"I think I'll pass." Good thing he can't hear the disappointment on my face.

"Oh, c'mon, Kay, you need to get out for a night. Let yourself have some fun."

I was planning on having some fun. At home. With Ben. Obviously that plan is a bust.

"Maybe I'll come," I say, even though it's the last thing I mean. Then I hear a shriek in the background.

"What's that?"

"Peyton just got a round of beers; mine's waiting on me."

Peyton. Of course. First she buys him beers and next, who knows. I know I should go there and put on a good face, fight for what I want—but I just don't have any fight left in me.

"I'll see you at home soon?"

"What, Kay? Sounds like you are in a wind tunnel."

"I said, I'll see you at home soon?"

"Yes!" Ben answers. My heart leaps. Maybe what he said earlier about finding a new place to live was a white lie, to appease my parents. Ben is good with parents like that. Maybe there is a chance my apartment will still be his home for the nearish future.

"I'll see you here soon!" he finishes. And my heart deep dives again. He only wants to hang out if it's in the relative comfort of a bunch of drunken coworkers. Which sounds like the opposite of comfort to me. I hang up the phone and put it in my jacket pocket and start on the long, cold walk home. Alone. Not even a seventh wheel anymore, I've been downgraded to just one: a lonely unicycle rolling my way down the Manhattan sidewalks by myself.

This is how the dolls are made: First, you melt beeswax. Then you pour it in the mold. Then you let it harden. Then you sculpt. Then you paint. And last, but not least, you take pieces of your own clothing, shred them up, and stitch them into miniature outfits that look like some semblance of what you actually wear on the street.

I'm talking myself through the process and this might be a sign of cracking up, but I don't care. It's more fun than I would have if I were shopping for a big, fat diamond at Tiffany's. It's more fun than I would have if I were sipping watery draft beer at the Hole. It's almost more fun than I would have if I were reenacting Simone-the-sommelier's pouty face when Brett said he couldn't believe his brother was asking for a ball and chain.

In the boxes my mom brought me were all the old dolls I had made in high school. I counted sixteen, but there might be more buried in there somewhere. Each one of them is wearing scraps of clothes I used to live in—all variations on the flannel-and-hoodie theme I still wear now. But every doll I pick up takes me back to the time when I made it.

Kay, graduating from high school with fabric from my real graduation gown.

Kay at her first concert, wearing a totally out-of-place cocktail dress because Kell and I thought the band was serious when they posted flyers around town that said "black tie." Remembering it now makes me laugh, but back then we'd hidden in the far shadows of the auditorium where the local indie act had set up shop.

Now I'm working on the Kay I started this week—Kay as a Manhattanite. I do her makeup the way I know Kell would instruct me, with thick black lines around the eyes and just enough blush to look permanently flushed. Not as in toilet flushed, more "I've been running down the avenue so I could throw my arms around your neck" flushed.

I find a long baggy sweater in the back of my closet that I don't think I'll wear anymore—and cut scraps for a heavy scarf. Hours are clicking by on the clock but I don't even notice. Every once in a while I listen for signs of Ben's boots dragging his drunk self up the steps, but for now the building is silent: Everyone is either in bed or out, letting themselves have some fun.

My phone rings and I jump. Maybe it's Ben? But no. It's Kell. Do I want to keep working or talk to her? Maybe I can do both.

"Hey, hey," I say as I answer the phone.

"Um, your brother is engaged? FaceTime, now."

Her familiar command makes me smile. Maybe I can make *her* smile. I take Manhattanite Kay and set her up on the kitchen table.

"Hold on, one sec," I yell into the speakerphone. Then I go to the kitchen, get a plate, napkin, and some silverware, and set the table all around the Kay doll.

I click the phone to FaceTime and position the screen so all Kell sees is the doll and the place setting. Then I put on my best sultry, seductress Manhattanite voice.

"Kellie darling, hellooo . . . I guess you've heard our family's *faaaabulous* news."

Kell starts cracking up. I can't see her but I know how she looks when she laughs. Your best friend's laugh is like your favorite pair of shoes that you could slide into with your eyes closed—there's nothing more comfortable in the whole world. I'm lucky my best friend laughs a lot.

"Your dolls are back! Kay, *c'est magnifique!*"

But I'm not going to answer her myself, this is too much fun. I start in with what Kay the doll has to say about her fancy Strip House dinner, but Kellie stops me before I can even get going.

"*Arrêté*, wait! I've got this new app that will record all the action on my phone screen. Take it from the top so I can get your whole show on film and play it back whenever I'm missing *ma petite* BFF. A little cinéma vérité, *oui?*"

Now it's my turn to laugh. Leave it to Kellie to want to turn my Kay doll into art. Spurred on by her enthusiasm, I scan the room for more props, then start improvising my heart out.

"Kells, darling, we had a *smashing* night at New York hot spot Strip House. I know what your dirty little mind is thinking but no, it's not that kind of strip house. Though they are also known for serving succulent but overpriced flesh."

I move my doll onto the dinner plate and stand the knife up in front of her, and between her legs so it looks like she's pole dancing.

"My brother's meat stick—I mean girlfriend—got us the best table, far away from the riffraff." Now I turn my phone and walk toward the bathroom door, zooming in on the toilet to punctuate my joke.

"Though you would think this city's It Girls would prefer to sit closer to the loo. Then they wouldn't have to hide their steaks in their napkins to make it look like they've eaten, if you know what I mean." I make a noise like I'm vomiting, then flush the toilet.

"Fifty dollars' worth of dinner down the drain. Of course that loss doesn't even make a blip on the radar if they're trying to keep themselves in diamonds and designer duds. And if you're a freak like me—without a man's arm to hang on—then you'd better pay up for a man to hang on *your* arm. Someone like Louis or Marc Jacobs, with Christian or Jimmy Choo at your feet and Provocateur on your ass."

Now I tilt my phone down toward the floor, homing in on Ben's pile of sneakers as I continue.

"But if you're stuck sporting Converse, they'd better be the limited edition John Varvatos ones, because why pay thirty bucks for a pair of sneaks when you can spend three hundred dollars?

"Yes, here no one cares who you are. It's all about who you are wearing. Or, in the case of some of the girls at Strip House, who you are barely wearing. Here's how to test if your skirt is too long: drape a dinner napkin over your lap. Can you still see your skirt? Then change into something shorter."

I rip off a tiny strip of napkin and tie it around the doll.

"What? You still can't see where my Brazilian starts? But, I bedazzled my vajayjay!"

Kell laughs, chiming in. "Postage-stamp length, Kay! Très très chic!"

"Yes, this look is the height of haute-cool-whore. Or maybe I should say, it puts the whore in haute cout-whore." Of course, it's best worn with heels, the higher the better. Because you just won't be comfortable unless you can look down on everyone else in the room."

Our favorite burrito joint in Jersey used to have a jukebox that only played the Boss and "The Roach Song"—as Kell and I affectionately called it. Suddenly "The Roach Song" comes at me out of nowhere and so I grab Doll Kay and start to dance, making her sing.

"La Coochie-cout-whore, la Coochie-cout-whore. Coochie, coochie, coochie cout-WHORE!" Doll Kay is tangoing her heart out around the stage—aka her dinner plate—when a well-timed breeze (that's actually me blowing out a huge breath of air) takes her napkin skirt right off.

"CLOSE YOUR CHILDREN'S EYES!" the Kay doll screams. "They shouldn't have to see this!"

Then I bring the phone right up to the doll so it gets a close-up of her face. "But they shouldn't have to see anything else in this restaurant, either. The girls in here are faker than my wax lips. A shot of Botox, a double shot of boobs, and kiss your shot at reality good-bye."

Next I pull the camera back so we see the Kay doll waving sadly. "So long, farewell," she sings woefully. "But you're making the right decision. Save yourself while you can. Me? I'm too far goonneee."

With that I raise up the fork and plunge it down into the shot so it looks like an ominous weapon coming out of the sky to punish her for being in that soulless place. And I stab Copygirl straight in the chest with it. Since she is made of wax, the fork's prongs spear right through her, and stick out her back, which I find hysterical.

Kell must agree, because she is wiping tears from her eyes when I get back to the phone.

"Masterpiece," she says. "I laughed. I cried . . ."

"Please, God, tell me you also farted."

Now Kell is doubled over in laughter again at our old high school joke. She starts waving good-bye. "I'm totally going to send you this recording tomorrow," she says. Then she blows a kiss at the camera and signs off.

Now that the fun is done I curl into my bed. Still no sign of Ben. I'm a unicycle wheel—all alone in my Shabby Chic comforter, but at least tonight I made my best friend laugh. And I made myself laugh. And that's worth something. Even—or especially—in this cement city.

valley of the dolls

"What is this, valley of the dolls?"

Ben's voice thuds through the thin wall of the apartment and in a millisecond, I'm awake but foggy. He *did* come home, after all. What a perfect voice to wake up to, except—what did he say about dolls? Shit. The dolls. I never cleaned up after last night's wine-fueled wax-working frenzy.

"Kay? Are you in there? Because there are a whole lot of little versions of you out here."

"Um, yeah, I'm here—I'm here." I jump out of bed in a panic and throw on my clothes from the night before. My mouth is dry and my head is pounding. I thought you were only supposed to get hangovers from cheap wine. I'll have to ask Simone about that next time before I keep topping up my glass like I'm getting free refills from McDonald's.

"Hold. One minute," I yell, stuffing my legs into my dirty jeans. Laundry must happen. Today.

"Almost ready! Don't touch anything. Unless, um, it's stuff that belongs to you."

I need an excuse to explain away the dolls, and fast.

"Those boxes you carried up last night were filled with old art projects from high school. Isn't that funny?"

I think back to the FaceTime with Kell, when the dolls actually were funny. Now they just seem massively embarrassing.

I throw open the bedroom door and there's Ben in the middle of the living room, surrounded by my emptied-out boxes and a sea of miniature wax versions of me. The small window to the right of the breakfast area is letting in just a little light—this is the only hour my apartment gets natural sun through the crack between the building next door—and it looks like Ben's face is glowing.

"You made it home last night!" I sound maybe a little too excited. Or a little too motherly. I haven't had time to slip into cool Kay mode.

"Ah, no, I slept at my new place." He looks right at me with an expression I can't quite name. "Kay, you look like hell. What happened here? I thought _I_ had a crazy night . . ."

My heart skips a beat. Crazy night? Tell me his new place isn't Peyton's place. Please God let his new place be anywhere but in Peyton's bed, and I swear I'll be at church every Sunday for the next year.

"Your new place?" I force myself to keep the bright note in my voice.

He is standing up, leaning against the breakfast nook. He is holding Kay the aspiring short story writer doll. She has a small pencil glued in her left hand. What a nice little fantasy I had back in high school—the thought that writers could be artists instead of cat food connoisseurs. Now I always have an Apple laptop attached to my hand, and my motivation is to boost sales instead of to inspire hope and joy in the human race. Times change, I guess.

"This is pretty cool." Ben turns the doll over. "It doesn't look exactly like you, but it's close enough that I know it's you."

"Like I said, high school art project. I'll probably take them all down to the garbage room tonight." I clear my throat, eager to get back to the most important question of the hour. "So, where's your new place? Are you relocating from the couch immediately?"

"Immediately and permanently—I won't be in your hair anymore." Ben says this like he's doing me a favor.

"In my hair?"

"Oh c'mon, I know you have to be tired of me hanging around—being in your space." He has already removed my extra key from his Swiss Army knife key chain and it's sitting there, alone, on the counter.

What's a girl to do? Is this my moment to admit that I want him in my space even more? No, no. Not this early in the morning. Not when there's a chance he's already sharing space with a female companion. I'm really glad my steak last night was the size of a quarter, otherwise the flips in my stomach might turn my embarrassment into actual physical mortification.

"So, like, where ya gonna be living?" This valley of the dolls is wearing off on me. I'm talking like a valley girl.

"The guys from work lost their fourth roommate. You know that guy, Matt, who was really into sculpture? He got into some exclusive artist community in California, so he just got on a Greyhound bus, left them high and dry. Pretty stupid life decision for him, but good opportunity for me."

My relief is slightly tempered by the "stupid life decision" comment. I remember when Ben thought the life of an artist was the goal. Times change for all of us, I suppose.

"I'll make us coffee," I say. It's all I can say because it's all I can think. The image of Peyton curling up to Ben is gone. I can handle losing him to an un-air-conditioned loft in Greenpoint with Joshjohnjay and their poop project, especially since we'll still be working together. Lots of late work nights . . . projects that keep us at work too late for him to make the trek to Brooklyn.

Maybe it's not as bad as I thought. And with coffee on the horizon, it could be okay. "We gotta get to work," I mumble as I boil water.

"It's Saturday," he reminds me, still staring at me with that nameless expression. Remorse? Pity?

"Oh yeah," I laugh, a little too loud. "All the days are blurring together."

I focus on rinsing out my dual-cup French press, a gift from Kell, and realize that very soon I'll only be making single servings. "You're going to have to learn to wash dishes if you're going to survive living with the boys' club."

"True." He nods. And then he puts Kay the short-story writer on the counter, next to the lonely key.

"You shouldn't throw the dolls out. They're cool, Kay."

"They're okay," I agree.

"O-Kay!" he chants while I measure out coffee grounds. And I have to laugh. Maybe it's all right that times change, as long as the important things stay the same.

I am calm inside for exactly three seconds, until Ben says, "So, then, can I use those boxes to pack up my stuff? Peyton rented a Range Rover to drive out to the Lululemon sample sale, and she's coming by after to help me move."

This time I actually try to channel my mother's flippant brightness when I respond. "Absolutely," I say. Then for the first time ever, I actually start counting the minutes until he's out of here.

I'd never realized how quiet weekends in New York City can be if you have no one to spend them with. No Ben to go on a bagel run with. No Ben to share sections of the newspaper with. No Ben, period.

I'd helped him pack up his CDs, his art books, his ironic trucker hats, and T-shirts and Converse sneakers. It didn't take long. What little he'd lugged to New York fit neatly into my three cardboard boxes, yet left an emptiness the size of the Grand Canyon in my tiny apartment and my hollowed-out heart.

Then I did the only thing I could bear doing solo on a Saturday in the city. I went to the laundromat. I had enough dirty clothes for three loads, and had to wait awhile for machines, but I didn't mind. There's no way I wanted to be home when Peyton pulled up to fetch the one thing in this town I'd been so sure was mine.

Ben and I didn't bother with formal good-byes since I'll see him on Monday. We're still a team after all, though now only in the work sense. And, in the cold light of the laundromat, it occurred to me that's all we probably ever will be. I'd had endless opportunities to reveal my feelings, speak my mind, and now it was likely too late.

Still, the whooshing and whirring of the washers was oddly

comforting, the promise of a clean start made palpable by the rinse cycle. As I sat there watching my jeans and underthings dance in circles of suds, I realized what an apt metaphor that was for my life so far in Manhattan. As the world around me danced, I sat and watched it all through glass, waiting for the buzzer to signal that my time was up.

I needed to act. Stop waiting and start making things happen. Find it in me. I fished in my tote bag for my notebook, flipped it open, and started to fill up the pages with my feelings. As usual, it felt good putting the thoughts into words. But this time I didn't stop there.

The minute I got home and dropped my basket of clean clothes on the living room floor, I ran into my room to retrieve my doll-making supplies. I'd hidden them and my dolls under my comforter on the outside chance that Peyton actually braved the six flights up in her Louboutins. It would be bad enough having her see *where* I lived. No need to let her see how.

Then I set about sculpting two new wax dolls based on sketches I'd made at the laundromat, working way into the night. The first would be a skinny girl with glossy black hair, thigh-high boots, and a barely there miniskirt. While the inspiration was Peyton, this doll would represent *all* the sleek, chic city chicksters who never give girls like me the time of day, let alone stop to help one of us up out of the gutter.

The next doll would be a guy, my first. I'd make him a fusion of Joshjohnjay, the quintessential urban hipster. For this, I would need baggy denim, a backward ball cap, and of course, designer sneaks, so first thing Sunday morning I walked myself up to the Chelsea Flea Market in search of fabric, dollhouse accessories, and other bargain finds. I can't remember the last time it felt this good to be out among the ebb and flow of city life. Clearly, this town is more palatable when you have a purpose.

Now I'm back in my apartment, dolls dressed, scene set, popping cashews like pills as I review the script I scrawled yesterday while my clothes cleaned themselves. Washing machines and tampons are two top reasons I'm glad to be a woman now and not a hundred years ago.

I've got my comfy sweatpants on, the ones I never would have worn if Ben were still living here. But they're perfect for recording another video to send to Kell.

My Manhattanite Kay is propped in front of my phone. I brushed her hair out and leaned her toward the camera, the way you'd stand if you were confiding in a best friend. Because really, that's what I'm doing. I want Kell to know how I feel, being forgotten like yesterday's news by the guy I like. Feeling stupid for thinking he could like me back. I want to tell her how boring and bland I feel when I walk down the street here, not that I want guys whistling at me like I'm a piece of meat—but a double take or two from a random stranger wouldn't be so bad. Acting all this out on video will be more fun than my usual whining.

I know I have posterboard and thick black markers around here somewhere, leftover supplies from all the nights Ben and I would work late in my apartment trying to come up with ideas to wow E-hole.

I *will not* let myself think about that now, him in a wife-beater and shorts sitting this close to me, sketching pictures on the posterboard while I shouted out possible taglines. Like Scattergories but more fun because we knew we were getting paychecks at the end. I thought maybe I was going to get laid at the end, too, but now I know that was just short of totally freaking delusional.

The posterboard is slid behind my refrigerator. I pull it out and bring it back to my "set" with some markers, and then I scratch out the title.

THE ADVENTURES OF IT GIRL AND CLUB BOY. I do a close-up of the card for my first shot, then throw that sheet to the side. Now I've got my camera rolling on Kay and she's whispering.

> *"I'm glad you're here,"* she confides to the viewer on the other side of the camera. *"I have a new frenemy I want you to meet."*
>
> *"Copygirl,"* I shrill in my highest voice, stretching the syllables so it sounds like Cooppyyygirllll. *"Oh, Copygirl, where are youuuu?"* It Girl bounces on the scene, and when she sees Copygirl she runs right over and leans in for a stiff doll kiss on both cheeks.
>
> *"Darling,"* It Girl says. *"For the moment I'm going to ignore the hideous outfit you're wearing because I have great news: I've met* him.*"*
>
> *"Who?"* Copygirl asks.
>
> It Girl's hands shoot up to the sky, exasperated. *"Him!"*
>
> I move Copygirl's hand up so it looks like she's scratching her head.
>
> It Girl, clad in scraps from some black fishnets I had in my closet, pulls at her shiny flat doll hair.
>
> *"The One*, Copygirl. *I met* The One!*"*

"That's good, right?" Copygirl says cautiously.

Copygirl stands and walks over to It Girl with her arms outstretched for a hug to say congratulations, but It Girl is in the middle of a cartwheel and catches Copygirl's head with her foot. Copygirl goes down with a thud I make from hitting my hand a little too hard on the hardwood floors. I did have that art teacher in high school who said if art didn't hurt, then it was just a canvas and some paint. Mrs. Studebaker has to be out there somewhere, still rocking her armpit hair and Jesus sandals. I bet she'd be proud to see me now.

"I didn't even know you had a boyfriend," Copygirl says from the ground.

"That's what I'm telling you!" It Girl shrieks again. *"I didn't until last night. But thanks to the fact that we drank all the tonic that came with our bottle service, I had to borrow some from the hottie at the next table and now I know the man I am going to marry!"*

On cue, a guy's voice is heard.

"Yo, yo, yo. Is my main squeeze in da house?"

Quickly I grab a piece of posterboard and scratch out: IT'S A BIRD HIPSTER! IT'S A PLANE POSER! IT'S SUPERMAN CLUB BOY!!

"Damn, you're looking fine," Club Boy says as he struts toward It Girl. Copygirl is still on the ground so he steps right on her but keeps going without looking down.

"Ooff," Copygirl says, but neither It Girl nor Club Boy notices.

"*Damn, did I tell you how hot that straight hair you rock is looking? My last three bitches had that exact same style.*"

It Girl runs a hand down her locks. "*Thanks, Club Boy. It's the latest straightening treatment—they slather your hair with sheep guts. It's like fifteen hundred dollars a pop, but Daddy gets the bills so it's, like, practically free.*"

"*Damn, hold up for a selfie,*" Club Boy says, and he pulls out a piece of lint. I zoom the camera close.

"*Like wow! Is that what I think it is?*" It Girl is breathing heavy.

"*Damn, if you think it's a cell phone so small you have to look through a Hubble telescope to see who you're texting, then yeah, it's whatcha thinking.*"

"*God, Club Boy,*" It Girl croons, "*we were made for each other.*"

Copygirl picks herself up from the ground as It Girl and Club Boy start to make out.

I'm doing the best slobbering dog imitation I've got, licking the back of my hand and sucking and making noises I imagine only come from brothels and Super 8 motel rooms in Daytona Beach at the height of spring break.

GET A ROOM! I write on another posterboard.

I stand Copygirl up and now she's just watching the couple while they continue to make out.

"*Hey, guys, I'm standing right here. And it's not nice to spritz your friends with flying saliva,*" she says.

I swivel Club Boy's head to look at Copygirl. *"Who's that?"*

"Oh, no one," It Girl says.

Then I zero in on Copygirl. Her doll face has the same expression as always, except I'm whispering, *"You bitch! I didn't even like you to start with!"* so everyone at home will know what she's thinking.

Then the camera cuts back to It Girl, who's now giving Club Boy a lap dance. She's thrusting and grinding at incredibly awkward angles that only a doll can do.

I cut back to a new poster.

WHO SAYS FOREVER CAN'T START WITH A LAP DANCE?

With the camera still on the poster, you can hear Club Boy's voice.

"Damn, girl, almost forgot. I got our names on the list for that club you said you wanted to hit in Hell's Kitchen. Poser Bar. Bottle service, baby."

Now It Girl lets out a long, prolonged orgasm. Obviously I have to guess at what this sounds like since I haven't had one in about a hundred years. While I fake it, I take a bottle of Mountain Dew I've shaken and open it so liquid explodes across the poster, mimicking It Girl's off-camera explosion. The spray blurs out the word FOREVER, which is a really nice touch.

When she's done moaning, It Girl croons at Club Boy, *"Baby, you just made my day—I've always wanted to try Poser Bar. I. LOVE. YOU."*

Copygirl pushes her way through the wet spot in the poster, surprising the young lovers behind it.

"Love? Really? It Girl, you've know him for like, what, five minutes?"

It Girl looks up, pulling down her micromini. *"Copygirl, ohmigod, I forgot you were still there. Don't be jealous. If you'd go shopping with me so we can get you clothes that don't scream lonely cat lady, you could totes come with us to Poser Bar and maybe my new soul mate could get you in. Then you'd meet your soul mate, too!"*

Club Boy laughs, looking Copygirl up and down. His baggy jeans are down around his ankles, so we're treated to a view of his hot pink boxers. *"As if. We might have to bribe the bouncer."*

"Oh wow, guys, what an offer. But I think I'm good." Copygirl's tone is sarcastic. *"My cat needs feeding and I need to take my soul—I mean my clothes—to the laundromat for a good scrub."*

"She'd be better off burning them," Club Boy says to It Girl like Copygirl's not even in the room.

"Who? What? Whatev!" It Girl shrills. *"Get her out of our way so we can take a sex selfie."*

Now I move my phone in close on Copygirl's face for the wrap-up.

"The moral of the story, friends? If you can't find true love, fear not—you can buy it. You just have to know where to shop."

And then I press stop.

I smirk, looking at ever-trendy It Girl and Club Boy still frozen in their lap dance, feeling cathartic. It's like I've exacted a small piece of revenge on Ben and Peyton—even though they'll never see this. I watch the playback on my phone and am happy with how the footage looks, even on my cracked screen. It's bitchy and pokes fun at all the girls who think The One might drop from the sky at any moment—and yes, I have to admit that was kinda me just a couple weeks ago—but the video is true. And that makes it better than anything else I've been writing lately.

Suddenly I can't send it to Kell fast enough. It's the kind of madness we'd create back when we were in pigtails in suburbia, taking the frustrations of our elementary school days out on our Barbies. After I message it to her, I collapse on the couch. Somehow it's the first time all day I've even noticed how quiet my apartment is and I don't mind in the least. I close my eyes and let my mind bathe in the silence. I have bigger plans, things I want to make happen in the real world. But that's for another day. Right now, I'm content to live in this universe I've created for just a little while longer.

"Top that, losers!" Elliott yells so loud that I look up from my laptop and glare at him.

They're playing the Tape Game, a popular office diversion invented by E-hole and adopted by the rest of his minions. The rules are simple. Holding a piece of blue painter's tape in your hand, you run down the hallway and jump as high in the air as you can, slapping your tape up on the wall. The goal? To stick your tape higher than anyone else's. The point? I'm not sure, but I suspect it's to let Elliott remind everyone how superior he is by being the recurring winner, due solely to the fact that he's so damn tall.

From what I can see, Johnjoshjay must have already taken their turn, because there are strips of tape way below Elliott's on the wall, and they are high-fiving his high jump with such fervor that I am fairly certain we will have to send in scuba divers to extract them from up the guy's butt. Even Todd has taken a break from pretending to work while he surfs furniture websites so he can watch the ruckus with the rest of the peasants.

Next on deck is Peyton, who rips the roll of tape out of Elliott's hands, making a big show out of the whole thing, as usual.

"Let me show you boys how it's done," she purrs, batting her ridiculously inhuman eyelash extensions.

I'd been secretly trying to write new taglines for Little Kitty to kill time this morning, but Peyton's wearing her boots with three-inch heels, so it's like witnessing a bad car accident; I can't look away. I'm hoping she twists an ankle and falls on her perfectly coiffed head, but who am I kidding? I'd settle for a really lame jump.

Elliott must be bloodthirsty, too, because he says, "*No way* you can catch enough air in those heels."

She looks him right in the eye and fires back, "You'd be surprised what I can do in these heels."

She may be flirting with E, but I'm sure it's to get Ben's attention. I glance at him, one desk over, and he's grinning like he's in on the joke. Just thinking back to that ShoutOut from the strip club, her boots wrapped around his waist, makes me pray she trips and falls right through the Sheetrock like an old cartoon character, leaving a Peyton-shaped hole in the wall and disappearing forever.

Once she's certain she has *everyone's* undivided attention, she starts sprinting effortlessly across the polished concrete like she's run entire marathons in heels. Which, now that I think about it, she probably has.

She leaps and slaps the wall, then sticks her landing like she's Kerri Strug, complete with arms raised triumphantly in the air. Her tape is stuck a few inches below Elliott's, but the boys all hoot and holler anyway, impressed with her crazy agility. No wonder Ben's into her. If she can do that with heels on, I can only imagine what she does when they're off.

"Got what it takes, Wildman?" Peyton hands Ben the tape.

"You know it!" he says, and I die a little inside, thinking that she probably does.

As Ben stands up and eagerly takes his turn, cheered on by Joshjohnjay, I realize he's becoming one of them, joining in their reindeer games. He sticks his tape close to Elliott's, but no cigar.

Suddenly, Suit comes walking out of the conference room and heads right toward the boys, with laser focus. I wonder if he's here to complain about the ruckus. I hope so. I really want to get back to work on my Little Kitty lines. I know I can come up with something better than E-hole's cattitude—even if the client *has* started running those dumb ads in magazines. I want to be ready for the next round. All part of my new plan to take action.

"Elliott, are you ready to start—" he begins, but E cuts him off.

"Not until you have a turn," Elliott tells him.

"C'mon, is this really—" he tries, but now his words are drowned out by the crowd, who've begun chanting his name.

"Suit! Suit! Suit!"

"Fine, I'll have a go!" he yells, putting down the document he was holding. He tears off a piece of blue tape, stretches his arms above his head, loosening up, then runs down the hallway. His stride is long and effortless. Was he on the track team at Tulane? I watch, along with the others, amazed as he takes to the air like an accomplished high jumper and slaps his tape a full two inches above Elliott's.

I can't help applauding right along with the gang. I mean, that was impressive. *And* he beat E at his own game! I could hug him! *If* he weren't Suit, obviously.

Hearing me cheer, he turns and gives me that crooked smile. "Kay?" he's asking me, eyebrow cocked, and I blush, confused. Has he read my thoughts again? Now everyone else is looking at me, too, and they're all saying, "Kay! Kay! Kay!" and I realize he's just offering me a turn at the Tape Game. I don't want to do this. I really don't want to do this, but the herd has me cornered. I have no choice but to play along.

"Go get 'em, Kaykay," Ben whispers as I pass, bolstering me slightly.

I stop at the end of the hallway and take a deep breath, acutely aware of every eyeball on me. Then I hear a sharp voice in my head—it's the voice of Copygirl, my wax alter ego. She's saying *Screw it, Kay! Go for it!* So I do. I tear down that hallway as fast as I can, tape in my hands, and take a huge, uncharacteristic leap of faith—landing right on top of Peter Schmidt, who has suddenly rounded the corner. He jerks back, taking the brunt of my impact in typical German stride, not even flinching, but I fall to the floor, tape still stuck to my fingers. Elliott yells, "Way to go, Special K!" and everyone—even Ben—starts laughing.

Everyone but me and Schmidt. He mutters something that is definitely not English but most certainly a curse word, and I just want to melt myself into the carpet. Suit rushes over to help me up, which is seriously nice of him, and the least he can do, since my embarrassment is all his fault. But before I can properly accuse, or even process what's happened, Schmidt is pointing at me. "You. At ze conference room. *Jetzt!*"

I stand there, paralyzed with fear, and watch as Schmidt walks down the hall, summoning others. "Todd. Peyton. Josh und Jay." He points at each of them, and they obediently walk past me.

I look at Ben and make eyes at him, and Ben makes eyes back, motioning for me to follow everyone else. And then Schmidt points at Ben. "You, Kay's partner. *Komm!*"

I feel a small prick of sadness for Ben. I know Schmidt knows his name—you don't get to be a crackerjack strategic planner by being stupid—but his choice of words, a German affectation, has no doubt left Ben feeling inferior.

"Come!" I mouth to him, repeating Schmidt's command, but Ben looks away, down at his feet, and reluctantly follows me down the hall.

If I had to make a list of the best-of-the-best in the agency, it would probably be the exact list of people getting corralled into the conference room. People act like they don't keep tabs, but the truth is that every agency person knows who is currently on top of the game—for that moment at least. The best account supervisors, who connect clients with the creatives. The best account planners, who devise strategy and also deal with clients. The production people, who help ideas get turned into actual ads. And us, the creatives, who think up those ideas.

Suit is here, of course, and Elliott. Peyton is next to Elliott, whispering something he actually seems to find funny. This is interesting as I'm not sure I've ever seen Elliott laugh at anyone's jokes but his own.

Joshjohnjay are on deck. I'm here. So is Ben, who still won't meet my gaze. Todd. Jess, the account supervisor, who always has her shit together. I take a seat far from the center seat at the table—where I assume Schmidt is going to be sitting—and wait.

The good news, I'm almost certain, is that this group isn't here to get fired. This definitely is not a room filled with people they can afford to lose. As I scan the place I do notice that Bouffa isn't here, so I hope the people Stalin left out aren't the ones getting fired.

"What's going on?" I whisper to Ben. He just shrugs his shoulders. When it comes to our agency's crazy, gangsta-rap-loving German leader, anything is possible. I let out a big blow of frustrated air and settle into my seat. I attempt to find a spot on the ceiling worth studying, but instead somehow get stuck in Suit's field of vision. For a second it seems like he's been staring at me, but I'm sure that's just coincidence. Should I smile and acknowledge the eye contact or just look away? I'm saved from the decision by the conference room doors slamming back against the walls, signaling that Schmidt has arrived.

He clears his throat, which always seems to be filled with phlegm, making me wonder if the German national anthem is sung to the tune of coughed-up mucus. Then he dives right in.

"You are here," he barks, "because you are ze core peeps on ze pitch of Kola."

Apparently greetings are only used when there is time to waste—times when the business of a billion-dollar soda company is not hanging in the balance.

"We are changing zings up for zis pitch. Heavy hitters are needed und as all you know, change has always been in ze DNA of Schmidt Travino Drew.

"We're going to mix up partners in the creative side to freshen ze talent oop, like when Jay Z verked with Alicia Keys, or when Mariah Carey sang on zat Ol' Dirty Bastard track, you know vat I'm sayin'? From here in oop, Josh vill verk with Elliott. You—" He points at Ben.

"Ben," Suit tells him.

"You. You vill be helping me keeps it real, because yes, some of you may not know zis but I have ze mad writing skillz."

Am I hearing him right, or was something lost in translation? Now Schmidt is a copywriter? And Ben's going to be his art director? Who will I verk, I mean work, with?

"Todd und Kay are verking together und I couldn't find her on the office but ze intern will be helping them, too. Und I expect everyone on zis core team to support we creatives in our mission to win zis business und establish Schmidt Travino Drew as the best mofo agency not just in America—but in ze world. Vord to your mothers!"

Oh my God, I'm going to start throwing things. At the very least I want to cry out in disbelief. Ben and I are no longer working together? Me with Todd? And Bouffa? This is not part of my plan.

Schmidt dismisses us by leaving the room, establishing that good-byes are now as irrelevant as hellos. Suit immediately takes over the meeting. "You guys hang tight for a minute; we'll take you through the Kola brief as soon as we get Travino on the line."

I don't even have the energy to search the ceiling for a safe spot, so I stare at the table. My whole world is spinning and all I want is the safety of the cubicle, the last thing Ben and I share. Though at the rate we're going, that will probably change in the next five minutes.

I turn to ask Ben what he thinks of all this only to find he's already gone, on the other side of the room queuing with the other guys behind Elliott's chair. My pocket is buzzing and it takes me a minute to realize it's my phone. *Back to reality, Kay, someone's calling.* I look and it's Kell—like I have time for her right now. I send it to voice mail, stand up, and walk as fast as I can back to my cubicle, but before I'm even halfway there my pocket buzzes again.

"What's up?" I answer the phone. Like Schmidt, I have no time for greetings. My dreams of launching my and Ben's careers into the stratosphere have just been sandblasted. All hope of working alongside him deep into the night on the pitch have been squashed! I can't be expected to say hello.

"Kay!" Kell shouts. I extend the phone from my ear, then gingerly pull it back.

"What?"

"Are you sitting down?"

I actually have to look around to assert that, yes, I am in my chair. This is my cubicle. My computer is in front of me. The partner I came to the agency with has been ripped out of my life but otherwise, everything is as it should be.

"So don't be mad—" she begins. She's so hesitant she doesn't even bother with her usual Parisian accent or crazy Frenglish. Not good for Kell. She's probably going to follow up with *but I'm having a spontaneous elopement with a multi-gazillionaire prince of Monaco this weekend.* It's one of those days when the world spins for everyone but me.

"I just thought your last video was so badass," she says.

"Fine. Great." I can't help my bitchiness. "It was badass and what."

"Well . . ." She trails off.

"Kell, I'm at work and life is sucking so hard I might as well be on the underside of a Dyson, do you need something important or can we do this chat later?"

"Geez, Kay. I just wanted to tell you that I put your videos online, um, on a blog I sorta set up for you. And then I maybe, kinda forwarded the blog link to a friend of mine at the museum. Who must have a shitload of friends somewhere because I just got woken up with a call in the middle of the night from *my friend* who said *her friend* called to ask when you were doing another video because people are eating it up."

"I'm confused, Kell. Eating what up?"

"Your videos! Copygirl! The blog I set up for it! I just checked it and you're getting, like, a shitload of hits. I guess from this friend of a friend who linked to you. I don't totally understand how it all unfolded but the point is—*people are loving you.*"

This is no time for a joke. "Kell, I'm sorry, but I can't deal with this right now. I have to do a pitch with this vet ad guy who's never even said hello to me before, and an ex-intern, and Ben won't make eye contact with me, and he moved out and—"

"What!" Kell screams again. "Ben moved out?"

"Gone. Packed up and drove away in a Range Rover, no less."

"Oh my God, Kay, you have to do a video about that. I'm e-mailing you the blog login info right now. "

All of a sudden Bouffa is here. Hanging over the wall of my cube like a Chia Pet of stylish disco curls.

"I heard I missed a meeting. And I am, like, so devastated about it. But I had to have a Diet Coke, you know? So, I like, ducked outside? And I didn't know there was a meeting?"

I tell Bouffa to hold on, and then go back to Kell. "We'll continue this prank call at a later date."

Kell is upset; I can hear it in her voice. "You're not being very cool, Kay. I want you to do another video—I want you to do a lot more videos—you can tell the world what you think about Ben and work and—"

I cut her off. I don't care if I'm making her mad, she's making *me* mad. What right did she have to put my videos online? And now acting like anyone out there cares about my stupid doll rants.

"How many times do I have to say it, Kell? This is a stupid idea, *comprends? Bête! Idiote! Stupide!*" I may not have retained as much high school French as my BFF, but I do remember how to put someone down.

Without saying good-bye, Kell just hangs up the phone. I can't remember her ever doing that in all the time I've known her. But I don't have time to worry that she's mad. Bouffa is waiting and she tells me we're wanted back in the conference room.

"So, I *cannot* believe I'm going to work with you! And Todd! OMFG!" She is literally squealing as we walk down the hall.

"I can't believe it, either." I say this without an ounce of her enthusiasm. But she's too jazzed to notice.

Apparently Todd's not thrilled either, because when Gina takes the empty seat next to him at the conference room table, he doesn't even look at her.

Suit starts the briefing back up right away, putting Travino on speakerphone.

"*Not flat water! Pellegrino!*" the boss man is barking at someone.

"Where is he?" Elliott mouths to Suit.

"Saint Barts," Suit mouths back, and Elliott nods knowingly.

"So Diet Coke is off the list, but Pelligrino is okay?" Bouffa whispers. She seems injured, but that might be her withdrawal symptoms talking.

"Fred, we're all here," Suit says into the speakerphone, interrupting some conversation between Travino and a deckhand. Or maybe a waiter.

"*That will be all,*" he says in a lower voice, then, much louder, presumably to us, "Today is the first day of the rest of this agency's life! For the past week, we've been meeting with the Kola clients, learning about their business, getting to the heart of what makes them tick, and what they want. And what is that, you ask?—*No, no ice, I drink it room temperature*—They want what we all want, to be popular!—*Not lemon. Lime. Just leave it, dammit! I'll squeeze it myself!*—What was I saying?"

"We all want to be popular," Suit says. He happens to look at me and I don't look away. Is Travino for real?

"Yes, right. Though challenging their biggest competitor, Coca-Cola, seems like the obvious route, Kola has other rivals. In the past year, they've lost significant market share, thanks to the huge growth of at-home carbonation systems. Brands like SodaFizz have stolen the limelight, making it cool for people to bottle and drink their own flavored bubbly drinks. But these drinks are not REAL SODA. They're frauds, fakes, me-toos, flat water in sheep's bubbled clothing—*Straw! Marius! I cannot drink this without a straw! Where did he go? Do I really have to get up off this lounger . . . ?*

Through the speakerphone, we hear rustling noises, a loud splash, and the thump of feet on a deck.

"Fred? Fred?" Suit calls into the phone.

Travino answers, but now he sounds far away. "I'll let you take over, my good man. You wrote the brief, so brief away! *Where's my towel?*"

And just like that, dial tone.

Elliott doesn't even try to suppress his laughter. *"Straw! Marius! But not this one. It's way too bendy!"*

Suit starts cracking up, too, and it's the first time I've ever seen him smile with his whole face. So the straight guy has a sense of humor?

"He's so cute when he laughs," Bouffa says so only I can hear, and I kick her under the table. I guess she's right, but he's still Suit. And Bouffa's a pretty girl, but next to Suit's lady friend, we're all vanilla pudding.

"Here is the creative brief." Suit quickly gets back to business. "I will be heading up the planning team, so along the way, please feel free to come to me with questions, or to check if your ideas are on track."

Todd passes me my copy of the brief, and I read along, yellow highlighter at the ready, as Suit continues.

"Our strategy, in one sentence: Kola is the original, the authentic soda, and being authentic is cooler than any fad."

Todd snorts loud enough for me to hear. I look down at his brief and he's scrawled BULLSHIT across the top. Great. My new partner is jaded and unenthused. Not exactly the traits of a pitch winner. I do my best to ignore his not-so-subtle body language for the next hour as Suit leads us through background information on Kola and I take copious notes.

When Suit gets done talking, Todd reaches over and takes the highlighter from my hand. He draws one, two, three bright lemon lines across the BULLSHIT on top of his page. Then he announces, "I think I've got what I need to get started. Kay? Gina?" And he stands up from his chair and turns to walk out of the room.

I turn to Ben, who would usually be my life jacket in such a situation, but he is staring at his page, not willing to save me. I don't dare make eye contact with E or any of his boys, and so I am left looking at Suit, who, I think, gives an ever-so-slight nod of his head, urging me to follow Todd.

"C'mon," I whisper to Bouffa, and she scurries after me as I leave the room.

The walk to where all of us creatives sit is short, but it's long enough for Bouffa to ask eight times if I think Kola is really the best soda out there. I don't pay any attention to her. It's all I can do to contain my frustration until I reach Todd, and then it's code red.

"So you think you're ready to get started?" I am seething. "Did you listen to anything they said about the pitch in there?"

Todd doesn't bother to acknowledge our arrival. He's sweeping books off his desk into his bag. The he unwraps his jacket from the back of his chair and slides into what looks like very fine black leather. I make a mental note to ask Bouffa later how much she thinks that baby costs.

"Hello?" I ask. But he is ignoring me and still won't look in my direction.

"Have you done one of these before?" he finally asks as he shuts down his computer.

"By *one of these*, do you mean *one of these* huge career-defining pitches? In that case the answer is no, I have not."

He's ready to go but can't leave without turning to face me and Bouffa. "The first thing you need to learn," he says, "is that the briefings for these 'huge career-defining pitches' are all the same."

"All the same *bullshit*?" I try to let the sarcasm flow but I know it is just dripping slowly; I simply don't have enough experience at being a bitch.

Todd intimidates me in a singsongy voice. "Yes, all the same bullshit. At the end of the day, the flashiest idea will win, so sound strategy, great thinking, solid client input . . . none of that matters. I'm going to head out for a couple hours and clear my head of all the filler they just tried to insert in my brain. Either of you creative gals care to join?"

Bouffa, who has not spoken yet, finally pipes up. "Are you going somewhere where they serve—um—Diet Coke?"

Todd looks past me to her. "Put on your jacket. Miss Kay, are you coming with us or are you going to stick around here and sulk about the loss of your beloved partner?"

How does he know that Ben is my beloved partner? Shit. Is that what everyone thinks? Is it so obvious?

"Let's go, Bouffa." I practically run to my desk and grab my things, then head in the path Todd has taken to the elevator.

When we get to the elevator bank, he is chatting up Veronique. "What do you think about curry powder with fish?"

"Oh, I don't believe in using store-bought spices for my fish, pumpkin. I buy 'em fresh and cook 'em clean. That way you get their spirit."

"Ah yes," Todd says, "and the true spirit of the fish is what I am looking for."

I look from Veronique to Todd and Todd to Veronique. Did she really just call him pumpkin?

"You ladies ready?" he asks.

"Where you headed to?" Veronique addresses Pumpkin, ignoring Bouffa and me.

"We're going to get some fresh air. Best way to get fresh thoughts, you know?"

Veronique nods her head in agreement. "If anyone calls, I'll tell them you are involved in a brainstorming session."

"You always know the perfect thing to say."

Both of them laugh again and I swear I see a sparkle in Veronique's eye. I realize I've never looked far enough from the incestuous circle of creatives to wonder what other friendships might be lurking in the agency.

Todd pushes the elevator button and raises a hand in a wave good-bye to Veronique. I raise my hand timidly and Bouffa jumps in the elevator; even the cashmere scarf around her neck bounces.

"See ya soon, Veronique!" she shouts. I cringe. It's obviously never occurred to Bouffa that maybe—just maybe—not everyone is her BFF.

Once the elevator door closes, Bouffa asks Todd where we are going. But her actual words are, "So where are we, like, going?" Again, I cringe.

"I was thinking manicures."

Bouffa can barely contain a squeal. "Are we allowed to do that?"

"We are allowed to do anything that gets us closer to cracking the Kola equation," he answers in a very deep voice. I think he is mocking Travino, but maybe it's Suit. I think back to Suit's voice. It isn't quite that deep. In fact it's actually kind of light and easy, calming.

Man, why am I thinking about this?

Todd snaps me out of it with his next bit of unsolicited advice.

"The second thing you need to know about these 'career-defining pitches'—as you call them—is that once you crack one nut, there is always another one waiting around the corner. If you burn yourself out on a sprint to the finish, you fizzle. If you take care of yourself and stay fabulously above the fray, you've got a chance at winning the marathon."

I say nothing and wait for the burst of icy winter air. I want to feel the burn of something besides anger—this guy has zero fight in him, and I know that to win Kola it's going to take a big fight. In one week I've lost my best friend in this city, my roommate, and my partner—who was the reason I wanted this big, badass ad job in the first place. If I don't figure out a way to rally this new "team" of Todd and Bouffa to somehow create a Kola ad that's unlike the other five million fizzy carbonated drink ads that have been done since the beginning of time, then I will seriously have nothing.

Of course I don't have any brilliant ideas during the walk to Soho. Todd turns a corner and pushes through the door of, yes, an actual nail salon, acting as if he owns the place. And he might as well, given the reception he receives. Everyone who works there turns to acknowledge his arrival. He is the George from *Cheers* of this Happy Nail Salon in Soho.

Pretty quickly he works the room. I've heard him talk more today than ever before, and I have to admit he's actually quite kind and funny. He doesn't roll his eyes or mention the word *bullshit* or seem jaded or cynical. When he's not lecturing me, he actually seems like a pretty cool guy.

People are shuffled around so the three of us can line up in three neighboring manicure stations. Quicker than they can tell us to pick a color, Bouffa has procured a straw and Diet Coke from her Marc Jacobs bag and is sipping away.

"Do you have a refrigeration pack in there?" I ask her. She seems confused, but Todd snickers. This is a good sign.

He finishes his laugh with a question, not a directive. Another good sign.

"Tell me, Kay, why do you think this pitch is so crucial?"

"Everyone says it's the most important thing to ever happen to the agency." *Hell, I think to myself, it's the most important thing to ever happen to me.*

"And you think if you listen to everything they say, you will have a great idea that wins the pitch for them?" Todd's tone is flat at best. At worst, he's patronizing the hell out of me. Maybe those good signs earlier weren't so good after all.

I bristle defensively and my manicurist flattens my hand so she can keep working.

"I guess, um, well . . ." *Now is not the time to stumble over words, Kay.* I take a deep breath and assert myself. "*Yes*, that's what I think."

"Is that what everybody told you in school?" Now there's no getting around his patronizing tone.

"I don't know if everybody told us that, specifically, but I got this job by working hard, doing the assignments that were given me. I don't see why this would be any different."

"You don't win the big games by playing by the rules," Todd says. "And in an agency, a pitch is the biggest game there is. You've got to come up with your own strategy, you have to do the idea that feels right to you. Blow it out. Make it larger than life."

From my other side I hear Bouffa practically squeal, "Go big or go home!"

"Um, yes, Gina. Go big or go home . . . I guess."

Bouffa takes a perfunctory sip of her Diet Coke, clearly pleased to have approval from Todd. Then she absorbs herself in micromanaging her manicurist with directives about her cuticles. Briefly, I feel guilty. There have been entire years of my life when I didn't even notice I had cuticles.

Todd keeps talking to me. "You're a good writer, from what I've seen. And you seem hungry enough. But you've got to look beyond what people lay out as 'the rules.' You've got to do things your own way."

"Your way is ditching work and getting manicures?" I'm skeptical.

"Sort of," Todd says, not at all offended. "My way is letting everyone scurry around like mice looking for teeny-tiny pieces of cheese, while I sit back and think about the big feast.

"Your little art director friend—what's his name, Ken?"

"*Ben*," I say. I know I am blushing but I can't help it.

"Oh, right, right, *Ben*." I don't dare look at Todd but I can hear the smile in his voice.

He continues, "Ben is running around looking for a piece of cheese right now."

"Maybe."

"Kay . . . do you wish you were that piece of cheese?"

"What? Ben's cheese? Me? Oh, you couldn't be further from the truth!"

I thought Bouffa was done listening but sure enough, now she pipes right in. "I thought for sure you had a thing for Ben."

"Um, no, Ben and I are—were—partners. For a long time. And we were roommates. But that's it. I don't even know who he's romantically interested in . . ."

I leave this hanging, hoping maybe somebody will give me some dish on what's up with Ben and Peyton, but now these two chatterboxes are quiet. I'm not going to come right out and ask, because I'm not sure I want the true answer.

"Well." Todd waves his hand. "Regardless of that. The point is that if you want to win, you are going to have to find a way to color outside the lines—you're going to have to get creative."

"You're talking about the pitch, right?" I am a little confused.

"Of course I am, Kay." He reaches over and touches the split ends at the edge of my hair. "Of course I am."

"When do we get to work?" I ask.

"When are you going to understand what I am telling you, Kay? If you want to have a fabulous idea, you have to feel fabulous first. I'm not getting a fabulous vibe from you.

"Gina, are you getting a fabulous vibe from Kay?"

Bouffa slurps the end of her soda. "Sorry, Kay, but not really."

"Thanks, Gina." I'm not sure how I ended up underneath this dog pile. Next time I definitely will not take the middle seat between these two.

I hear my phone buzz and, glad for the distraction, I reach in my purse with my free hand. My manicurist makes a face and Todd tells her, "There's no polish yet, Qi. Just give her a second."

The manicurist shrugs her shoulders and then starts speaking to the other manicurists in Korean—I hate it when they do that; I always feel like they are talking about me.

The ShoutOut is from my brother. He's uptown, in the middle of Central Park.

"Friends and family, in one week we will be having an engagement party right here, in the park where Naomi and I first met. The best park in the world in the best city in the world and we want you to join us. Strong cocktails. Cocktail attire. And lots of merriment. Boathouse. Eight p.m. Cheers."

I sigh. Cocktail attire? That's what people say when they don't want you to wear flannel.

"Sounds like a party." Todd is on me like a bloodhound.

"Yeah! Sounds like a party!" Bouffa repeats.

I ignore both of them, sit back up, and give my hands back to Qi. She seems put out that I thought my phone was more important than my manicure. Since half the people in this city walk around with their phones attached to their ears I seriously doubt I am her first customer to cause such a delay—but since the rubdown she's doing on my arms feels like I'm putting my wrist through a meat grinder, maybe I'm wrong.

"Gonna take a date to the party?" Todd raises one eyebrow.

"Might be working, might not be able to go." I am so not having this conversation with them.

"What are you going to wear?" Bouffa perks up, more interested than she's been all afternoon.

"Like I said, I might be working on this Kola pitch—since

you two aren't concerned about it at all. *And maybe I won't be able to go to the party at all.*"

Todd clucks his tongue and all the manicurists look at him. They smile. I guess this cluck is a universal language for *Clearly this girl knows nothing.*

"You're acting like you're five minutes behind already, Kay. That's not fabulous behavior—that's mice-chasing-the-cheese behavior. I'll make you a deal, you try one week of working my way, where you actually enjoy yourself, and see what kind of big ideas flow. And by the time this party comes around, if you don't feel better about the pitch, then we'll spend the second week of our work time doing things your way. Very stressed out. Trying to please Elliott . . . or is it everybody . . . or is everybody Elliott?" He looks to the sky as if the answer is hanging up there, somewhere near the *As the World Turns* reruns playing on the television.

"Oh," he adds, like he just remembered in the nick of time. "And making googly eyes at our partners—can't forget that part of your winning strategy."

"I don't make googly eyes at my partners." I am extra defensive.

"Not anymore, I guess," Todd concedes.

"Fine," I agree. "It's a deal. One week your way and then we'll try it my way."

"Great." He's just getting a buff and no color so he pulls a hundred-dollar bill out of his wallet and hands it to his manicurist. "This should cover all three." Then he stands to leave.

"Wait! Are you going back to work without us?"

"To work? We're done with work for the day. Today's a brainstorm day. We'll meet back there tomorrow and see if we feel like 'working.'"

I start to protest but he cuts me off. "My rules for one week—we made a deal."

He's got me there. I did agree. One week of fabulous living for fabulous ideas. I don't have high hopes, but at least I got fabulous nails out of the deal.

Only one week until I can prove that work hard, write hard is the only way to win.

"Hey, Kay," Bouffa suddenly spits out. "I've always wanted to ask if Kay is short for anything? Like, are you really Kayla or Kaitlin . . . or maybe a Kami?"

I steel myself. This is going to be a very long week.

being bubbly

Day seven of Todd's plan is finally here. Don't know how well it's worked, but I do know that I am more comfortable in my apartment than I've ever been. Seems like before this week I had never spent much time here unless I was sleeping or watching TV with Ben. But with us being out of work pretty much every day "to brainstorm," I've logged some serious hours inside these four walls.

I guess Todd told the big guns that he wanted our team to work on our own and they said that was fine. Can't believe he got such an extended hall pass, but he did.

I *did* pop into the office once, midweek, but it was only to bring Ben his mail. Okay, that was a bit of a ruse. I really wanted to see him, and also to show my face in front of the partners and Elliott so they wouldn't think I was slacking. But none of them were even there. Veronique told me Travino was still in St. Barts, Schmidt and Ben had gone to Café Noir to concept, and E and the boys went to a matinee of the new Quentin Tarantino flick at the Angelika.

Veronique even scolded me for coming in!

"Girl, ain't you supposed to be working *off-site*?" she said while feverishly stitching her latest muumuu. "What you doin' coming by here, trying to look all goody-goody in front of the bosses? Or are you trying to make googly eyes at that old partner of yours? Get on out of here before I tell Todd I saw you."

Then, I kid you not, she stuck her sewing needle into that voodoo head thingie on her desk and I swear I got a kink in my neck five minutes later. I wanted to ask Todd about Veronique and her alleged black magic but I didn't dare. It would only give me away.

Back on the street, I was feeling down about missing Ben, and guilty for breaking Todd's rules, so when this little Asian street vendor whispered, "Pssst . . . Miss. Mahk Jakub bag?" I didn't ignore him like I normally do. Instead, I nodded yes, because what could be more fabulous than a Marc Jacobs bag—even if it was a knockoff? And Todd did say if I wanted to write fabulous, I needed to feel fabulous. But feeling fabulous has never been my strong suit.

The vendor motioned for me to follow him down the block, and led me to a gated door next to a Chinese grocery. *Is this a little weird?* I wondered He removed the padlock, opened the gate, then looked left and right like he was checking to see if the coast was clear. That's when I knew, this was mega weird. The streets of Chinatown are lined with tables of fake bags with misspelled logos, like Channel, Luis Vitton, and Mark by Marc Jakobs. What were we doing here?

Against my better instincts, I followed the little man through the door, where we stood together inside a dark windowless room the size of a walk-in closet. I started to freak out. What if the man locked me in here and sold me into slavery? No one would even know where I was, and I'd be on a ship to China by dinnertime. See? This is why I don't like taking risks.

Then the man turned on the lights and I realized the room was filled with shelves and shelves of purses. Every designer any city girl worth her salt would know enough to drool over. He pointed to a row of studded satchels and said, "See. Mahk Jakub. Very nice." And all the logos were spelled correctly.

"Are these stolen?" I asked, flabbergasted.

Ignoring this, he said, "I give you very nice price. You try," and handed me a black Astor hobo bag that I'd seen in *Lucky* magazine for four hundred dollars. I slung it over my shoulder, fingering the buttery leather and shiny studs. Suddenly, I understood why Bouffa lists Marc Jacobs as her religious denomination.

"Look very nice. Fifty dolla. You buy!" the man insisted, and before I knew what was happening, I was forking over the entire contents of my wallet. I only had forty-two dollars, but he took it anyway and released me back out into the safety of daylight carrying my contraband bag. I couldn't wait to show Todd and Bouffa my first foray into fabulous when I saw them the next day.

Gina shrieked, "Marc Jacobs Astor hobo! Nice job, Kay!"

Todd nodded. "Hot bag. Very hot."

I told him, "You have no idea."

We've been meeting for coffee every day at ten and talking about life. Every day I try to steer the conversation back to Kola but Todd reminds me we're working by his plan. And then we end up talking about his futile attempts to turn his relationship with his boyfriend into a long-term commitment and about Bouffa's dream to one day open her own purse store. Actually, a purse boutique, specializing in handbags for people who have assistants that carry around their heaviest things. They ask me about my life but I don't open up much. Instead of talking about Ben or my dolls—the only two things really on my mind other than winning the pitch—I just turn the conversation back to them and neither one of them seems to mind that much.

But at home I've been all about my ex-partner and my wax creations. The dolls have actually been helping me get over Ben in their own way.

I've got six new ones now—and a very ruined manicure to prove it. The super-tall creative genius who I named Evil Leader of the Free World. I guess that one's kind of Elliott inspired. Two twin girls dressed as wannabe fashionistas from the burbs, wearing UGG boots and velour sweats that read *Juicy* on their ass. Each repeats everything the other one says, adding a question mark to the end of every sentence. And I did the perfect couple—guess that would be Brian and Naomi. They look very Upper West Side with just enough downtown mixed in to prove they believe in life below Union Square. As long as life is a five-star restaurant or the squeaky-clean insides of an art gallery. Of course I had to do another Kay doll. It's Kay as I am right now: lonely and confused. I drew a question mark on her chest instead of putting her in clothes, but she does have Converse on her feet.

Lonely Kay is the star of the first video I did for my website this week. It's all about how she develops an unlikely relationship with her newly purchased handbag, and finds that it fulfills her needs better than any boy ever could. The suburban twins, Bridge and Tunnel Girl, come to her for love advice, so she takes them to her black market purse dealer and introduces them to Louis and Marc.

I actually shot part of that one on the street in Chinatown, and it gave the film such a cool look and feel, I decided my next video would have to be done on location, too. And what better place to film the Evil Leader of the Free World than in front of the United Nations? So I packed up my dolls and props and hopped a subway train up the East Side. The last time I'd traveled above 14th Street was with Ben, the day we ditched work to go to Central Park. Remembering that afternoon bummed me out some, but I'm proud to say I saw four different ads for Dr. Zizmor during the commute, yet I only cried once. And the trip was totally worth it, because I really love the way the creative genius video turned out. First the Evil Leader of the Free World charms It Girl and Club Boy into believing the world is flat after all. Then he gets into a pissing contest, literally, with Copygirl. Thanks to the water pistol I brought, it really looks like he's relieving himself on the UN lawn. And of course, Copygirl loses, because unlike Evil Leader's male minions, she never even had the right equipment to compete in the first place.

But my crowning achievement of the week is the video I dedicated to Kell. I still haven't talked to her since she got mad at me on the phone the other day. I've been calling her, but all I get back are texts saying she's really busy at the museum.

So I put together a video that had all the different Kay dolls talking about one best friend through the years.

"You know, if it weren't for you holding my hair back I totally would have puked peppermint schnapps all over my Doc Martens and I never would have forgiven myself."

"You know, if it weren't for you I would have totally been embarrassed by those aprons we had to wear that summer we were checkers at Larry's Grocery—but you held your head high and showed me how to look right past the haters . . . and shake their sodas when I ran them over the scanner, of course."

"You know, if it weren't for you I never would have had the courage to move to this place and start a life I could really call my own."

Sort of a sappy, sweet Hallmark-moment kind of film. But it should get my apology across, and maybe let Kell know that even if she is on the other side of the world, she's still the best friend a girl could have. As for all her talk about people actually visiting the site she set up for me—well, she's always had a tendency to dramatize. I'm pretty sure I'm the only person in the world entertained by these balls of wax.

I'm hoping Kell will see my video and call me. But I don't have any kind of plan on how to get Ben to call me. He's sent me a couple ShoutOuts this week, mostly just telling me how slammed he's been working with Schmidt as his partner. But one of the video posts was actually from a table at the Hole and I swear I heard Peyton's voice in the background. That was enough to make me seethe. That girl is always lurking around. But in his ShoutOuts Ben is distant and quick, and nothing feels like it used to.

My phone buzzes and I look. I guess because I'm thinking about Ben I immediately hope it's him. But no, it's a text from Suit.

The longer I'm out of the office, the more Suit texts me. It's nice of him, I guess, to keep me posted on Little Kitty. In a vote of confidence, the client has apparently doubled its media budget and has started running the "This Kitty Don't Cuddle" work in every major magazine cat lovers could possibly read. They're even talking about doing TV commercials. It's weird; I've been spending zero hours in front of my computer but I have all these scraps of paper all over my apartment where I've been writing some killer ads for Elliott's stupid tagline. I haven't showed it to Suit yet—and I probably never will—but I even rewrote the tagline itself and developed a new campaign complete with, like, twenty headlines around the idea of "Love 'em Big with Little Kitty."

It's kind of Hallmarky, I'll admit . . . Maybe I've just been in a sappy mood. But I think it makes so much sense for them. If I had cats—and one day I probably will have at least eighty, given how my love life is going—this new campaign would make me want to buy Little Kitty.

Suit texts that he has a big client lunch today to discuss consumer feedback on the new ads.

Not sure why he's telling me that, but okay. I text back, *Great.*

You guys working hard on Kola?

Ah, so he's just trying to pump me for info on what our team's up to. Can't exactly tell him the truth: nothing. Instead I write, *Of course.*

I assume our texting conversation is over but in a second my phone lights up again. *Todd's got a great head on his shoulders.*

Cryptic, much? And why are you telling me this, Suit?

I don't text back because I don't know what to write, so I am totally shocked when my phone lights up yet again. *Will I see you at your bro's party tonight?*

Oh yes, my bro's party. Tonight. At the Boathouse. Couldn't be less excited. No date. No cocktail attire. No place to hide.

I'll be there. And he'll be with his supermodel, I'm sure. The prospect of awkward conversation with the two of them makes the party seem even less appealing.

My phone beeps. *See you then.*

Ugh.

Should I take Todd's advice and try to up my fab factor for tonight's party? It's almost time for daily coffee with him and Bouffa. Maybe after our lattes she can help me find a dress. If Bouffa knows anything, it's how to shop. I wonder if it's time to do a Kay the Fabulous Girl at the Party doll . . . but instead of having her be wax, she'll actually be me.

I'm sitting at the Starbucks on Spring Street, halfway through a mocha latte and three notebook pages into a brain dump on Kola. I'd gotten here early, eager to start coming up with scripts. After taking a week off from actual writing and spending most of it playing, I can't believe how ripe my mind is with ideas. Maybe Todd's method *does* have some merit. But there's only a week left until the pitch, so now we have to focus.

Todd saunters in at 10:20, five minutes behind Bouffa, already carrying a Starbucks cup that he must have procured from another location on the way. I'm in the middle of reading Gina my ideas, but to my annoyance, she interrupts me, mid-sentence, to call him out on it.

"Like, is there something wrong with the Starbucks at *this* Starbucks?"

"No, Genie," he trills, "but the barista at the one on West Broadway is just so good with his hands."

"Does your boyfriend know you have a thing for bean grinders?" she teases.

"Until Gael puts a ring on this finger, I'm free to get my beans ground by anyone I choose."

"Okay," I interrupt. "Todd, I was just taking Bouffa through my Kola thoughts. Can we get down to business?"

"NoKay, my little worker bee, not until I tell you the fabulous news. Gael had a cancellation after lunch, so I've gotten him to agree to fit you in for a cut and color. On the house!"

"Ohmigod, Gael does Blake Lively's hair!" Gina shrieks.

"Ohmigod, am I that much of a charity case?"

"Nohmigod, Kay. There's a pretty girl in there *somewhere*. We've just got to let her out." Todd eyes me up and down like I'm a couch he wants to reupholster.

Apparently Gina agrees. "If anyone can find your fabulous, Todd's boyfriend can. He's, like, a magician, but with scissors? Make sure you bring him a picture of what you're wearing to the engagement party . . ."

I take the lid off my latte and stare down into the cup, wishing there was room in there for me to hide.

"So, like," she continues, "*what* are you wearing?"

"Can we please talk Kola?" I plead.

"You don't have anything," Todd guesses.

"*You don't have anything?*" Gina repeats.

"*We* don't have anything." I hold up my Kola brief.

They look at each other, then back at me, speaking at the same time: "*Bloomies!*"

Then Bouffa reaches for my hand. "It's only a block away. Come on. We're going dress shopping."

"No!" I yell. "I mean, fine, I do need a dress, but *we* need to work even more. I'm not going anywhere unless we come up with some Kola ideas first."

Bouffa gives Todd a look. "Can you believe her priorities?"

Todd pats her hand. "It's fine, G. I have to finish my cappuccino anyway."

"So, I wrote some concepts based on the strategy . . ." I start to tell Todd, but friggin Bouffa interrupts me *again*. At least this time, she doesn't change the subject.

"I like that one line you had," she says. Then she puts her finger to her lips. "What was it you were saying, like, about bubbling?"

I have to roll my eyes. "Be Bubbly," I say. "The line is 'Be Bubbly.'" If Bouffa wants to be a freaking copywriter, she has got to start paying attention to words.

"That's it!" Todd's face lights up like a runway at Fashion Week.

"That's what?" I ask.

"That's the big idea!"

I shake my head no. I must be missing something. "But I haven't even read you any of the concepts I worked out."

"Oh, that's so cute—concepts. Well, why don't you just put those in your pocket and when you get home you can file them away with everything else you learned in ad school. *Be Bubbly*! It's the perfect tagline for this a-may-zing film technique I found! Take a look."

Todd flips open his laptop and hits play on a YouTube clip

that's up on his screen. It's a Swedish music video that starts out in black and white, with a band playing crazy techno beats, but the picture starts to bubble up all over as if someone has poured acid on the film, transforming the footage into Day-Glo colors. Todd's right. It *is* a really cool effect. But . . .

"But what is the *idea*?" I just don't see it.

"*This* is the idea." Todd's enthusiasm is building. "Imagine young, hip kids dancing to an a-may-zing song as the film bubbles up."

"We could use music from that hot indie band that hangs out with Josh and Jay!" Bouffa says. Todd has already sold her on this technique of his—hook, line, and sinker.

I try again to make them see that there is no real idea in there. If all we have are flashing lights and a line, then we've got nothing.

"I don't see what the dancing has to do with Kola?"

"Be Bubbly! Get It? The kids are bubbly and cool. Then Kola is bubbly, so automatically it's cool," insists Todd.

"Cool." Gina nods. "Automatically, totally cool."

"So then, if you don't drink Kola, you're totally flat?" I wonder out loud, not really buying into any of this. But the powers that be don't keep Todd around the office because he's Mr. Congeniality; the man does have a few pitches under his belt. More than the goose egg I've got tucked in mine.

"Oooooh, that's so smart!" Gina nods even more violently. "I get it. Like, Don't be flat. Drink Kola and be bubbly."

In a voice that isn't very convincing, even to me, I point out that the 'idea,' as visually interesting as it may be, is completely off-strategy. Todd tells me to stick my strategy where the sun don't shine because it's pictures, not planning, that win pitches, bitches. Then he reminds me that we're in show business, and it's our job to make Kola look fabulous.

And, at 11:05, we are officially done working for the day. At least, in my opinion. Because *now*, as we are standing on Broadway, outside the doors of the Soho Bloomindgale's, retail playground of the fierce and fabulous, Gina says to me, "Let's get to work!"

Four floors up, the contemporary-designer department is sparse and scary-chic. I want to run back down the up escalator but Bouffa starts grabbing items off racks as Todd pulls me by the arm. He introduces me to the manager, Olé, who's a personal friend and thus kind enough not to look down at my baggy black hoodie and black high-tops, seriously out of place in this pantheon of posh.

"Olé, she's a diamond in the rough, but we need you to help her shine. And hook Kay up with my employee discount, 'kay?" Todd says and I look at him, confused.

"Toddy helps design our holiday window displays," Olé explains. "Last year, he came up with the Nutcracker dancers wearing gas masks. *Brilliant!*"

Wow, what is up with all my coworkers and their high-profile side projects? They would laugh if they knew about the stupid wax videos I've been moonlighting on. But I'm thrilled about the employee discount. Even with it, I'll have to take out a small loan to afford any of these dresses.

"And you'll get an *extra* twenty percent today if you open a Bloomies charge account," Olé tells me as if reading my mind.

Todd excuses himself—he's off to a get a seaweed wrap—telling Bouffa to make sure we ShoutOut him with options from the fitting room. She's already got an armful of outfits to show me, but not one single dress.

"Brian said cocktail attire, G. I can't wear leather leggings and sweaters," I tell her.

"Maybe not tonight, but your whole look, like, needs an update?" she pleads, begging me to just try on some of her picks. As the daughter of a wealthy dad with mob ties, she's not used to taking no for an answer, so I humor her by slipping into the leggings, a black cashmere sweater, and a pair of black motorcycle boots that she thrusts at me.

It's hard to believe that the cool girl in the mirror is me.

"See, Kay?" Gina is pleased with her work. "It's like the stuff you always wear, but like, better fabric, and more fitted, to show off your bod? If you want Ben to notice you, you've got to start packaging the goods in a better way."

I cringe when she say *Ben*. I've never admitted anything to her. I must be really transparent.

"*Come on!* I've seen how you look at him. Ask him to go with you tonight? Like, you've got nothing to lose, you know? You're already friends?"

Here in the dressing room, looking at the me I could be, I know she is right. I have vowed to take risks, so why not?

She promises to bring me actual dresses, and I promise I will text him. I try on a few of the fitted plaid shirts Bouffa scoped out, procrastinating, then take a deep breath and pull out my phone.

I text, *Hey.* He pings back right away, *Hey you! Where ya been?*

I type, *Bri's engagement party is tonight! Boathouse. Free booze! Tag along?*

He texts back, *Sure. I could use a drink.*

And like that, I've got a date for tonight! I'm super stoked, so much so that when Gina returns to the dressing room, I try on every dress she hands me over the door.

Each one is prettier than the next! Nina Ricci! L'Wren Scott! Derek Lam! I'm twirling around, admiring myself in a Chloé sheath that Bouffa and Todd have declared a winner, when Olé comes in to check on us.

"Have you decided?" He eyes me up and down with professional scrutiny.

That's when I think to check price tags. The dress I have on is $2,400. Is Bouffa out of her spoiled-rich-girl mind?

"They're all very nice . . ." I start, "but I don't think they're for me . . ."

"But, Kay, you look so good?" Gina whines, oblivious to my embarrassment.

Olé stares deep into my eyes and frowns. "You're right, Kay. We can totally do better. I have just the thing."

He vanishes for half a sec and comes back with a short gray tweed dress with leather sleeves. "It's our own label, normally $425, but the hem is torn, so I *just* marked it down to $169."

I obediently change into the C by Bloomingdales dress and a pair of black leather booties, and everything fits perfectly. I look sleek and sophisticated. The epitome of NYC cool.

"It's not as fancy as the others but you look like a rock star?" Gina concedes.

"All the other girls will be trussed up like overdone Thanksgiving turkeys in their silk and chiffon. Boring. Next to them, you'll be a tall glass of premium vodka," Olé promises. Then, as if again reading my thoughts, he adds, "And this, you'll even be able to wear this to work. When you want to look like the most fabulous ball buster in the room."

"Yeah, but the ripped hem look is, like, not gonna work for tonight?" Gina pouts. She does have a point.

Todd waves her off, pressing the intercom button on a wall phone. "Reneeeee! We need your magic in the fitting rooooom on Four!" he croons into it. Then to us, "Our seamstress Renee is *brilliant*! Used to be a custom dressmaker—the most perfect fit in town. Doesn't need to work—*this lady is loaded*—but she just does it to get out. She'll have this fixed in a jiff and we'll messenger it over later."

This satisfies Gina, who's familiar with Renee's work, but she's upset that I'm not buying anything else, and I have to console her. "All those outfits you picked are great, but after I buy this and the booties, I'm maxed out."

"Really?" She is shocked. "Then, like, you need to have the spending limit upped on all your cards."

Clearly she is incapable of fathoming a life where people have to pay their own bills. Sometime during our debate the seamstress must have walked, in because I hear an older woman's voice. "Hello, dear. So we meet again."

Gina responds, "Hay, Renee. I just saw you last week? This is Kay . . . I'm off to look at purses, 'kay?"

I turn around and see immediately that the woman was actually talking to me. And it's not just any woman. It's the woman from McDonald's. Of all the dressing rooms in all the world, she walks into mine!

This time I do smile and say hello, making sure to look at her, to really see her.

"So, Kay"—she smiles back—"have you found what you were looking for?" I'm not sure if she means the dress or something much deeper.

"I'm working on it." I'm a little taken aback by the randomness of this repeat encounter, and by the fact that she's not in the least surprised to see me.

"This is a much better look than the last time I saw you." Her eyes lock with mine, and again I get the feeling she's referring to more than my attire.

"I have a party to go to," I tell her. "My brother's engagement. To Naomi. A fabulous girl. Everyone there will be fabulous. But I have a date. And now I have this dress. So I'm happy. For my brother. And tonight will be fun. I'm planning on having fun." I'm rambling like an idiot, trying to cover my confusion with conversation. But Renee just smiles at me like she's grateful for even this ridiculous slice of human contact. Then I remember all the questions I had about her after I left McDonald's, and think to finally ask her about herself.

"So you've been doing this a long time? I mean, I know you used to be a dressmaker."

"Yes, dear. I've worked here for ten years. Early retirement didn't suit me. This city doesn't wait for those who sit around on the sidelines." She bores a hole into me with her eyes as she says this. Am I in the twilight zone?

Just then, Gina returns, waving her phone. "Todd just buzzed, Kay? Gael's, like, expecting you in ten minutes!"

I still have to change back into my old clothes, open up a Bloomies charge card, pay for my purchases, and get myself to Nolita. As much as I hate to leave this woman, I absolutely have to.

"Please excuse me, Renee," I say with more politeness than I've shown since I moved to New York. "I have to go, but it was so nice seeing you, and thanks in advance for the quick turn-around on this dress."

"Of course, dear." She smiles brightly but cryptically. *"I'm happy to help."*

Later, as I'm walking back to my apartment, I replay the whole scenario in my head, trying to find the hidden meaning in her words. Though walking isn't exactly what I'm doing. I'm practically bouncing. Gael has given me such a great haircut—Bouffa was right, he's a magician with the scissors—and even though he chopped off three inches, I don't even care because this new, shoulder-length, asymmetrical style accentuates my formerly lifeless waves in a way I'd never dreamed possible. He insisted on golden highlights, too, said they'd bring out the green in my eyes, and they really do.

Just when I think this day can't get much better, I leap up my stoop at exactly the same time a messenger is ringing my bell. Must be my new dress!

"I'm Kay Carlson," I tell him, and he hands me not one, not two, but *three* garment bags, plus *two* shoeboxes.

"Must be a mistake? I'm not expecting all this."

But he shrugs, shows me that it is indeed my name on all the items, hands me an envelope, and asks me to please sign because he has two more stops to make before he can get to his bowling league. I scrawl my initials on his clipboard, lug everything inside my foyer, and rip open the envelope. There's a handwritten note inside:

Dear Kay. Kindness is the cure for this city. Have fun. —Renee

That dear, sweet, and very rich old woman bought me the outfits Gina had picked out for me, even the motorcycle boots! I'd always sneered at fairy godmothers in the movies as some lame fictional device, but not anymore. If I were writing about this in my journal, the whole page would be punctuated with kittens and hearts.

I just want to hug Renee and this whole darned town.

Up in my apartment, new clothes strewn across the couch Ben slept on not so long ago, I crack open a Kola to sip while I get ready. I don't normally drink them—I prefer my caffeine at least 40 degrees hotter—but I'm hoping some big brand insight will seep into my brain through osmosis. *Be Bubbly?* It's okay for a tagline, but it's hard not to call bullshit on the promise that this attitude can be created by a soda. By a fun shopping spree, on the other hand? Maybe. By a killer dress? For sure. By an amazing hairdo? Most definitely.

And so I am feeling more bubbly than ever when I stand outside the 72nd Street entrance of Central Park at 8:12 p.m., waiting for Ben. "Like, tell him how you feel, Kay?" Gina had urged me earlier. "Peyton always says you don't deserve anything you don't reach for." Seems to be working for her. But just thinking of Peyton's name proves to be a jinx, because now I get the text from Ben that just a week ago I would have certainly expected.

Schmitty wants to work late over dinner at Balthazar. Can't disappoint the crazy German. Or pass up that free meal.

And just like that, my bubble is burst. Of course Schmidt can't concept at Starbucks like the rest of us. And of course Ben didn't care enough about our plans to say no. We all want what we want, and in Ben's case, it's definitely not me. I drag my deflated self over to the Boathouse and scan the room full of little black dresses for someone who'll be happy to see me no matter what I'm wearing. Dad hugs me hello, so glad that I wasn't stuck at work after all like I'd warned. Even Mom seems pleased by my presence.

"Thank God, Kay," she offers as a way of greeting me. "I was worried you'd show up in jeans."

It's Naomi who actually compliments my new look. "I love *love* the hair and dress. You look fabulous!" she gushes sincerely as she hugs me, and I'm so grateful that I hug her back.

"There's someone who could use some cheering up," she whispers in my ear, motioning to Suit, who's sitting alone at the bar staring miserably into his drink. "He and Cheyenne are over. This time, for good."

I don't know what I'm supposed to do with this news. I've never been privy to the details of Suit's personal life, and I'm not sure I want to start now. But Naomi and my brother have more guests to greet, and my parents are schmoozing with the future in-laws, so I am standing here alone, with no one to talk to anyway. Renee's note said kindness is the cure for this city. I guess it wouldn't kill me to be kind. Even to Suit.

"This seat taken, stranger?" I maneuver onto the stool next to him, offering my brightest smile. But he doesn't look up or smile back, not even a lopsided grin. He just shrugs and mumbles, "Suit yourself," which under any other circumstance would make me giggle. But he is uncharacteristically down. And a little drunk.

I plop on the stool and forge ahead with Operation Cheer-Up, trying to divert him from his apparent girl troubles. Referencing his earlier text seems like a good start. "Must have been some Little Kitty meeting! You guys celebrate with a three-martini lunch?"

He snorts and downs the rest of his cocktail. "I wish."

Wow. He's obviously taking his breakup hard, and why wouldn't he? Girls like Cheyenne are the kind you marry if they let you. Can't be much fun getting dumped by her. Now I feel stupid for feeling sad about Ben. My relationship wasn't even real.

"Want another?" I wave the bartender over. "My treat!" Which is funny, because it's an open bar, but I can't even elicit a smirk.

"Vodka seltzer, lemon," he fires out, and I order the same. We sit there sipping our drinks, when our silence is interrupted by my brother's voice.

"Thank you, friends and family, for coming," Of course Brian is perfectly calm and collected at the microphone and Naomi is tight at his side. "We are so thrilled you can share in the happiness of our engagement. I knew the moment I laid eyes on Naomi, dancing there in her Rollerblades in the Skate Circle, a stone's throw from where we are now, that she was my one true love. And when you find true love, you have to hold on to it with all your might. Please raise your glasses and join me in a toast. Here's to holding on to true love."

As all the glasses but ours clink, I see Cheyenne come up to give Naomi and Brian a hug. She looks as beautiful as ever, and is wearing the same Chloé sheath from Bloomingdale's that I could not afford. Surely Suit must see her, too, and I suddenly feel bad for him. Really, genuinely bad. He may make me crazy at work, but he's a real person with real feelings, and he deserves happiness, too, doesn't he?

"Maybe it's not too late?" I jerk my head toward Cheyenne. "You have to hold on with all your might when you find true love."

Now Suit looks at me. Really looks at me. And starts laughing so hard I think he might fall off his stool.

"You think you know everything, Miss Copygirl? You wouldn't know love if it was staring you in the face."

He may be laughing, but there's a strange resentment in his tone. My head is whirling. At that moment, Cheyenne comes over and says hi to both of us, touching Suit on the arm. "Nice to see you laughing. Got your message about what happened at work, and I'm so sorry." He kisses her on the cheek. I know I don't have a ton of experience in the relationship department, but this definitely seems like an odd way to greet someone who just broke his heart.

"Take my seat, Chey. I need some air." Suit gets up and walks out of the restaurant, leaving me there with his girlfriend, or ex-girlfriend, or whatever, and for some reason I can't explain, I want to make things right in his world.

"I've never seen him like this," I tell her. Normally a woman so chic would intimidate the bejeezus out of me, but luckily I'm speaking before I can talk myself out of it. "He's obviously reeling from you just having broken up with him."

Now Cheyenne laughs. What in hell is going on?

"I didn't *just* break up with him, Kay. I didn't break up with him at all. The split happened a month ago and it was mutual. We'd been friends forever and we tried to make something more of it, but it wasn't meant to be. He loves me like a sister, but that's not enough to make a relationship, is it? We both deserve something more. Something like what they have." Then she throws her shining mane in the direction of Naomi and Brian.

I take this all in, confused but enlightened. Friendship vs. relationship. It's not the same thing. God. I am so dumb.

"Then why is he so upset tonight?" I ask her.

And what Cheyenne tells me next upsets me as much as it did Suit. His lunch meeting with Little Kitty did *not* go well. And there certainly was not any celebrating. Apparently, the early consumer feedback on the new campaign is in, and it's not good. Cat lovers most certainly do not want kitties that don't cuddle, and they hate the new work, claiming it offends animal rights. PETA members have been picketing outside the cat food factory, threatening to boycott the brand if they don't pull the ads immediately. The client is throwing Suit under the bus, blaming his poor judgment for selling them the campaign that they wholeheartedly lapped up. And they are threatening to fire the agency. Without Little Kitty's revenue, STD will have to fold, unless there's some miracle. A miracle like winning the Kola pitch.

I look down into my drink and watch the ice melt for a second. I feel like one of those ice cubes, turning into mush on the inside.

"I'm going to need something stronger than this." I hold up my drink.

I half expect Cheyenne to look down her perfectly triangular nose at this suggestion—getting schnockered at an open bar in Central Park might be the sort of thing a Southern gal is not accustomed to doing. But Cheyenne doesn't hesitate for a second before she agrees.

She throws her head in the direction Suit just left. "I just can't stand seeing him upset. It really gets me down." Then she waves the bartender over to us and bats her eyelashes a few times. "Think you could pour us a couple shots?"

The bartender scans the area around us to make sure no one is looking. "Technically I'm only supposed to pour mixed drinks—but I imagine two shots won't hurt anybody."

He pours a heavy finger of scotch into two glasses and he's right, it doesn't hurt—in fact it helps. At least a little. I can't stop thinking about what will happen if Little Kitty leaves the agency.

"I didn't mean to ruin your night," Cheyenne says. Rather kindly, I have to admit.

"It's just how my luck's been going lately."

"Ouch." Cheyenne grimaces. "Things are bad, huh?"

"Could be better." Things had been looking up for me a little, it's true, but still, this news about Suit and the agency reminds me that the road ahead is still paved with land mines.

"The sad truth is that this city isn't easy on anybody. It makes you work hard, doesn't it?"

"How long have you been here?" I don't want to pry but I am curious; she seems like such a natural at handling New York.

"Fastest two years of my life." She shakes her head. "I thought

I would only stay for two, but now that the time's come and gone, I can't imagine leaving. Sometimes I wonder if it's possible I'll stay forever."

"Forever?" That seems like an unbelievably long time. I know people do it—figure out how to keep up with the break-neck pace—but it would take a lot of figuring out for me to make Manhattan a permanent home.

She laughs at my reaction. "You sound like that's the worst idea I could suggest."

"It's not a bad idea, it's just so hard to feel on top of your game here. Well, not your game, maybe. But for me, I just always feel like a fish out of water."

"Of course you do. I do, too."

The scotch is flowing through my veins and I feel myself finally loosening up. My melting vodka seltzer tastes even better than it did before. The lemon flavor is an especially nice chaser on the heavy scotch.

"I doubt you ever feel like a fish out of water." I laugh.

"Oh it's definitely true." She motions in Suit's direction again and continues. "I think that's why we stayed together for so long . . . The idea of being alone here was just too scary for me. And he knew that; he was willing to stay with me until I felt okay on my own."

"Seems like he's a pretty good guy," I agree. And I am not just saying it to agree with Cheyenne—I'm starting to see where he is a pretty good guy. If he weren't a good guy he wouldn't take the Little Kitty blow to heart . . . He would assume it was somebody else's problem, somebody else's fault.

"He's the best," Cheyenne asserts. "If it weren't for him I wouldn't ever have gotten my head shots done."

"What do you mean?"

"Oh, it's silly . . . It's nothing." I can tell she's embarrassed, because now she's the one studying ice cubes.

"You can tell me. Trust me, I'm not going to judge you."

"I just had this dream, you know? I'd always dreamed of being on a cover of a magazine. I think it started back with *Seventeen*? Did you ever read that, or were you too young?"

"Oh no! I read *Seventeen*. Like, religiously. Of course I was only ten when I read it."

She laughs. "Yeah, I think that was the deal. The only ones of us who read *Seventeen* were the ones who wanted to be seventeen. The actual seventeen-year-olds were probably wishing they were twenty-five and reading other magazines.

"But yeah, it started with *Seventeen*. They had this model search and I remember being in my bedroom back in New Orleans and dreaming that maybe I could win the contest. I fixed my hair on top of my head and had my little sister take a picture of me. I put the picture in an envelope and we walked to the post office . . ."

"And?" I ask.

"And I never heard back."

"Oh no!" I can't believe they would have ignored a girl like Cheyenne. "Well, I'm sure about a million girls entered the contest."

"Yeah, I know. But sometimes you get disappointed and it just stops you. I checked the mailbox every day for a reply, and when some other girl won the contest I gave up. But not just on the contest, on the whole darn thing."

"But now you've done head shots and you're going for it?" I ask.

She nods her head. Her whole face is lit up and so I guess there's more to the story.

"Did you already get a modeling job?"

She shakes her head yes, but is staring at her ice cubes again.

"Are you going to be on the cover of a magazine?"

"Even better!" She grins like a toddler who got a new puppy. "I think I'm going to be on a billboard ad in Times Square!"

"You're kidding!" I accidentally slosh my drink so that the last of the ice cubes tinkle against the glass.

"I can hardly believe it myself. And really, if I hadn't been convinced to do the head shots, it never would have happened. That's why I hate to see him so down, because he made this whole dream work for me."

"That's so cool, Cheyenne." I am genuinely psyched for her. I mean, she's gorgeous, so it makes sense. But I can also see in the way she talks about it that she doesn't necessarily realize how gorgeous she is—obviously it took some convincing on Suit's part.

"This calls for more shots!" I announce. I wave the bartender over and he smiles, then produces two more scotch shots.

"To making New York your home." I raise my miniature glass. She raises hers, too. "Cheers!"

After we throw back the shots she lets out a mini-burp and even that doesn't sound repulsive coming out of her mouth. We both giggle like little girls, even though we're drinking the big boy drink.

"So maybe all you need is to find your thing here." She stops to think for a second. "Do you think your thing is advertising?"

I shrug my shoulders. "It's kind of my thing. But I'm so stressed out, so much of the time. Everything is—as you know—sort of falling apart at the agency."

"Is there anything else? A side hobby or a guy you are interested in?"

I think about mentioning Ben. But his rejection tonight is still so fresh and, frankly, I'm tired of thinking about him. He used to be what lifted me up, but now he's more of a burden than anything. But there are the videos . . .

"Well, I do have one thing going on, but it's kind of silly."

"Oh, come on!" Cheyenne says encouragingly. "I told you that I lost a decade of my life to disappointment after a failed model search; what could be sillier than that?"

If you'd asked me an hour ago, I would have guessed that Cheyenne and I had nothing in common. But now I could imagine me and her and Kell sitting around, hanging out. She's so easy and sweet . . . not at all intimidating.

"Okay, I'll show you. But only if you swear not to laugh." I take a big sip of my cocktail through the straw, then fish my phone from my Marc Jacobs-ish bag.

"Nice purse." She fingers the metal studs.

"Oh, this old thing?" I make a mental note to tell Kell about how smooth I pass it off. If I ever speak to her again, that is.

"I really do love your dress," I say. "And I'm *not* just saying that to return the compliment."

"Thanks. Yeah, I'm lucky. I could never afford a dress like this, but my roommate's got great taste and a credit card her parents pay off every month. Walking into her closet is like cruising the streets of Soho."

This is a surprising bit of information; apparently I was wrong on every assumption I made about Cheyenne.

I cue up the blog that has all the Copygirl videos on it and pass the phone to Cheyenne. "Sorry about the cracked screen, but you'll get the general idea."

Cheyenne watches all the videos one by one. At first I am mortified, just guessing that she is going to think they are so lame. But after the first one is done she pops her head up and says, "This is so creative. I could never think of doing something so cool. Do you make these dolls?"

I tell her that I do.

"And you write the scripts?"

"I do. But that part's not hard at all; it's stuff I would actually say. So the words come pretty easy."

When she watches the It Girl video at the bar with the vomit she laughs so hard that she snorts, and at that moment, every last bit of my apprehension falls away.

Then she goes through my more recent ones. When I get to the part in the subway video where the Kay doll begs the audience not to be a Copygirl, I even hear Cheyenne lightly repeating those words: *Don't be a Copygirl.*

And when she's done she hands the phone back to me. "These are online for everyone to see?"

"Yes. But I don't know if that many people care."

"That's awesome. Really awesome, Kay." Then she raises a glass. "I propose a toast."

"Okay." I raise my glass to meet hers.

"To finding your place in this big bad city," she begins.

"And to *not* being a Copygirl," I add.

We cheer and both drain our drinks.

"Okay." Cheyenne pushes her empty cup out of reach and slaps her palms on the bar. "I have to go find Naomi. I haven't gotten to talk to her at all and she is going to be a total diva about it tomorrow if I don't give her due attention."

"I get it," I say. "But you'll keep the videos a secret, right?"

"I promise I won't tell Naomi or Brian about them." She puts up her scout's honor fingers.

"Perfect." I stand up from the chair at the bar and I'm only a little wobbly. *Nice tolerance, Kay,* I congratulate myself as I grab my purse. I guess I'll go check on my parents. Surely my dad is tired of hobnobbing by now. Don't think my mom ever gets tired of that, but with a couple drinks in me I can even put up with her social chatter right now.

We're about to go our separate ways, when Cheyenne stops and looks at me. "Hey, Kay, will you do me one favor?"

"Sure." I'm thinking maybe she wants me to talk to Naomi and Brian with her. Which would be boring, but all right. Or maybe she wants me to meet her for drinks after the unveiling of her fifty-foot billboard in Times Square. That would be more than all right, that would be super fun.

"Will you go check on him for me?" She nods to where Suit used to be standing. "I just know Naomi will talk my ear off and I might be stuck for a while. I want to make sure he's okay."

She wants me to check on Suit? Right. Like he wants to see me. He couldn't get out of here fast enough earlier.

"I don't know if that's a good idea," I say.

"Actually," Cheyenne answers, "I think it's a great idea."

Then she leans over and gives me the two-cheek kiss goodbye. I'm definitely not savvy enough to totally pull it off but I do manage to lean the right way so our noses don't clink. At the very least that's a step in the right direction of being cool.

If I'm going to track down Suit and force him to talk to me, I might as well arrive with the gift of a drink. I order one more vodka seltzer from the bartender and then, as he's pouring the first drink, I think better of it. "Actually, make that two more," I say.

After all, I'm taking a cab home. And I'm pretty sure I'm so low on the radar of everyone here that getting sloshed will hardly be of notice. I'll just check on Suit, drink this drink, catch the cab home, and sleep peacefully.

With beverages in hand I head to the far border of the party and repeat these instructions to myself: *Find Suit, drink this drink, catch that cab, sleep peacefully. Find Suit, drink this drink, catch that cab, sleep peacefully.*

I don't see him in the crowd so I walk just a little farther, still muttering: *Find Suit, drink this dr—*

"Talking to yourself again?" I know it's Suit's voice but I don't see him anywhere. I'm at the very edge of the party, looking out into a very dark Central Park.

"I've been talking to myself some tonight, too." His voice reaches me again but I have no idea where he might be.

"Where—um—are you?"

I hear him laugh. "Forward, forward—walk forward, Kay."

I step into the dark, away from the people. This might very well be the beginning of a *True Crime* story: On a dark early-spring night, a drunk girl meanders into Central Park with two vodka tonics . . .

But it is Suit's voice I'm following. He's more Disney Junior than *True Crime*. And actually he's not cartoony and silly like Disney Junior, he's got a little more sophistication . . . maybe more Nick at Nite–ish.

"Has anyone ever told you that you remind them of a Nick at Nite character—Ward Cleaver–ish, but in a good way?" I ask.

Now he starts laughing hard. "I can never guess what's going to come out of your mouth next, Kay."

I've walked far enough by now that I can see him, sitting underneath a huge oak tree. His tie is loosened and his blazer is in a crumpled pile next to the tree. My heart twists up and I feel . . . I don't know, I guess it's pity? I make a mental note to reexamine the feeling later, even though I'm not sure I will remember anything I tell myself right now.

"The party's over there." I point to where I've just come from.

"Not in the mood for people right now." He *does* sound pretty down in the dumps.

"This kitty don't cuddle," I mutter.

"Exactly," he says. "This kitty don't cuddle."

I can't think of anything else to say, so I offer him the drink and take a seat on the grass. I'm absolutely sure that Bouffa would have a coronary if she saw me sitting in my Bloomie's dress right on the lawn of Central Park. I guess you can take the girl out of her jeans, but you can't take the jean-wearing attitude out of the girl.

"You plan on going back in there?" I ask Suit.

He's quiet for a minute. "I like the view from here."

I find myself blushing for reasons I don't understand. Luckily my face is mostly hidden in the dark.

I force myself to focus on our view of the party from the distance, and it does have a certain magic. Usually I have the feeling of an outsider looking in, all awkwardness and bumbled edges, but tonight I can actually just sit back and appreciate the lights.

"You did find a pretty good spot," I agree. When he doesn't say anything, I venture a little further. "I really like Cheyenne."

He does speak to agree with this. "She's a great girl."

"I'm sorry it didn't work out for the two of you." Instantly I wish I hadn't brought this up. Cheyenne doesn't think it's a sore subject, but what if Suit disagrees?

"Not every couple is meant to be," he says.

"I like that philosophical spin."

"You can use it for yourself if you want," he offers.

"Oh, I'd have no reason to use it. Never seem to be part of a couple." Ouch. This may be too much to share with someone I only know through work. But Suit doesn't seem to mind.

"Is that by choice?" he asks.

I wonder if I should be embarrassed. What if he's like Todd and thinks that I am all googly-eyed over Ben?

"I like being single," I say, maybe too strongly. But it is the truth. Here, in the middle of New York City, wearing my new dress, with the memory of Cheyenne actually loving my videos, it's easy to believe I am 100 percent totally and completely single by choice.

"Single looks good on you," Suit says. "But you always look good."

Now I blush so much I am sure he can see, even in the pitch black of night. I need to change the topic.

"Do you think it can work out with Little Kitty?" I ask. "I hope you don't mind, but Cheyenne told me what's going on. Are we—is the agency—going to make it?"

Suit is quiet for a long while. "It might take magic, Kay."

Magic. I think of Veronique's pushpin voodoo doll. I think of my fairy godmother at Bloomies. I think of Cheyenne's face in Times Square. I reflect on how badly I need to keep my fucking job—there could be nothing worse than asking my mother to help me make rent.

"Magic," I repeat.

The stars really are shining, and combined with the lights of the party I can see Suit's face fully. I look at him and he looks at me and says, "But yes, I think it can be done."

And more than anything else, I want to believe his words are true.

there's no "k" in team

Magic, Kay! I love this new direction for Little Kitty :-)

A smiley face. Suit actually texted me a smiley face. I can't believe it. Any more than I can believe I actually e-mailed him my "Love 'em Big with Little Kitty" idea over the weekend. Without speaking to Ben, who's technically still my partner on this account, and without running it past Elliott, who's definitely supposed to approve any work I do before it leaves the creative department. What in hell was I thinking?

It's just that Suit looked so defeated sitting there under that oak tree on Friday night when my mom came outside to drag me back into the party.

"There you are, Kay! Your dad's been looking everywhere!" Mom was accusing. I started to tell her we had a work crisis, but she interrupted, saying she couldn't believe how nice I looked for a change, and she wanted to get a photographic record of it, with the whole family. "Not in five minutes, *now!*"

"I'll be there in a sec," I told her, before turning back to Suit.

"Wow, is your mom always so . . . intense?" he asked me after she marched back into the Boathouse.

"That was actually her way of giving me a compliment."

He nodded at me with an odd look of either understanding or pity. I didn't have time to figure out which. "You coming with?

"No, Kay, I'm going home," he sighed. "My job—hell, all our jobs—are in jeopardy. I can't go back in there and pretend everything's okay."

I knew how he felt. Pretending takes so much effort. That's why the next words came pouring out of my mouth before I could think to stop them. "I always thought the Little Kitty work we sold was total bullshit but I was too afraid to speak up. I have this other idea I've been working on, something that feels right for the brand. Maybe you would want to take a peek?"

And suddenly Suit's face flickered back to life, full of something that looked an awful lot like hope.

So that's why I sent him my new ads that next day, behind everyone's back, without thinking. I wasn't trying to be sneaky. I just thought, maybe, if there was a chance of saving the account, saving all our jobs, then the risk might be worth it.

And now it very well may be. Suit called the client on Saturday afternoon to talk them through my idea, and they agreed it made sense! He convinced them to put the campaign into testing, and if research goes well, they'll run the new ads and stay with Schmidt Travino Drew. Like he said: magic.

Suit's in the conference room now, at the Monday status meeting, bringing the partners up to speed on everything that's happened since his Friday client lunch. I can see through the glass windows that it's going okay because Travino just smiled and patted Suit on the back.

Out here in the creative wing, things aren't as jovial. Ben's been giving me the cold shoulder all morning, acting like I betrayed him. Apparently, Suit promised the Little Kitty execs that they would get our new campaign right away, so he called Ben yesterday to come into the office to design the layouts. Ben was NOT happy about working on a Sunday, being "the fucking wrist, yet again, for your ideas," as he so poetically wrote me in a much longer, scathing text.

I'd tried calling him to apologize and explain the situation so he wouldn't think I threw him under the bus, but he kept sending me to voice mail. Grumpy bastard even had the nerve to text, *Guess there's no "K" in team.*

Now Elliott's here, in my cube, ripping me a new one about my breach in protocol.

"So, you wanna be the creative director, Special K? Think you're fucking special? *All* work is supposed to go through me . . . you *know* that . . . Pull that shit again and you'll be lucky to get a job writing ads for the phone book."

I'm staring down at my new motorcycle boots, speechless, fighting back tears during this tirade, when Travino comes over and comes to my defense.

"Elliott, if we lose Little Kitty, you'll be doing phone book ads with her." Now Travino almost smiles at me. "Nice save, little girl. Let's hope it works."

Elliott slinks off, seething, and I know I'd better watch my back. In ad school, they sure as heck don't teach you about office politics, and I wonder if maybe I'm in way over my head here. It's only ten thirty a.m., but I wish I could go back home and play with my dolls. I'm hating this whole adulthood thing. Plus, this scenario might actually be funny if I could reenact it all with wax figures.

At least Kell *is* talking to me again. She saw the BFF video I made for her, and finally reached out to me. Only texts, because she's so busy with her Louvre internship and all the local artists she's been meeting. Glad one of us is actually living the dream. But she did manage to give me one of her patented pep talks—in a fifty-word typed phone message—telling me all my hard work at the agency will pay off soon and this Little Kitty coup is proof of my talent. To further boost my confidence, she sent me a screen shot of the analytics from the Copygirl website. The numbers were pretty phenomenal, though I'm pretty sure most of my followers are in France, thanks to Kell's artsy connections.

I seriously hope Kell is right about work. If I follow my gut on the Kola pitch, maybe, just maybe, everything will work out. For me. The agency. Everybody. I look over at Ben, wanting to try one more time to explain. But he's got his headphones on, rock music blaring out of the earpieces, and he's working on the Little Kitty layout that's up on his enormous monitor. I tap him on the shoulder, but he actually shoos me away.

Dejected, I unplug my laptop and walk over to Todd's office, anxious to fix something that's within my control for a change.

"Look at you, all fierce in your new designer clothes!" Todd gives my Bouffa-picked outfit his stamp of approval. "And obviously I love love *love* Gael's haircut."

"Wish I felt fierce," I admit, sinking my microsuede leggings down into his buttery leather sofa. "Elliott just scolded me something awful . . ."

"Oh, don't let big bad Elliott blow your little house down. Girl, I heard what you did, and good for you coloring outside the lines! Thanks to you, we're still getting paychecks, at least for now!"

"For now," I repeat. "Todd, we *have* to win this pitch. Whatever it takes. I think our Be Bubbly concept has lots of style, but now we have to give it substance—style *and* substance will make it bulletproof."

"Fine, Miss Thing. We'll do things your way now. A deal's a deal. Plus I have zero interest in dusting off my resume."

"Like, *what's* the deal?" Bouffa comes bouncing into Todd's office clicking her three-inch heels. "And, Kay, I thought you were only buying the dress?"

"Long story . . ." I start, but Todd keeps things focused.

"G, we're getting down to business. Be a love and go fetch us some huge Starbucks lattes. From the one on Spring. Tell Jorge I sent you. We need primo fuel if we're going to find genius."

"I can totally do that!" Gina squeals, happy to serve some actual purpose. Twenty bucks says she'll make a pit stop at a bodega for a big bottle of her Diet Coke fix.

"You know she's not an intern anymore, right?" I say to Todd after she clicks off.

"Of course. But you and I need to put in some serious think time. Once we nail the idea, Gina can help us polish it."

"She *does* love her polish," I laugh, "and her well-trimmed cuticles!" I'm thrilled Todd is finally on board for hard work, even if his ultimate motivation is saving his own big salary.

Apparently, keeping himself in buttery leather is expensive, and unemployment ain't gonna cut it.

As fabulous as last week was, playing hooky and recharging the old brain cells, this week's been even better. Todd and I have been cranking on our Kola work like we've been partners since ad school. I never dreamed I'd find another art director I gelled with as well as Ben. But it turns out Todd is a total pro, and once you've ignited his creative fire, he's one hell of a flamethrower. And Bouffa has been more than happy to fan the flames, whether procuring the best coffee or takeout, or finding the perfect art book, film short, or other inspiration to make our good ideas great.

"Did you ever consider becoming a producer?" Todd asks her now, impressed with Gina's talent for choosing both dim sum and directors.

"You mean, like Peyton?" She gets all wide-eyed as she sets up the Asian office picnic she's brought in. "Sure, but Daddy didn't know anyone in the movies . . ."

"G, I think you've got what it takes to break in on your own." I am 100 percent sincere.

And, though, *like*, this *totally* never occurred to her before, now she must think it's truly possible, because she hugs me so tight I think I might choke on my pork dumpling.

"That would be even cooler than opening a purse store! Like, being on film sets, hanging with actors, plus all those wardrobe, hair, and makeup people!" she gushes.

"I *do* love going on TV shoots," Todd chimes in. "Especially in LA. I always stay at Shutters."

I nod like I know what he's talking about, although I don't. I've never shot a commercial. Or even been to LA. I would have guessed a place with a name like Shutters offered by-the-hour room rentals.

Apparently not even my fancy new threads can hide all my cluelessness because Todd informs me, "Shutters on the Beach is the most fab hotel in Santa Monica. Frette sheets, cozy bedrooms with balconies overlooking the Pacific. And the. World's. Best. Oysters."

"You get to stay at the beach?" Now it's my turn to be wide-eyed.

"Of course. Why do you think I *always* put a beach in my script? Or, at the very least, palm trees. You *could* stay in Hollywood instead—Chateau Marmont is super fun—saw Lindsay Lohan puking in the bushes there once—but I like waking up by the water and rollerblading down to Venice Beach for break fast burritos."

"You saw La Lohan!" Gina shrieks. "Who else? Tell us more!"

"The last Superfine sneaker shoot, I was out there for two weeks," Todd continues. "Gael came to visit for the weekend and we hit the flea market on Melrose, and then the Fred Segal boutique, and guess who was in the fitting room?"

"Who?" I ask.

"Brad Pitt?" Gina guesses.

"Better. Sharon Osbourne! With *Mr. Chips*! You know, her fuzzy Pomeranian?"

Gina nods knowingly. "The one with a face like a teddy bear?" I know nothing about Sharon Osbourne, her dog, or the fact that she has more than one of them.

"Exactly," Todd affirms. "Well, Mrs. Ozzy was trying on the ugliest Hermès scarf, and *she asked my opinion*."

"No!" It's Gina's turn to choke on her dumpling.

"Yes! So, of course, I couldn't lie to her. That would be a crime. So I said, "'Sharon, you are far too fabulous for paisley. Do yourself a fave and try colorblock instead.' And then Mr. Chips peed on Gael's penny loafer."

"Really?" Gina gasps, successfully dislodging the undigested pork bite from the back of her throat.

"Uh-huh. We bronzed the shoe and it's on a mantel in our bedroom."

"Do you think we'll get to go on a shoot if we win Kola?" I ask Todd.

"Of course! Kola's ad budget is *huge*. If we pick the right director, maybe we can even go to a Caribbean island. But Elliott will probably insist on coming along—the big bad creative director. He acts like he needs to put his thumbprint on every decision. Really, he just likes going on shoots for the girls. You should see the way he chats up the actresses and makeup artists."

Now this is the kind of gossip *I* find interesting. "But isn't Elliott married? With kids?"

"Ye-ah. But he's married more to his work, or so he'd have you think. Last shoot, he bailed out early on the pre-production meeting, saying he had a stomachache, then later I saw him leaving Shutters with the receptionist from the production company. Girl couldn't have been more than eighteen."

"No!" Bouffa says again.

I'm speechless. I knew Elliott could be a bit of douchebag,

but this was beyond douchey. I've been avoiding him all week, hiding out in the bubble of Todd's office, but that hasn't stopped his reign of terror. He keeps texting me screen shots of phone book ads, and yesterday he left a crumpled-up box of Special K cereal on my seat with a Post-it note that read, *See how easily you can be replaced.*

"Get my present?" he sneered when Ben and I had to go to his office to get him to sign off on the new Little Kitty comps. "Special K! Get it? Benny, my boy, wasn't that a good one?"

Then E-hole put his hand in the air for a high five—*and Ben actually gave it to him.* I wanted to crawl up in a ball on the floor and die. But Suit was there, too, and must have sensed my embarrassment, because he started telling Elliott how great the new ads look.

"Kay's direction is so smart. Elliott, you've really taught her well."

This made Elliott puff up like a smug little rooster, reversing his approach to give me a compliment so backhanded that if I didn't know better, I would have thought it came from my mom.

"Yeah, she has potential. By the way, Kay, I like the new look. You get picked to be on some reality show, like *Extreme Makeover: Jersey Edition*?"

I wonder if his wife knows what goes on during his business trips. I'd love to borrow his bug camera, get a little video proof of his extracurricular activity to use as leverage and get him off my back. How great would that be?

Even just thinking about the trip part gets me excited. If we win Kola, I'll maybe get to do *that*. Go on a trip and "shoot a spot."

Now that Todd and I have written some great scripts together, it's not just a pipe dream.

So much has been happening at work, it's a good thing I have the dolls or else I'd probably go schizo. Like Jack Nicholson's character in *The Shining*, we all need a change of scenery. Not that talking to dolls is completely sane, but at least it's a break from talking to ad people.

My latest masterpiece is inspired by Todd and Bouffa. By anyone, I guess, who has lived in this place so long they instantly know the year of the vintage Chanel bag a woman is carrying. And will judge her based on that information. I love me some fine leather on motorcycle boots, but I want to keep said boots firmly planted on the sidewalk.

And Copygirl was due a night shoot. *Especially* after listening to Todd hammer *glamour, glamour, glamour* in my head the whole freaking time he and Bouffa were doing my makeover. (*A little part of everyone wants to be Elizabeth Taylor circa* Giant. *It's not just gay men, dear.*)

But finding a night to steal time away from the comfort of my Shabby Chic comforter was harder than I thought it would be. It actually hadn't taken long to adjust to sleeping in a Ben-less apartment. I really liked walking around in my cotton nightie with my hair on top of my head, working on wax dolls and singing bad 90s love songs until it was time to call it a night. But then one day on my way home from work I saw a bolt of sequin yardage leaning against the window in a Chinatown shop and I knew the universe was saying—in a sparkly kind of way—that tonight's the night for Copygirl.

So I bought a quarter yard, then I took it home and worked it until I had a miniature dress that was red-carpet ready. I also did some face painting on a couple of the dolls that could either go scary cool or total fashion victim. And at about ten p.m., I grabbed one of my million effing totes and stuffed it with the dress and all my dolls.

Walking in Soho at night is so different than during the day. All these stores I usually got intimidated by had been put to bed by the shopgirls. The boutiques weren't definitive lines in the sand between me and everyone who could afford couture—nope, just a bunch of dark squares inhabited by mannequins. Not very scary at all.

I went to what Bouffa would have labeled no-man's-land, though she really means every-woman's-land when she says that. The H&M zone. If you really want to see eyes crossed, you should use the words *Old Navy* in a sentence to Bouffa or Todd—he won't even waste the energy of rolling his eyes, he'll just immediately stop listening.

Forever.

I figured the storefront of Zara would be perfect for the night shoot. Plenty of light from street lamps, and the windows were dressed in all black and white—*très chic* as Kell would say. It was stylish, yes, but what was even more important to me was that it would cast some shadows.

All the film footage I'd been watching at work this week had me in the mood for something even campier than usual. I set up

the suburban twin dolls so they were staring up at the mannequins in the store window. Both were dressed in mall-bought
fashions from days gone by, with faded blue jeans ripped at the
knees. The first doll, the one I'd nicknamed Bridge, wore a tube
sundress over her jeans. The other doll, Tunnel Girl, was sporting a T-shirt with a men's vest over it. I made her speak first.

> Tunel Girl: *"Bridge, can you believe we're in New York
> City? This is nothing like home. All the fashion is so awe-
> some, there's not a pair of velour sweatpants in sight!"*
>
> Bridge: *"I know! Look at all these a-may-zing out-
> fits!"*
>
> The camera panned over to the mannequins in
> Zara's window.
>
> Tunnel Girl: *"I wish we could buy one of each! We'd
> be the most stylish girls in Jersey!"* Cackling laughter
> erupted behind them, then a snooty voice snarled,
> *"Bridge & Tunnel Girls, shopping at Zara is NOT going
> to make YOU stylish. As if it were that easy for you sub-
> urban twits!"*
>
> Bridge turned to Tunnel Girl, squealing. *"Ohmi-
> god, it's HER!"*
>
> Tunnel Girl: *"Ohmigod! Who?"*
>
> Bridge: *"Queen Copygirl! Duh! The one who sets all
> the trends."*
>
> Then the camera zoomed in on a pair of high heels,
> moving up to a sequined dress and leather moto jacket.
> I shot this doll in shadows, so we couldn't make out
> her face.

Queen Copygirl: *"So you know who I am? Well, that's a promising start. Too bad you haven't been reading my fashion blog, because if you did then you'd know everything you have on your body is WRONG. You, Bridge, that dress-over-jeans look got canceled back when* Sex and the City *did. And Tunnel Girl, the nineties called. They want their men's sport vest back. Yawn . . ."*

Bridge: *"You're right, we're hopeless, we know. Please say you'll help us, Queen Copygirl?"*

Tunnel Girl: *"Like, yeah, Queen Copygirl? Please? We weren't born perfect like you . . . I mean, look at us, we have, like, cellulite and stuff!"*

Queen Copygirl: *"I guess I can help you. If you immediately start following me on all social media and pledge that you will stop thinking for yourself. First, walk this way."*

Then I moved the Queen in a few steps. Bridge stumbled after her.

Bridge: *"Walk this way."*

Tunnel Girl wasn't far behind.

Tunnel Girl: *Like this? Walk this way?*

Queen Copygirl: *"No questions! Do you understand?"*

By leaning my iPhone against my tote, I could reach both hands in and move Bridge & Tunnel Girl's heads so they nodded in unison. I wanted them to seem like they were in a trance. I would edit out my hands later, and make their voices sound shaky and dronelike.

"*Walk this way*," they both chanted. "*Talk this way*," they said.

"*Good*," Queen Copygirl replied, her voice becoming singsongy and witchy.

"*You must do what I do, go where I go, and wear only what I approve. You'll be such precious Copygirls! And when I have enough followers, you'll be part of my Copygirl army. Ready?*"

Bridge and Tunnel Girl nodded again. "*Ready!*"

Queen Copygirl stepped closer to them, into the light of the store window, and now that we could see her better, it was revealed that I'd painted her to look like a zombie! Pale gray skin, black circles around her eyes, red gashes on her cheeks, and oozing blisters all over her flesh.

As campy horror music played from my phone, she began to gnaw at the flesh of her two fashion victims. I shook the camera to simulate a scuffle, punctuated by ridiculous screams. Bridge's arm went flying in the air, then Tunnel Girl lost half her face. Queen Copygirl was on top of them both, red ketchup dripping down her lips. I paused the camera for a sec to swap out dolls, then Queen Copygirl stood up, pulling her mutilated followers to their feet. They were both now wearing the exact same sequined skirt and moto jacket as their leader, their bloody faces also painted like zombies.

"*We love to be Copygirls!*" they both droned—and I knew how to distort their voices using an app I

**found, making them sound ultra-zombie-ish. I could
see the final screen I would splice in right there—all
red with electric words that appear as a warning for
all the people in danger of following the crowd . . .
First DON'T, then BE, and A COPYGIRL at the end.**

**DON'T BE A COPYGIRL—then static, my favorite
last gasp of a homemade horror movie.**

This video is definitely the biggest statement I've made yet
on the Copygirl site. And I guess maybe that's got me stressed
out, because I can't stop thinking about it. Wondering if all the
dialogue was right and whether or not people will like it. Even
as Todd and I are putting the finishing touches on our Kola
work, *Fashion Victims* is the script my mind keeps running over.

Todd notices that I'm not all with it, but he probably thinks
that has something to do with Ben. He never mentions my googly eyes anymore, but when Ben walks by, Todd always gives me
a knowing look. As an answer, I focus harder than ever on the
scripts he and I are developing.

Finally, at the end of the week, Todd says he thinks we are
ready. And not a moment too soon, because our internal creative review is on Monday morning.

"You know Travino," I practically whisper—working in such
close proximity to all the other creatives who want their idea
picked for the pitch makes me feel like I'm guarding a national
secret. "Do you think he'll like Be Bubbly?"

"Darling, I think he'll swoon for it." Todd makes a gesture
like he's fainting. "You should go out to celebrate."

"Just me? Don't you want to celebrate?"

"Oh, I'll celebrate, but not with all these clowns"—Todd waves to the boys' club, E's office, and the general vicinity of Ben with a disparaging swat of the arm. "I saw on ShoutOut that they are all going to happy hour. You should go and show you-know-who how much fun you can be. "

"You know who?" I say this with a blank face. If he wants to be catty I'm going to make him work for it.

"Want me to shout it?" He's just as blank-faced.

"Okay." I give in. "You win." It's not worth explaining to Todd that Ben really doesn't cross my mind nearly as much anymore. I don't want to sound like I'm trying to convince him (or myself) of this truth. So I let it go.

Bouffa pops up at this very moment. "So . . . happy hour . . . who's in?"

Todd sings in a falsetto, "Like, not me, G."

I look at her and roll my eyes to make sure Bouffa doesn't take his brattiness seriously. "We were just discussing happy hour. Todd isn't going."

"But you are, right, Kay?"

I was actually hoping to go home, work on videos, and psych myself up to show the work to Travino on Monday. But it feels like it's been a gazillion years since I've been to the Hole.

"One beer," I agree.

"Um, awesome!" Gina is already on the move. "Let me go find Peyton and see if she's ready to go."

I do my best not to groan, and swivel back toward Todd, who's watching me again.

"Peyton's not exactly your bosom buddy, I take it."

"I'm going to ignore you now." I start to load up my stuff.

Now that we're done with Kola for the day, my brain automatically clicks back to Copygirl. I think it's time to do a script about mean girls and why the world is a better place without them.

Just as I'm thinking that, I hear the voice of Copygirl coming from outside Todd's office.

I pop up.

"What's wrong?" Todd eyes me curiously.

"What is that?" I jut my chin in the direction of Joshjohnjay's cubicles.

And Todd shrugs. "What is what? The boys are probably working on another one of their pigeon poop videos." As Todd says this, he shudders.

"I don't think that's a poop video," I say to him. But he's not listening. He's logged on to the West Elm website and is frothing at the mouth over a sofa that looks, to me, as comfortable as sitting on a cinder block.

I wander into the hall so I can eavesdrop on Joshjohnjay. The closer I get, the less I can believe what I am hearing. It's my voice—or the voice of Copygirl—coming out of John's massive two-foot monitor. Even more amazing than the fact that they are watching the videos is that they seem to have no idea that the videos are mine.

"My girlfriend can't get enough of these films; she made me watch all of them last night," Josh is telling the others. "It's, like, a compulsion with her and all her friends. She says they constantly check back on the site to see when a new one has been posted."

No friggin' way—Josh's girlfriend is obsessed with the videos? I know her. She's a Billyburg girl—I thought the only people watching these videos were Kell's Paris people.

"Well," Jay says in a voice much kinder and less defensive than he ever uses when speaking to me, "the doll *is* kind of cool."

I can't believe it I can't believe it I can't believe it. I MUST talk to Kell now.

I race past Todd and tell him to have Bouffa wait on me when she gets back, and I rush to the ladies' room. I do my customary check for feet under the stalls and then FaceTime Kell from my phone.

"Answer, answer," I say to no one but the porcelain thrones. My Jedi mind trick works and somehow Kell picks up the phone.

"*Allo, étranger.* I was actually just about to textez *vous.*" Kell's face beams through my splintered screen.

"Kell! You'll never believe it! People in the office are watching my videos!"

Kell has a smirk on her face. "*Un*, your haircut, *c'est fantastique. Deux*, people everywhere are watching your videos. *Tout le monde!* That's what I've been trying to tell you. Duh!"

"You have been telling me, but I guess I was just too stuck in the STD world to understand."

"*Voici* what I was going to textez *vous.* Voilà!" Kell flips her phone down to her chest and there, across her ripped vintage beige T-shirt in hot pink letters is the Kay doll's slogan: DON'T BE A COPYGIRL.

"Kell! You made that?"

I don't know if I am flattered or impressed or just thankful we ended up standing next to each other at kindergarten enrollment and our parents decided to make us friends. She really is the best pal I could ever hope for. I could kick myself a million times over with Bouffa's pointy heels for having been such a bitch on the phone last week.

"*Oui, il a été fait* by moi! But one of the interns here really likes it and her boyfriend, Yannick, has his own screen press so we are going to *imprimez beaucoup plus.*"

"You're kidding!"

Her smirk is back. "Not kidding *du tout,* Mademoiselle. Kay."

"Will you *imprimez me* one?"

"*Bien sûr!* You're the first person on the mailing list," she promises. "Now *s'il vous plait* tell me you will go out tonight to *célébreiez?* You are a freaking Internet sensation. *Va s'amuser,* dammit."

Geez. Am I such a pathetic wallflower that everyone I know has to beg me to be social? I promise her I will celebrate and then we promise to talk again soon. I walk out of the bathroom slightly dazed and head back to my seat, where Bouffa is waiting next to Todd.

"Did you, like, see the new sofa him and Gael are going to get? H-O-T." Bouffa flashes me a picture that's up on Todd's phone.

Before I can even answer, Todd has snatched back his phone and is on his feet. "Well, ladies. I'm off to burn some cash. It's how you'll both celebrate when you have cash of your own."

"Whatevs!" Bouffa can't take a comment like his seriously. She has no idea the difference between the cash in her wallet right now and cash of her own.

I'm too pumped up to care, though. "Are we leaving?"

"Peyton says to go ahead and she'll meet us soon; I guess she's putting in overtime on Schmidt's Kola work."

This does scratch the surface of my joy, just a little. Of course Peyton would be helping Ben and the crazy German.

Todd gives me a pointed look. "Maybe the feeling's mutual." I ignore him, not sure if he means Ben, or Peyton, or both.

"What are you talking about?" Bouffa asks. Then it's his time to ignore her.

"Ta-ta, ladies!" Todd makes like a tree and leaves.

"Should we see if Josh and them want to walk over with us?" I'm feeling uncharacteristically friendly.

Bouffa shakes her head. "They already left. They walked by here talking about whether dolls were the new poop, or something like that. Boys!"

And then she's off, chattering about the newest collection of menswear she is in love with. If only she could find a boyfriend so she could dress him in it. I don't even mind listening to her chatter. Copygirl is taking off and I am going to revel in it—none of the irritations of this office are going to get me down tonight.

The Hole is not technically in Soho. It's east of Broadway, on Grand Street, in the no-man's-land near the Williamsburg Bridge. But until the scenesters who hang here decide the Lower East Side is cool, they'll refer to it as a Soho bar anyway.

The floor is littered with pistachio shells—the hipster equivalent of peanuts—and the bar top is lined with help-yourself bowls of the uncracked nuts, which is something I really like. It's rumored that Jack Kerouac's smack dealer used to live one floor up, so the beat poet and hipster god spent a lot of time here back when the place was a coffeehouse. Needless to say, the Hole is always packed with all the wannabe novelists, artists, directors, and deejays who haven't yet headed back home to Billyburg for the night, and like to pretend they don't spend their days writing ads, waiting tables, or driving cabs. This, I like less.

Usually, I can't hang here without suffocating from the "hipocrisy" of all these posers, but tonight the affectations don't bother me. I'm here to have fun. And so far so good. I'm sitting down one end of the bar, near the out-of-place fish tank, hanging with Joshjohnjay, Jess the account exec, and Bouffa, who's impressing us with her ability to crack pistachio nuts hands-free, using only her tongue ring. They've commandeered this corner strictly for STD coworkers and friends, many of whom have been trickling in. I wonder where Suit is? Elliott's not here either, and that's a big relief. He'll probably come over with Ben, whose nose has been so far up E's butt since they've ganged up to hate on me that the two practically see eye to eye.

I don't know if it's the booze, the recent shift in office alliances, or the fact that they like Copygirl, but I'm not ticked off by Team Boys' Club as much as usual. Turns out, Jay's really funny. He just told a story about paint splattering all the pigeon droppings in the Museum of Modern Art courtyard, and he had me laughing so hard that Corona Light came out my nostrils. There were so many pigeons, he said, showing us pics on his iPhone, that he was literally covered in bird poop and people thought he was part of his own art installation.

Now, John and Josh have us taking turns spitting pistachio shells at the fish tank, trying to see who can hit the glass. My first two attempts fall short, but the next shell I spit soars above the tank and plonks in the water.

"Nice one, Special K," John says admiringly, throwing me a high five.

Josh fist-bumps me. "Not only are you an amazing writer, but you can spit with the best of them!"

I'm shocked by the sincerity of their praise. Have I misjudged these guys and their sophomoric teasing?

"I can do that, too," Jess slurs, reaching for the bowl of nuts.

"Get your own trick," Josh tells her. *"Don't be a Copygirl."*

Hearing him mimic my video makes me spit out my pistachio more forcefully then ever. At this moment, the bartender Rory, a tall blonde with short hair, herself an actress, sidles over with a round of clear-colored shots, and I miss hitting her boob by one-eighth of an inch.

"Compliments of those guys over there," she says. We look over and see some of the creatives from Blood Pudding nodding to us, holding shots of their own in their hands.

"A peace offering for our foes on the Kola pitch. May the best agency win," yells Nigel Davies, their head creative director, from across the bar, and it occurs to me our own Elliott would never do anything remotely so nice. Then my coworkers and I join the competition in tipping back our little glasses, and I down my cool, flat liquid, waiting for the burn, the bite, the aftershock that typically accompanies white spirits like Everclear, Rumple Minze, or Patrón. But it tastes smooth the whole way down, like none of the above, and I realize we've just been given plain shots of water!

If we were in a musical or a movie, now's the time when one of us would pull a switchblade or start a wicked fight by smashing someone over the head with a stool. But we are in advertising, and would hate to get our ironic T-shirts and laptop bags all bloody, so instead we laugh outwardly while inwardly vowing to beat those Brits bad in the pitch.

"Sorry for the prank, mate," someone with a British accent says now to Josh. I turn and see a tall, slightly older man with a ridiculously handsome face that I recognize from a recent cover of *Ad Rage* magazine. "Been a long week and we're just looking for some fun. Let me make it up to you and your friend here." He hands us both a proper shot—this time tequila—introducing himself to me as Rupert.

Rupert Walker! The award-winning copywriter and Nigel's partner at Blood Pudding NYC. I'm not surprised Josh knows him, since I heard him bragging about interviewing at Blood Pudding when they were first staffing up stateside. I am surprised we're all drinking together now, like we're not rivals on the biggest pitch on the planet. You'd never see players from the Jets hanging in the same space as the Patriots. Or even Microsoft employees hanging with the guys from Apple. Just goes to show you how incestuous the ad scene in Manhattan is.

"Kay's an amazing copywriter," Josh tells Rupert, and mentally, I hug him. "One of the best at Schmidt Travino."

"I had no idea STD actually employed any attractive creatives." Rupert winks at me and I wonder if he's flirting. Then he asks Josh, "Is she the one to beat on Kola?"

"Well, I don't know . . . Elliott and I have a *rockin'* campaign. Two words: pitch winner," Josh tells him, and I remember that we're not just out to beat the Brits. We've got to beat each other, too.

The realization must not sit well with me, because Rupert sees me frown. "I think that's enough shoptalk, don't you, Kay? We need more Cuervo, straightaway!"

Josh gets a call from his girlfriend and excuses himself to answer it, so Rupert takes his seat and we do another shot.

"Do you think this counts as dinner?" I hold up my lime and shake salt on it.

"Fruit juice. Sodium. Agave. Perhaps it's more like breakfast?"

"The breakfast of champions!" I quip, and *the* Rupert Walker is laughing along with me, a perfect white smile. I thought the British were supposed to have bad teeth?

"How is it I've never seen you here before among all these ugly mugs?" he asks, and now I know he's flirting. It feels nice to have someone so good-looking interested in me. It feels even nicer not to be butchering my words.

"I prefer to do my concepting in the office, unlike some of these clowns."

"Ah, a hard worker. The good ones usually are." He leans in closer to me. "You *must* come here on a Monday for heavy-metal karaoke night. It's a bit of a blast."

"Tell me you perform? Let me guess, Def Leppard!"

He shakes his head. "Led Zeppelin. 'Stairway to Heaven.' My air guitar is not to be missed."

He gives me a little demo now, fake strumming while singing the famous hook, and I grab my phone to video it. Why should Peyton be the only one to ShoutOut her fun? Before I can hit record, I notice I have a new text. From Ben.

Is that his presentation for Kola? Don't let him steal your ideas!

WTF is he talking about? I haven't even posted any videos yet. Wait, is Ben here?

I look up and Ben is indeed watching us from one of the tables, a half-drunk beer in front of him. Peyton is there, too, but she's sitting on Elliott's lap, playing with his bug camera. No wonder Ben looks miserable. She must be trying to make him jealous.

I put my phone back on the bar and give Rupert my undivided adoration, clapping extra hard. "Not bad. Did you learn that at Oxford?"

"Nah, in prison . . . How'd you know I went to Oxford, anyway?"

Oops. Here I thought I was being so cool. Can't admit I read about him in *Ad Rage.*

"Just a guess. It's the way you hold your pinkie when you're sipping tequila."

"My turn." He grabs my hand. "No rings. Could mean you're an amateur boxer—don't want that hardware getting in the way . . . And a botched manicure. Obviously, you do more work with your hands than just writing . . . I know . . . You're an organic farmer from upstate New Yawk, and you spend your weekends milking cows."

I laugh, pulling my hand away to applaud him again, when suddenly someone is grabbing me by the arm. It's Ben, looking absolutely pained.

"Kay. We need to talk. Now."

"Wha? Rupert, this is my partner Ben. Well, ex-partner . . . No. Sometime partner. I guess I have a few partners!"

"How promiscuous of you." Rupert winks.

"My other partner is gay!" I laugh.

"Sounds like that would make for a very nice office threesome!"

"Yup, our receptionist answers the phone, 'Hello! STD!'"

Ben is the only one not enjoying this repartee. "Please, Kay. I need to talk to you."

"Sorry, Rupert. Work calls." I reluctantly abandon my stool to be led away by Ben.

"A writer always writes, right?" Rupert winks again.

"Right! Thanks for the concert." Ben is actually pulling me toward the door. What gives? "Wilder, that could have been our future creative director. We've got to go back and show him our portfolio!"

"You're drunk. And he wanted to see way more than your portfolio."

"I'm not drunk," I lie. "I just didn't eat enough pistachios for dinner."

I glance back toward the bar one last time and, through my boozy haze, I realize Suit has joined the gang. He is watching me leave with Ben. I wave but he just looks away.

Now we are outside. Ben buys us hot dogs from a guy on the corner, and we sit on a stoop to eat them.

"What were you thinking, chatting up the competition's creative director in front of Elliott?" Ben demands. "Are you *trying* to get yourself fired? He's pissed enough at you as it is."

"I didn't even see you guys come in. And I told you both I was sorry about Shitty Kitty. I was just trying to save all our butts . . . I don't want you to lose your job any more than I want to lose mine, Ben. You're the reason I came to New York in the first place." And there it is, out on the table, finally. I focus hard on my hot dog, like it's the most interesting thing in the world.

"What do you mean? I thought you wanted to live here, too. Set the ad world on fire?"

Now I backpedal. "No. I mean, yes. I mean, I do want the big career and everything, but New York was always *your* dream. I thought we'd find fame together if I came here, and now we hardly talk anymore and you're working with one of the big bosses and you're totally leaving me behind."

Ben snorts. "Yeah, right. I didn't ask to work with Schmidt . . . hell, I'd get out of it if I could. The crazy German should stick to account planning. Man can't write a tagline to save his country. *Driiiiink Ze Kola or Ve Vill Blow Oop Your City!*"

Ben's impression makes me laugh. It's like old times. Him and me. Against the world.

"I bet you have something brilliant for the pitch." Ben looks directly at me with his gooey eyes. "You always do."

I tell him all about my "Be Bubbly" campaign. Must be something in his deep green peepers and my need, still, for his approval. It's nice to have my guard down, even if it took many shots to get here.

"It's really good, Kay," he tells me, with this look of admiration. "You amaze me."

The next thing I know, I'm leaning toward him, and I kiss him. *Me*—I do it. *I* lean forward and put my lips on the mouth I've been watching for years. And amazingly, he kisses me back.

It would be the best moment of my whole life if it weren't for one teensy-weensy, non-amazing fact . . . It feels like I am kissing my brother.

kiss of death

Some ideas are bad but you don't know *how* bad until you're looking back on them later. Like eating Indian food before you go to a movie so you have to sit two hours with curry stewing in your stomach. Or getting a perm—any perm. Has any woman in the history of women ever looked back at a picture of herself with a perm and said, "Damn, I look good in frizzy curls"?

The other kinds of bad ideas are the ideas you know *immediately* are headed south—that was how it felt kissing Ben.

All weekend I've been trying to figure out how that could be. I've been waiting to kiss Wilder for a mini-eternity. I thought he was my one—the Neo to my Trinity, the Simba to my Nala, the conc for my vanilla.

It took serious work to figure out the issue. Specifically, six pizza slices, four cupcakes, and one new video where a doll goes on a search for the perfect man and ends up with an overpriced pair of hand-knitted leg warmers from a boutique in Brooklyn. As I was putting the final editing touches on the film Sunday evening—the doll is actually quite pleased with the leg warmers once she realizes they will keep her warm at night without hogging any of the bed—I realized that the kiss with Wilder wasn't a bad idea, it was just a bad set of circumstances. That's a weekend of work worth doing.

Of course my intuition would be screaming *No, No, No*, when our first kiss was floating in a sea of *cerveza*. Who wants to stand up at their rehearsal dinner to give a toast that goes a little something like, "I knew it was love from the moment I took that tequila shot." My gut reaction was about *how* it happened, not the fact that it happened.

All weekend I felt nervous. I couldn't get that feeling of wrongness out of the pit of my belly, but as soon as I figured out that the kiss was still right, every worry I'd had went out of my brain. I slept like a baby last night and that's probably why I bounced out of bed early, took extra time with my makeup, and now feel like a million and one bucks as I'm cruising through the doors of STD. Of course the fact that Todd and I—oh, and Bouffa, too—are about to present our winning idea to the management team might have a little something to do with the good mood . . . but the big picture is that Ben and and I will be together forever, and that little glitch I felt on Friday night—nothing but a speed bump. Next time we see each other I know sparks will fly and we'll be speeding off to forever—just like I always knew was meant to be.

It was slightly weird that when I texted him to say hey on Saturday he waited an hour to write back and then answered *At the office probably all weekend . . . see you Monday.* I had expected at least a little nod to our shared saliva. But Ben and I have been like two peas in a pod for years now. If I felt hesitation, then he did, too. I'm sure that hesitation was at the root of his short response, and there are two things that will erase his concerns: 1. How hot I look today and 2. Our second kiss, which will be sober and therefore stellar.

I'm in such a good mood I even venture to make eye contact with Veronique as the elevators open. Usually I just cast my eyes to the floor and do a shuffle through the front corridor, but today I look up and, to my surprise, I find her looking directly at me. I do the first thing that comes to mind, I smile, and even though she doesn't smile back she does cock her head slightly to the side with a thoughtful look. I decide to take that as a positive and scurry for my desk.

"What the heck are you guys doing here?" I stare from Todd to Bouffa and back, amazed. They're scurrying around Todd's office like they've been drinking triple espressos since sunrise. Bouffa is straightening papers—maybe the first time she's actually cleaned anything in her life—and Todd is throwing empty acai berry juice bottles from behind his monitor into the trash can.

"There aren't, like, any Diet Coke cans back there, right?" Bouffa is serious.

"If I find any I'm going to put them on Elliott's desk—we definitely don't want the bosses sniffing out your habit." Todd's tone is so snarky I think he might actually be without caffeine at the moment—not his best side.

"Um, hello? Are you guys spring cleaning a month early?" I almost don't recognize the place.

From behind the monitor Todd's voice comes through loud and clear. "Where have *you* been?"

"What are you talking about?" I am *always* the first person here. Except for today.

Bouffa doesn't even stop wiping down the surface to talk to me. "Didn't you check your ShoutOut last night? Travino told us to be ready to go at 9 a.m. Him and Suit and Schmidt and *who knows* who else are going to come around to all our offices and go through our work."

"What? We're not presenting in the conference room?" I guess I'm late to the party.

"Look." Todd stands up in front of his monitor. "The showdown starts in five minutes and we are not going to use that five minutes to get you up to speed. I'm going to get our printouts from the studio. Bouffa, you do finishing touches around here. And as for you"—he turns my way—"why don't you take off your jacket and try to make it look like you've been here longer than five minutes. You might think you're hot shit now that a Blood Pudding creative director is ready to jump in your pants, but that don't mean shit in these four walls, so get ready to earn your dinner."

I'm so stunned my jaw actually drops and I can feel air coming in through my mouth. Todd wasn't even at the bar on Friday night. How would he know I was talking to Rupert? And why the hell would someone tell him that—that Rupert wanted to get in my pants. Unless . . .

"Hey," I whisper and run up to Bouffa. "Did you think that Rupert wanted to get in my pants the other night at the bar? That's the craziest thing I've ever heard!"

"Of course he did." Bouffa rolls her eyes. "It was totes obv. And he's hot, but just a little old for me . . . Are you into old guys? I never took you for daddy issues."

Now I have to take Todd's advice. I throw my jacket over the back of a chair and take a seat. I feel like I need to put my head between my legs but Todd's back in the cube with our mocked-up work. The only good thing about his arrival is that Bouffa stops talking. Did she tell Todd about Rupert? What was I thinking going all weekend without checking ShoutOut—there's probably a damn video on there where someone's talking about it. Someone like E, the eternal asshole. Oh geez—maybe that's why Ben was so short with me on text!

"Hello in there." Todd's face is right in front of mine and he's snapping his fingers in front of my face. Why is it that gay men wear such better cologne than the straight ones?

"I'm here, I'm here," I snap back. "And I'm not retorting to your *way* out-of-place comments now, but later we are going to talk."

Todd leans in. "You know what's riding on this pitch as well as I do—if we don't nail this there may not be a later."

Luckily Bouffa doesn't hear him or it would be twenty questions about his cryptic comment, but I got it loud and clear.

I straighten my shirt and smooth my hair and try to get back to the hot vibe I had only five minutes ago while Todd divides the work and gives us each a part to present. I'm responsible for the unveil of "Be Bubbly" and all the selling points of the line. That's something I believe in, it's something I can do with my eyes closed. Hell, it's probably verbatim what I actually told Ben the other night when I was schnockered before our kiss. I know technically Ben and I are on opposite teams this morning but I'm not used to presenting without him; it would be nice to see him and just get one reassuring look.

But there's no time. Before I know it a small army of people led by Travino, Suit, Elliott, and Schmidt are heading over to Ben's cube.

Travino raises his voice so the whole creative department can hear. "I assume you are all in your cubicles, ready to present. Wait where you are and we'll come around so each group can take us through the work. We want this to be informal, relaxed, creative. It's supposed to be a working session—so continue your working."

Of course none of us do that. Who can work on command? That's like trying to be happy on command.

On cue Bouffa does her damnedest to prove me wrong. "So what should we get started on?" She's happy and trying to work, all at once. I watch Todd slowly slide both hands under his body so he is sitting on them. This is likely a cautionary measure to ensure he does not reach out and slap Bouffa. I can make this guess with a fair amount of certainty because that was my first thought, too—and *I've* had my coffee this morning.

"We aren't going to work," Todd whispers to Bouffa. "We're going to eavesdrop."

Bouffa looks confused. "On who?"

"On Ben!" I realize that maybe I said that too quickly. "And Schmidt, I guess. They are presenting their work first."

"How will we eavesdrop on them?"

"Have you looked up lately?" Todd asks her. Bouffa drops her head back so that her shimmery hair brushes against the back of her chair. She's like a walking shampoo ad, but you have to love her for it—the idea that she could be anything less than shimmery has never occurred to her.

"He's trying to make the point that these are open-air cubicles. And so we can hear everything that goes on over there as long as people stay silent," I say.

"Which they will," Todd says. "Because they are doing what we're doing."

I can tell Bouffa is still confused, so I grab the board of work Todd assigned her to present. "Study this, okay?"

There's light chitchat and laughter coming from Ben's cubicle. This is likely only because Schmidt is presenting work with Ben, and Travino can't intimidate him like the rest of us since he's a stakeholder. I try to imagine Suit in the cube with all those bigwigs. When he walked by I noticed he didn't look like he had slept much. Maybe he's still stressed about work. I hope he's not jumping into another relationship too fast . . . That's always a bad idea.

"Wipe those googly eyes off your face," Todd warns me.

"What? I was thinking about work! Why are you being so mean this morning?" I whisper back at him.

"That new sofa I bought? I had to sleep on it last night. Gael was being a real jerk."

"I'm sorry, Todd."

"Yeah, well maybe I'm a sucker for staying with him . . . always believing in him even when there's no reason. I feel like a dope, you know?"

"And now you have to be bubbly," I say. He nods his head yes.

But the jokes seem to be slowing down in Ben's cube, so Todd puts a hush finger over his mouth. It's time for their show to get started.

Schmidt starts talking and it's his usual smug tone of voice, in broken rapglish. *Zis* is what they were told about Kola. *Zis* is the strategy they were using. They *were* following zhat lead *until* they had *ze* major creative breakthrough that was "da bomb." And then, most uncharacteristically, Schmidt actually gives Ben some credit. "Mad props to *Ben* for having ze lightbulb." My heart leaps for Ben because I know what that will mean to him.

But of course Schmidt won't sell himself short. "*Gott sei Dank* I had the bangin' words to match his idea und now we have ze campaign to blow Kola sales and customer lovin' into za muthafucking roof."

I find myself holding my breath—no way Schmidt could have written something better than me. I'm 99.9 percent sure I can outwrite that guy any day of the week, with a blindfold on, and my right hand tied behind my back, and not just because English is my first language.

"Yo check zis'" Schmidt says, "our idea is whack simple. Und in ze simplicity is ze genius. I'll give you the tagline und let Ben take our show from here. Our line is . . ."

Okay, I am 99.5 percent sure I can outwrite him. If only he would say his damn line.

"More Bubbly," Schmidt finishes. "It's more than a description of ze drink—it's ze way you roll when you drink Kola . . . *everyzing* you do is more bubbly, you feel me?"

I can hear Ben start talking but I can't focus on a thing he's saying. I lean over and put my head between my legs, bracing for impact. Todd leans in close and says, "That's our line, Kay."

I can't even speak, I just shake my head yes. Yes, that is our line. Crash and burn. Bouffa looks up from the page she's been studying, a true look of heartbreak on her face. "Guys, it's not *exactly* our line."

Todd answers her but keeps staring at me. "It's close enough to ours and they presented first. Game over. I wonder where they came up with that idea? Any guesses, Kay?"

"I-I-I-I . . ." The stammering was back. I really had nothing to say. I couldn't tell him the truth—that I had told Ben about our idea. And I couldn't come up with any excuses. Ben had stolen my line . . . after everything we had been through. The eight-tiered wedding cake I'd baked in my imagination was collapsing.

"I-I-I," Todd mocks. Then he finishes in his own voice, "Did you steal it from him or did he steal it from you? You know what? I don't care. I don't have time for these childish games."

Todd starts packing his bag with his books.

"Todd, wait!" I unpack his books. "You can't leave—you can't leave us here. Where are you going?"

"I'm not staying to present this work; it's already been presented."

I look at Bouffa to see if she can help me, but she is biting her nails. In her world, that's a code red.

"We still have to show what we've done. All our scripts. All our print ads. They don't have work that's the same as ours—maybe we can still win."

"This isn't my first rodeo, Kay," Todd assures me. "When your line matches the line of the COO and head strategic planner who thinks he's also a copywriter—his version will win. I'm not staying for the bloodbath. There's a couch in the West Village calling my name."

Todd is already walking out of his office when Bouffa semi-yells in his wake. Half good-bye, half grasping for hope. "We'll see you tomorrow!?!"

Todd doesn't answer, he just gives half a salute as he walks off toward Veronique. God knows what he is going to tell her about me.

But I have bigger problems than what someone can do to me with a voodoo doll. I am about to present to a team of people who can fire me on the spot, and my only backup is Bouffa and a line that got stolen out from under me by a man who, five minutes ago, I would have said that I loved as a friend, as a brother, as a guy I wanted to marry . . . all of the above. Todd was right; there isn't a damn thing to be bubbly about when you finally discover what a dope you've been.

I will not cry I will not cry I will not cry.

I'm talking to my reflection in the bathroom mirror. Any minute now, Bouffa will be here to retrieve me for our presentation, so I have to get a hold of myself. Gina had done her best to talk me down off the ledge in Todd's office and even though it didn't work, she was actually quite sweet.

"Like, Kay, you're the best writer in the agency, and Schmidt isn't even a real writer anyways?" she said while I tried to stop my whole body from shaking. "Your Little Kitty save was epic, and the bosses totally need your talent for this Kola pitch. They're going to love this work as much as they love you."

Then she hugged me. It was a nice moment, and I thanked her for being a real friend, which now that I think about it, is actually true. There are few people I can count on in this city of fakers and clones, and even though Bouffa looks like she fits in with all of them, she's actually good as gold. I was about to tell her how Ben betrayed me—I desperately need someone to confide in—but just thinking about it made my eyes flood with tears, so I excused myself for a trip to the powder room.

"Gotta go touch up my makeup," I lied to her.

"Totally. Use your hotness to sell the work to those boys, Kay. Good idea!" She handed me her lucky Chanel "Flirt" lipstick, the shade she'd worn the day she landed her internship by beating out ten other hopefuls who also had daddies that golf with Travino.

So far, I have not applied the lipstick. I *have* kicked a toilet. Twice. I *have* screamed in silence. For two full minutes. You know, the kind of scream where your face gets all red and your fists clench up and shake, though nothing but air comes out of your mouth.

I even texted Kellie, though I know she's in class and can't respond for hours: *Am total fool. Ben sold me out to help his own career. What took me so long to see the truth?*

The one thing I haven't yet done is full-on cried, and there's no way I'm going to. Not here. Not today. Not with the whole boys' club on the other side of this bathroom door and a killer presentation to make. The office is still a no-cry zone for me. I will not crumble or show up on Game Day with red rings around my eyes. I will never let them think they've gotten to me. A girl's got to maintain her pride—soon I may not have anything else.

I hear the click-clack of Gina's heels outside the door, then she's opening it, so I quickly uncap her Chanel lipstick and start applying "Flirt," willing it to help me feel something other than "Defeat."

"They're almost ready for us?" Bouffa points down the hall. "They're just finishing up with Elliott and Josh, and ohmigod, their idea is *the worst*. Like, it's not even an idea. They want to hire that famous rapper? DJ Jizz Whizz? And have him record an original song? And they don't even have scripts. They just showed Travino a montage of Jizz Whizz's music videos."

"Shooting a music video? That's their pitch winner?"

"Yeah I guess. But, like, I just read on TheInsider.com that DJ Jizz Whizz supposedly runs a prostitution ring? Which would make him more pimp daddy than puffy daddy."

"You know what this means?!" I hug Bouffa. I am amazed Elliott would hand us a spot so easily.

But Bouffa doesn't understand how Jizz Wizz helps us.

"We're still in the running!" I explain. "G, let's go win ourselves a place in this Kola pitch!"

Though it's my first time leading a creative presentation without Ben and his humorous, easygoing saves at my side, things are actually going kinda well. Sure, Schmidt and Elliott were ticked that Todd "came down with a stomach bug"—Gina's quick thinking—but Fred Travino owes God knows how many pitch wins to Todd, so he shrugged it off, saying, "I'm sure he would be here if he could." Then he actually gave Schmidt a look that said, *Loosen your lederhosen.* The moment was so cool, I almost want to forgive Todd for leaving us. Almost.

I start off by showing the "film test" Todd made, inspired by the Day-Glo bubbling technique he found, which everyone agrees "feels really fresh." Even Elliott gives his hipster-approved grunt of assent. Then I read them my first TV script, spurred on by all the enthusiasm. I sound confident and smart, like a famous talk-show host delivering a riveting monologue, instead of wallflower Kay struggling to emit actual sounds. The room is silent, but I can tell that Travino and Suit are really into it. At the end, they're both smiling and Travino says, "Powerful work, Kay. First, Little Kitty. Now this. I'm impressed. And trust me, I am very difficult to impress."

I glance at Bouffa, worried she might feel slighted, but she's sporting a toddler-sized grin, relieved that we're not dead on arrival after all. "I can't take all the credit," I say. "Todd, Gina, and I all worked really hard on this."

Peter Schmidt is nodding, his face pensive. "Yes, vell, I would compliment Todd if my dogg actually was in da houze. Strong concept. I just wish there was some vay to link zis campaign to my strategy, tie it up in a knot . . ."

Um, doesn't he mean a bow? And geez. Does the guy want to be a strategic planner or a writer or rapper or just an asshole? If he wasn't one of the agency's owners, I'd ask.

Elliott had been slumped back on Todd's couch, flipping through a graphic design book while I presented, acting disinterested. But now he sits up, fluorescent white teeth bared, grabbing onto the bone Schmidt just threw out with a rabid look in his eyes. "Of course you're right, Schmitty. Kay's campaign needs a great tagline to hang its hat on. You've been working *so hard*, why don't you have one?"

Great. I had left that part out, praying we wouldn't have to go there. *E-hole.*

"Um, well . . ." I start off, my spastic speech impediment threatening to resurface. *Don't fumble now, Kay. You're so close to a touchdown.* I take a deep breath and continue. "We do have a working endline, but it's not quite right yet."

"So let's hear it." E is relentless.

"Now that you're on board with the concept, we can spend more time nailing the line," I say. I send Suit as much of a pleading look as I'll dare with all the eyes on me.

"Why don't you read another script?" Suit suggests. "That will help us see how your idea works as a campaign." He may not know what the problem is, but I love that he's willing to help. Unfortunately, E-hole is foaming at the mouth and won't be distracted.

"Why don't you read us your tagline first?" Elliott dares. "What are you so afraid of, Kay? Gina?"

Gina has been clenching the print layouts to her chest.

"Like Kay said, it's not right yet?" she attempts.

But E, that futhermucker, grabs the ads from out of her hands, and reads one. *"Be Bubbly."* It takes him a moment to realize what's so familiar about the line and you can see the realization spread across his face in a wave of joy.

"Be Bubbly! Be! Bubbly! Oh yes, girls. That's a *great* line. Pitch winner. Too bad another team came up with it first."

Schmidt swoops in like an overprotective parent. "Actually, *my* line is More Bubbly. Which verks even better."

I cannot believe the schizophrenic talentless hack is actually taking credit for my work. Just because he dresses like a creative person does not mean he is one! Those eight-hundred-dollar jeans aren't fooling me; the man couldn't even write a good order at Waffle House. But of course I can't say any of this.

Suit is the only one who says anything in our defense. "Both versions of the line are equally strong, but *this* work is more on strategy than what Peter and Ben have. And it will appeal more to our most important target audience: Women twenty-five to forty-five. Remember, our research shows teenage boys may drink Kola, but it's the moms and girlfriends who influence purchase decision, and Kola was clear in the briefing that the work must resonate with females, too."

Once again, I'm filled with a strong desire to hug Suit. But Schmidt isn't feeling the same affection for his right-hand man, because he turns to Suit with venom in his tone. "Don't tell *me* about ze strategy, dogg. I'm ze one who came oop with it. You were just my typewriter. *More Bubbly* is da shizz, the clear winner. Though I do like Todd's film schnizzle. We can use zat for my scripts."

"The melting bubble effect works better for my campaign," Elliott counters. "Can't you see Jizz Whizz rapping music video–style, covered in bright carbonation?"

The discussion that ensues would be comical if it wasn't my big idea being defended and dissected like a science lab frog, its insides alternately gutted and offered up for grabs. For a minute, I think Travino will side with Suit, but his partner Schmidt pulls him back to the dark side, and I cannot believe how quickly my high-speed train to the pitch meeting has been derailed.

The bigwigs wander away to the front of the room, still discussing all the ways they can take our ideas and twist them around to look like their own.

Todd was right. It's a total bloodbath. In the end, all my work lies dismembered on the coffee table, and I'm waiting for someone to bring in the body bags.

Finally, Travino clears his throat. "Everybody, listen up. We've got our decision on the work. Every one of you will be expected to work around the clock until this pitch is won—I will not walk away from the Kola meeting with anything less than a new client. If I do, heads will roll, and make no mistake about it—those heads will be yours. *More Bubbly* and *DJ Whizz* are the winners that we will be taking to the pitch."

"Kay," Travino continues, "since you don't have any work moving forward, you can help Peyton do the visual blowout for Peter and Ben's idea. When Todd feels better and is back in the office—send him to me, I'll assign him to a job then."

For a moment there is silence, no one moves.

"Well what are you waiting for?" Travino screams. "Get to work."

Clearly shaken, Bouffa leans over to me and asks what she's supposed to work on. "Travino, like, didn't assign anything to me."

I don't answer her, not because I'm trying to be mean but because I can't breathe. The final nail in my career coffin has gone in, and I'm headed six feet under.

This is the dream: I wake up in my bed wrapped in other people's clothes. Shirts and pants all sewn together—some kind of mad hobo quilt. Where has my Shabby Chic bedspread gone? I don't have time to figure it out. First, I must find out what else has changed. I walk into the small living room of my apartment and instead of my furniture—it's all tables and chairs from work. Veronique's desk is there with her phone and her sewing laid on top, and the chair Jay is always leaning back in when he tosses his football in the air. What the hell? I think. I'm starting to panic, so I run into the bathroom to splash water on my face. This isn't happening. My life is under control. I know who I am. Then with water drip-

ping off my face I close the faucet, stand up, and close the medicine cabinet that was open. Once it is shut I have a clear view of the face looking back at me—and it isn't me, it's a wax me. And behind me is an army of other wax people—people I don't know, strangers who have silently tiptoed into my apartment and now they are laughing, all of them shaking with laughter and their wax heads teeter-tottering as if they are bobble dolls. They are laughing at me, I realize. The laughter gets so loud I can't think. I would scream but I am too overwhelmed, so instead I just barely open my lips and a light, feeble "Mayday" escapes my mouth and floats away from the crowd, into the night.

"Are you sure you're all right?" Peyton asks. This might be the fifteenth time she's repeated the question today. I guess that's better than the fifty times she asked me yesterday and the day before.

At first I thought telling her, "Sure, I'm fine," would get her off my back, but obviously half-ass attempts at passing myself off as a functioning human being aren't getting the job done. Now I just answer by reminding her how much work we have to do.

Since Monday morning we've been holed up in the editing studio, going through clips to make a two-minute "anthem video" for the More Bubbly concept. The project sounds easy— it's just a montage to get the clients pumped up and give a glossy summary of the concept—but every day the projects snowballs into something more difficult.

Every day at four o'clock Schmidt "pops" in to see how we're doing. Usually we're doing as well as we can with his muddled directions and lame script that I attempt to rewrite—because, regardless of my ego, we still need to win this. But the crazy German keeps changing half the words back so they'll be his own, even though they don't make any sense. I guess the fact that he didn't actually come up with the original vision means he has no clue how to clearly execute it.

The grunts he makes while Catherine, the editor, plays our cuts indicate his dissatisfaction. When each video ends he usually attempts a moment of silence, but really can't hold himself back—quickly launching into generic, unhelpful feedback along the lines of "I'm imagining *something more positive*" and "Do you think you could cheer that up?" Then he leaves, and we decide to lean into the cheesiness we had been trying to avoid, and when he shows up the next day to check progress, he announces with disgust that it's time for us to pull our heads out of the Hallmark channel and get back to reality. Didn't we listen to a thing he told us?

Schizophrenia is not a desirable trait in a boss, but this is a man who qualifies for the senior discount at Denny's yet insists on dressing like an eighteen-year-old breakdancer. So we are used to his thin grip on reality.

"I'm just worried about you," Peyton is now saying.

"I've told you—nothing to worry about."

"I know you've told me," Peyton said. "You insist over and over again that you're fine, but the circles under your eyes tell a different story. Ever since you started working here you've been focused and driven—on your game. And now there are times when I talk to you and you don't even hear me."

"You're exaggerating," I say.

Catherine called in sick today. I have a strong suspicion she's just sick of Schmidt's insanity . . . but I can't blame her for that;

we all are. So Peyton is sitting at the edit bay—a huge dashboard of keys and devices with five different monitors set up on top. She swivels her chair around so she is facing where I sit in a recliner a few feet behind her. From here I can see all the screens and can give her feedback on how the pictures fit together—I steer the story line of the video and she oversees the execution.

Every time I make eye contact with Peyton I'm amazed all over again at how perfect her liquid eyeliner is. She's one of those girls you imagine living at the MAC counter. Right now those thick-edged globes look worried.

"I know it sucks your idea didn't make it, Kay. But really, it's just one loss. You're still here—at one of the best agencies in the city—shake it off."

This is where I almost tell her the whole story . . . but then I remember Peyton on Ben's lap at the strip club, Peyton picking Ben and his furniture up from my apartment with her Range Rover that hopefully gets horrible gas mileage. God knows what else they've done together in the last few weeks—she's probably just warming me up to pump me for information she can pass on to him. At this point I wouldn't put anything past Ben or anyone in his manipulative reach.

"Thanks for the pep talk, Peyton. Really. Girl power and stuff—it works."

Peyton just shakes her head. "This isn't how I expected you to be."

I look at my watch. It's three thirty, which means Schmidt will be popping in soon .

"Our daily visitor is going to be here any second, and we don't have his last mood swing translated to film yet."

Peyton starts to smile, but then the largest wave of sadness yet washes across her face. She swivels back to the screen and expertly begins splicing and dicing all the stills we've chosen so they sync with the music. I have to admit, there's not much the girl can't do, and she's not afraid to jump in and get her hands dirty.

There's nothing for *me* to do at the moment, so I close my eyes. I can't let myself nap—even if I doze off for a second there's the chance I'll wake up sweating and on the verge of tears. Since Monday—when I had the dream for the first time— that's what happens every time I fall asleep. In seconds I'm waking up under the mismatched-clothes comforter and the whole nightmare is starting over again.

The little voice inside that I used to trust (before I realized that trusting anything is a futile enterprise) keeps whispering that I should turn the dream into a Copygirl video . . . that maybe if I bring the dream into reality, *Poof,* it will lose its power.

But doing another Copygirl video is impossible. I've washed my hands of it. Copygirl was a silly project from a girl who was silly enough to believe that someone out there might find inspiration in her words. But if the last week has taught me anything, it's that words are plentiful; billions of people utter tens of thousands of them every day—and that's enough to ensure that anything you say has probably been said already by someone else.

Be Bubbly, More Bubbly, Bubbles R Us . . . it's all pretty much the same. So from here on out, I'm going to let other people strive for thought-provoking originality. I'll just do what it takes to stay above water. Follow all the rules. No striking out on my own. I'll be happy with Little Kitty and my junior copywriter title, and as soon as I have the time and energy I'll trash the dolls once and for all. Maybe I'll burn them all in a big old wax bonfire.

I tried to explain this to Kell; of course she didn't get it.

FaceTime, she texted immediately. But this time I did not heed her order.

Not now Kell, working around the clock, will call when I can.

Kay—Mon Dieu—nombres on your site shot through le roof this week. Je ne sais pas what happened. A link from some kind of massive blogger???? You MUST continué.

When I didn't text her back she started sending me regular texts that say: *Ne Quittez Pas*. I may not be practicing my high school French quite the way Kell is, but I do know the translation: Don't quit.

Apparently she and Peyton are in a race to see who can nag me to death first.

And on that note, an insistent beeping from my phone forces me to open my eyes so I can see who's trying to contact me. I look at the phone and—oh splendid!—it's the black horse coming from behind to wring me around the neck with one big old nag. With a sigh, I pick up the phone.

"Hello, Mother."

"Kay! I must say, I am surprised you answered your phone."

"That's funny, I was just thinking the same thing."

"Can't talk for long—am just jetting from a charming lunch

with Naomi and her mother at the country club to a house show-ing, and then I have a meeting with Mercer County Women in Commerce and—"

I can't believe it, but I actually cut her off. "So you can't talk for long, what exactly did you need?"

"Well I was just telling Naomi's mother that you would have TV commercials in next year's Super Bowl and she wanted to know if there would be anything on sooner. Naomi said she assumed you probably would get something on TV before next year rolls around—goodness that's an eternity! And I agreed with Naomi—isn't it wonderful that she does always seem to be right, so much like me I have to pinch myself sometimes. So I am calling to have you e-mail me a schedule of when I can watch your TV commercials. Then I'll share that schedule with the pertinent people, of course."

I close my eyes again; this can't be happening. Why does she insist on not paying attention to me when I deserve it and also overselling me when I don't deserve it? I vow then and there never to procreate, so that I will not drag another female through the mother/daughter dynamic that always leaves me in an emotional gutter.

"It's going to take me a while to put that together for you, Mom."

"Oh look! I'm already at the house. I'll look forward to the schedule, thanks, Kay."

I hang up without saying good-bye. There's a chance she was saying "Ta-ta" to me, but there was a better chance she was say-ing hello to someone named Tatum. My mother has a habit of starting new conversations before finishing old ones.

"That your mom?" Peyton asks without turning around.

"Yup."

"Sounds like you get as many words in with her as I squeeze in with mine."

There's something we have in common. I guess. I throw her a tiny bone of acknowledgement. "It's exhausting."

Now Peyton swivels around to meet my eyes. I look away, down at my phone, to check the time. It's 3:48.

"What is up with your iPhone, Kay? Are you ever going to get that screen fixed?"

I wish she would zoom out, focus on something or someone else. So I change the subject. "Peter is probably marching our way. You think we're ready?"

"As ready as we're going to be. It doesn't matter, we're just chasing our tails here."

Chasing tails for a bunch of tail-chasers, I want to say. But that's the snarky edge of the old Kay.

The phone next to Peyton rings and she answers it. Then she turns so I can see her face, and rolls her eyes exaggeratedly.

"Of course. We're on our way." She hangs up the phone then stands up, perkier than she's been all day. "We've been summoned."

"By who?" I'm hoping against hope she's going to tell me someone manageable, like Suit.

"That was Elliott on the phone—but he's in Travino's office with Schmitty."

There's no choice; we have to go. So I stand and follow Peyton out of the room.

Travino's office isn't far and we're there before I want to be. I have managed to stay hidden in the editing bay during working hours, so I haven't seen many faces around the office lately. I have no idea if Todd has resurfaced. Bouffa got assigned to putting together some kind of goodie-bag-party-favor bullshit for the Kola clients, so she's been running around Manhattan looking for tissue paper. Every once in a while she does a ShoutOut with a question about which bag or mini–champagne glass or vintage-soda T-shirt Peyton and I like best.

Bouffa seems slightly stressed but it's good for her to be out of the office—she dodges the bad vibes and has easy access to all the Diet Coke she can drink.

Peyton swings her mane of hair back when she arrives in Travino's doorway. I note that I haven't seen her do that in the editing bay much. Maybe it's less of an unconscious habit than I originally thought.

"Hello, boys," she purrs. I definitely haven't heard her purr in the last week. Yet another person you can't take at face value.

Through the fogged glass I see Travino wave us into his office. The space is bigger than my apartment. I bet with his decorating budget I could buy my whole freaking building.

"Peter tells me you ladies have been struggling with the video."

Schmidt leans forward with a slimy, thin-lipped grin. "I didn't use ze word 'struggling,' I just said the bidniz vas whack."

I can feel fury boiling in me again but I consciously push it down. Getting mad won't change a thing.

Peyton doesn't skip a beat; she completely ignores Schmidt and stays eye-locked with Travino. "I've actually been saving all our drafts. You can watch a comprehensive list of where we've been if you're interested."

"I wouldn't mind seeing that." Elliott smirks.

Travino remains on course. "Yes, well I'm sure it would be educational but I don't need all the versions. Actually you're here because I don't need any versions. Instead of doing a typical mood video for this concept, I will just deliver an opening speech. For Elliott's campaign, they are going to get a DJ Whizz look-alike to show up and speak—it's a good idea and I want that human element in both."

I steal a glance at Elliott, who looks like a little boy, practically glowing from Travino's compliment about his good idea. Oh yes, *Elliott*—single-handedly spreading the warmth of humanity through advertising.

"I'd like you to spend the rest of the day working on a background visual to flash behind me while I speak—something ambient and relaxing but Kola-esque."

Schmidt's starting to twitch. Obviously keeping his mouth shut is wearing on him.

"Kola-esque and also . . . you know, positive and—"

Oh my God, he's not going to say it, I think to myself. *No way will he say it.*

But of course he says it.

"—bubbly," Travino finishes. "More Bubbly, More Bubbly, More Bubbly. It should infuse every aspect of the presentation. From the first speech to the finale."

The fury I pushed down has mutated in my belly into a generally unrecognizable ball of emotion. I feel a dangerous burn behind my eyes.

Oh God, not here, not now.

"Yes and when you finish that—by the end of the day, please—I want you to check in with the Little Kitty team. Apparently they have some video work that needs to be done, and you two will do it for them."

Suddenly there is a knock right behind where I am standing. I turn around to see a woman and a small child standing in the doorway. She is unlike the people I usually see in the office—she seems genuinely cheerful and has an easy smile. She's so petite that her toddler son is almost to her hips.

I step out of her way so she can see the whole room. Behind me, Travino speaks.

"Teresa! It's been so long, but of course you are as beautiful as ever." Travino's charismatic charm can be turned on in a millisecond. I'm trying to figure out which client would show up in off-duty mom clothes, because if this woman isn't a client then she's a one-in-a-million case—I've never seen Travino gush over anyone who didn't have a pen ready to sign a million-dollar monthly retainer.

"Elliott, you didn't tell me we were having such a wonderful surprise," he continues.

Elliott? I turn to see his face and he's smiling more warmly than I thought was humanly possible for someone of his species.

"Hey, Carter." Elliott stands and the little boy runs from behind his mother's legs for his outstretched arms. So this is Elliott's ever-elusive family. I'd heard of them but they sounded too good to be true. Now they look that way, too.

"Where's Sissy?" E tousles Carter's white blond pageboy.

On cue, a little girl shows up in the doorway. She seems older than the boy, but not by much. She's holding someone's hand and when I look up to see who it is, I come face-to-face, for the first time since we kissed, with Ben.

"Look who I found wandering through the creative cubes."
Ben releases the girl's hand and she runs over to Elliott, too.

"Mr. Ben showed me the skateboards," Sissy announces.

Ben leans over and gives Teresa a greeting kiss on the cheek.
I had no idea he knew Elliott's wife so well, and from the look
on Peyton's pasty face, she was clueless, too.

When he's done with that hello, Ben finally notices me. Our
eyes lock for a moment and I stare a hole through him, scanning
for signs that he's even aware of how badly his transgression has
hurt me. But he just waves and smiles sheepishly, and suddenly I
can feel all the rage I've been holding down. The tears that were
coming up earlier are back with a vengeance, and I'm too tired to
fight. Too physically tired, too emotionally tired.

To myself, too quiet for anyone else to hear, I whisper, "Mayday." Then I mumble to the room, "Excuse me," and slide out.
Travino was done with our assignment anyway, and they've all
moved on to fawning over Elliott's beautiful family.

I walk as fast as I can toward the bathroom. From the corner
of my eye I see Suit coming down the hallway that's about to
intersect mine, and the voice inside me wants me to slow down
so I can talk to him. But self-preservation is my bigger priority
so I speed on. If I'm going to break my rule about the no-cry
zone, it sure as heck is not going to be in this open-air office. At
the very least I will make it to the privacy of a bathroom stall.

I push through the ladies' room door and head for the back
toilet. Even before I can get the door closed the tears are rolling
down my face and I can feel my nasal passages blocking. My
phone is in my pocket and even though my hands are shaking, I
still manage to pull it out.

There is one new text message. Out of habit I open it and *Ne Quittez Pas* flashes up across the cracked glass. The shattered screen really works with the message to accentuate all the ways I am a quitter. If it weren't for my ridiculous rent I'd probably walk out of this job, too. That's slightly amazing, since just two weeks ago I thought maybe I really had a chance to make a career in the ad business.

Too late, Kell, but thanks for trying.

What a joke what a joke what a joke, I say to myself. But it is not a joke. At the rate the tears are falling I'm going to be here for a while, so I put down the toilet cover and take a seat. God, if my mother could see me now. How can I tell her I'm not going to have commercials on TV anytime soon, if ever at all? What a cruel joke. My idea has been bastardized into my boss's cheesy scripts and is going to the pitch without me.

Mom would probably blame me. But it's not my fault. My work was good—good enough to steal, apparently.

Finally I decide to hell with everything and just relax into my sobs, letting the waves of despair wash over me. It actually feels good to give in to a good cry. Suddenly I hear the bathroom door push open and I tense up, my whole body on silent alert.

"*Sniff! Sniff!*" Whoever walked in has been crying, too. I peek through the crack in the stall. It's Peyton! She's struggling to pull a paper towel out of the dispenser.

Veronique comes in behind her, handing her a box of Kleenex.

"Here, sugar, wipe with these. Those cheap paper towels will give a girl wrinkles for sure."

"Thanks, Veronique," Peyton sobs, mopping up her tears with the tissues. "How could I be so stupid?"

"He ain't worth the tears, child." Veronique hugs her. "You are so much better than this."

"You should have seen the way he looked at her. He *does* *love* her. I was just a stupid fling."

My mind is racing. They must be talking about Ben. And me? She obviously knows about the other night. He *loves me*? No way. He *loves* my ideas. That's true. And the way they help him get ahead. But that passionless kiss we shared and his subsequent betrayal proved love for me was never part of the equation.

I wipe my face with my sleeve and before I know it I am hopping out of the stall and confronting Peyton.

"My kiss with Ben was a mistake." I catch her completely off guard. "He's all yours if you want him."

"Ben? I don't want Ben, Kay." Peyton is seriously floored. "My God. Is that what you think?" She pauses for a moment and even through her red splotchy skin I can see realization creep across her face. "Is that why you've been such a bitch to me all this time?"

"No . . . I mean, yes . . . You mean, you're *not* sleeping with Ben?" I stammer.

"God, no," Peyton sighs. She looks down at her studded boots, then up at Veronique, as if searching for something. Permission? Strength? What finally comes out of her mouth completely blows my mind. "I've been having an affair with Elliott."

"Elliott?!" I repeat.

Peyton nods. "I know. How could I be so stupid?"

Oh. My. God. I feel so stupid, too. How did I get that one so wrong? Now Veronique is eyeing me compassionately. "Looks like you could use one of these tissues, too."

roach army

"It's not whether you get knocked down, it's whether you get up."—Vince Lombardi

That's the text I got from Peyton before bed last night. Leave it to her to quote famous football coaches. The amount of stuff she stores in a head I thought was filled with fluff is staggering. Almost as impressive as her roach-like knack for perseverance.

"Cockroaches don't give up, Kay. They don't die," she's telling me as we grab stools at the Genius Bar inside the Apple Store in Soho. "They can even survive nuclear blasts."

"So can Twinkies," Todd chimes in.

We're waiting here while Todd's friend Etsu, a Mac Genius, repairs my cracked iPhone screen. Todd arranged the free repair job. It's his way of making it up to me for leaving Gina and me in the lurch at our Kola internal review.

The mere fact that I agreed to finally fix my damn phone should be a sign that I'm getting back up and moving forward. But Peyton's pushing me for bigger action. Like figuring out how to fix my damn career.

Since her confession in the office bathroom, we've been growing tighter. While spending our waking hours sifting through footage for Schmidt's stupid mood video, she told me all about her tryst with Elliott, and how he had her believing he had separated from his wife. But when Peyton saw Teresa and the kids there in the office, in the flesh, she realized that not only was Elliott's perfect family still perfectly intact, but that she didn't want to be the home wrecker who tore them apart.

"The crazy thing," she admitted the other day while we waited for a version of our video to render, "was I really thought I loved him. I had totally convinced myself he was the one for me. Did I like the attention? Was it how he made me feel? Why did I turn into such an idiot?"

Those are the only answers Peyton doesn't seem to have. Along with me and maybe every other girl in Manhattan at some point or another.

Maybe that's why I confided in her about my feelings for Ben, and how hurt I've been by his betrayal. As devastated as I was, I, too, am realizing love and wanting to be loved are two different things. The Ben I built up in my mind was a far cry from the guy who slinks past me in the office, unable to even cop to his role in me losing my pitch berth.

It feels weird to be outside the office while it's daylight, but there are only a few days until the Kola showdown and our paltry part is done, so when Todd proposed this little field trip, I didn't even hesitate. Peyton tagged along because she needs a new Michael Kors iPhone wristlet, and I don't mind. It's nice to actually have friends who are living on my same continent.

"It should only be a few more minutes," Todd tells us now. "Etsu is the fastest screen replacer in Manhattan. They call him the iPhone Fairy. You should see the magic he works with that tool of his . . ."

"TMI, Todd," Peyton says. "Don't you have any straight friends?"

"I have you witches," he laughs. "Let's check out the new MacBook Air. If those clowns botch the pitch, I'll be needing one to properly launch my freelance biz. Man cannot live on unemployment alone."

Ugh. I hate being reminded how dire the situation at STD is. Wish I had more confidence in Schmidt and Elliott, but after the b.s. that's gone down lately, my only hope is that Kola's taste in work is mediocre, too.

Peyton and I trail behind Todd as he pushes his way through a group of teenage girls who are hogging the demo MacBooks.

"Your five minutes are up, girls. Make way for a paying customer." Todd shoos them with a wave of his hand and they move over, letting him have a machine.

Several of the girls are huddled around one screen, watching something and laughing.

"OMG I love this one!" a perky blonde shrieks. "Cecily, Zoe, you have got to see this." Their friends come over and suddenly it feels like a sorority slumber party with all the giggling and gawking.

I glance at their MacBook monitor and think I catch a glimpse of Queen Copygirl standing in front of Zara at night. I look closer. *No effing way!* They are watching my latest video!

"My God, my God, my God," I mutter to no one, but Peyton hears me anyway.

"What?"

"I don't believe it." I watch as Bridge and Tunnel Girl get attacked and turn into zombies.

Peyton turns to follow my line of sight. "Oh yeah, Copygirl. Have you seen these? They're totally fun."

The perky blonde is repeating my endline. "Don't! Be! A Copygirl!" and her friends start begging her to play the film again.

I must be in a state of shock because I don't even notice that Etsu has been tapping me on the shoulder. "Kay! Earth to Kay! Your phone is all done!"

"*You* know about Copygirl?" I finally say in Peyton's general direction.

Etsu thinks I'm speaking to him. "I heard about it from my cousin in Japan. Those dolls are so creepy cool. Girls there are dressing up like them."

I walk away for a moment, forgetting to take my phone, and sit down on a stool, trying to process this information.

Peyton follows me, teasing. "What's the matter, Kay? Do you have a fear of talking dolls?"

"How could it be?" I wonder aloud. "Do you think they're really watching the videos in Japan?"

"According to Etsu's cousin they are. It wouldn't surprise me. All the girls I know here watch them."

All this new information is so much to take in. I repeat after Peyton, "All the girls you know here watch my videos."

"Wait, wait, wait—what?" Peyton's eyes widen. "What did you just say?"

So Kell tells her friends in Paris. Who have friends in Manhattan. And maybe someone from Japan is visiting Manhattan, sees them here and shows them back home. How do these things happen? Are people in Brazil, Russia, maybe even Australia watching my videos? Holy shit—have they made it to Jersey?

"Kay." Peyton reaches over and gives my knee a shake. "Pay attention, this is serious. Did you just say the Copygirl videos are *your* videos?"

"Remember that little side project I mentioned that I no longer had the heart for? The video blog?"

She scans my face for clues and sees I'm staring at the gaggle of teenage girls. Now they're watching the video with It Girl and Club Boy, and damned if they aren't doubled over with laughter. Suddenly, Peyton puts two and two together. Copygirl is your *little side project*?! Holy crap, Kay!" Now she sits down, too, to absorb the news. "I *thought* the voice sounded familiar . . . and, well, now that I think about it, I can see the resemblance between you and some of the dolls. Is that on purpose?"

I shake my head yes.

"This is huge, Kay. Do you realize how huge it is?"

I think about this. Kell has been telling me for weeks that the Copygirl videos were big, but I wouldn't listen. Hell, I was ready to give them up. But not with these screaming girls, not if people actually want more of what I really have to say.

"Now I do," I tell Peyton.

"Amazing." She smiles, obviously impressed. "You really do have a truly creative mind."

Then Peyton turns to watch the girls, who are starting to plan their next move in Soho. "First," one of them says, "let's swing by Zara and all take pictures in front posed like Queen Copygirl."

Shouts of "Totes!" and "Yes!" come up from their little crowd.

"You know . . ." Peyton shifts into producer mode. "This is the kind of thinking that could win us Kola."

I'm about to ask what the heck she's talking about when Todd pops up with my iPhone in his hand. "Try holding on to this better than you did our tagline," he says to me. And then to Peyton, "What could win us Kola?"

"Something like the Copygirl videos." Peyton motions to the pack of teenage fans.

I look down at my phone. It's all fixed up, good as new—you can't even tell the screen was ever shattered. My mind is reeling. Could Peyton be right? Is that *impossible? Possible? Is there a way to fix my career, too?*

"That *would* be cool," Todd says to Peyton. "But nobody knows who's behind Copygirl."

My mouth opens and I speak without any hesitation whatsoever. "Actually, Todd, we do know. And I have an idea . . ."

"Here is the topline report from the all focus groups we did." Suit hands me a deck of papers. "And here are my notes from the client dinner. I wrote down everything their chief marketing officer said. I tried giving them to Schmitty, but he waved me away, insulted that I might be insinuating he wasn't paying attention."

"This is so great!" I smile, scanning through the pages. "You've been a huge help. I really can't thank you enough."

Suit just shrugs. No return smile. Lately he's been all business, which is weird because ever since the Boathouse and all the Little Kitty drama, I thought we were becoming friends, or at least cordial coworkers. At the moment, he seems anything but cordial.

"Is everything okay?" My tone is soft, concerned. "You don't seem like yourself."

"Be careful, Kay." He's brisk and ignores my attempt at personal conversation. "What you're doing could get you fired. Now if you'll excuse me, I am about to jump on a call." He picks up his handset, signaling that our tête-à-tête is over.

Geesh. I wonder what's gotten into him. As I exit his office, I think about his warning. It might be true, but if I do nothing, we may all wind up unemployed anyway. No time to worry about that now, though. I've got far too much to do.

I spend the next hour absorbing the research Suit gave me, and the next few hours after that writing in my cube. It's unusually quiet out here because the boys are all locked in the conference room, rehearsing their presentation. But someone could drive a Mack truck through the office and I wouldn't notice. I'm in a flow state, hyperfocused, and the ideas come easy. It's all starting to come together.

My team of roaches has been busy behind the scenes figuring out how to put my plan into action, and now we've got a jumping-off point. I hit print on my laptop, grab my pages off the printer, and head to Todd's office to brainstorm.

"It's really cool, Kay," Todd agrees after I take him through my thoughts.

He starts sketching out scenes, freehand, on a large sketchpad. It's old school, the way art directors worked before computers took over the advertising world, and it feels like we're really creating something, not just coloring pictures in a book that someone else wrote.

Bouffa walks in as we're hashing out the sequence and asks, "Do we have a script?" She's been acting as Peyton's assistant producer and she looks the part. Clipboard in hand, Bluetooth in ear. All that's missing is the Diet Coke, but I don't dare tempt her by saying that.

"We're just finalizing it now," Todd tells her. "But we need to find a great piece of music."

Gina writes *great music* on her notepad and circles it twice with a scented pink pen, then hands us both a sheet of paper. "Here's the schedule. We prep tonight, then tomorrow we put it into production."

"Thanks, G." I scan the schedule. "Lookin' good. Where are we with the props?"

"Veronique will sew the little costumes based on Todd's sketch. She obviously knows a thing or two about dolls, what with the voodoo and all. She says there's a fabric stall two blocks away she can hit on her lunch break to get what she needs?"

"Yeah, I know the one she's talking about." I still can't believe Veronique actually offered to help us out. *Ain't nobody in this agency as good at getting things done as me*, she said.

I agree with her. But after watching Peyton all week, I have to admit she's right on Veronique's tail.

"Hey, hey, hey!" Peyton breaks in to the conversation. She

has on her jacket and I swear I can almost feel the cool spring air still coming off her body. In a flash she repositions where Bouffa is standing so their backs are together and facing the rest of the agency—like a wall.

"Looky what I got!" She's talking to all of us, but she's looking directly at Todd. Then she opens her black messenger bag so that we can see the high-def video camera stashed inside.

"Yes!" After weeks of shooting with an iPhone, through a cracked screen, I know the difference this camera will make.

"Peyton! You got it!" Bouffa shrieks, clearly enamored with the procurement skills of her mentor.

"Who'd you go to?" Todd raises an eyebrow.

"I happened to know of an assistant at a production house in town who felt a little . . . how should I say this . . . jilted? Or maybe jizzed and whizzed? By a creative director we all know and admire."

Bouffa is the only one stumped by this hint. But we don't stop to explain.

"When are you going to be ready to shoot?" I ask Todd.

He pauses for a second and I hope—I really hope—this isn't something he's going to delay for a placenta facial or reservations he has at the latest pan-Asian-Latin-fusion restaurant. If I ever doubted his commitment to the Copygirl project, my doubts go out the window when he looks at me and says, "I'll call Gael and tell him to DVR *Dancing with the Stars*. If Veronique can have the costumes done by dark, let's get it done tonight."

"Catherine gave me the key to the editing suite, so we can use that after hours." Peyton holds up the coveted key ring.

"Good." I give her a thumbs-up. "We don't have much time left but it looks like it can come together."

"There is one answer I still don't have," Peyton sighs. "Those 'Don't Be a Copygirl' T-shirts would be so perfect—like the cherry on top of the double-scoop sundae."

"There's no way Kell could get them made and ship them over here by the pitch," I say, managing not to point out Peyton has probably never indulged in an ice cream sundae in her whole life—you don't get air between your thighs because you've got a thing for hot fudge.

"How many do we want?" Todd asks.

Peyton looks down at her notes. "At least twenty. And they all have to be originals—screenprinted and then ripped and sewn in different ways. The whole point is that each one is unique, you know? So no copies."

"That's a big favor to beg for," Todd admits. "I don't think Veronique has time for that with all the stuff Travino's got her doing for Pitch Day."

I am about to strike the item from the wish list for our presentation, when Bouffa speaks up. "Um, guys, I think I have an idea."

She's practically whispering, so I have to lean forward to hear. "Whatcha got?"

"There's a girl I went to high school with who has a screen-print machine. She does these T-shirts for pregnant moms that have quotes on the baby bumps? And the baby bumps say things like 'Future Bergdorf's Lover on Board' and 'I'd rather be in St. Barts' and they're super cute and she sells them for like eighty-five bucks a piece—"

Peyton clears her throat to encourage G to move along.

"Right." Gina talks even faster. "So. She owes me because her high school boyfriend asked me to prom after they broke up but I turned him down and so the two of them went together in the end and now he's a trader and she vacations in Barbados—"

"Gina!" Peyton insists. She simply can't handle delays.

"And I can have her do the screenprinting! I know she'll say yes! And for free because God knows she doesn't need the money!"

"Excellent!" Peyton gives a little golf clap. "Good thinking, G." And Gina practically glows.

Then Peyton goes on, "But there is still the problem of a seamstress who can handle such a big order in no time flat and with no budget."

Bouffa scrunches her eyebrows and I can see it dawning on her who we can turn to at the exact same second as I do. Renee.

She looks at me and I give her a little nod the rest of the group won't notice.

"I got that part covered," I tell them. "Bouffa, will you call your friend and see if she can get started immediately on the shirts? Make sure she's not in a cabana somewhere being fanned and eating bonbons?"

"Oh God, Kay. People spend January and February away; this is March."

I have to smile. The occasional sneak peek of the world according to Bouffa is simply delightful.

"So everybody knows what they're doing? Let's meet in front of the agency at, say, eight thirty tonight—ready to shoot?"

They all agree. Peyton and Bouffa rush off and Todd turns back to his computer.

I'm still facing out toward the agency. This place pisses me off, but I do love it here, too. At least I think it's love. I definitely love these people I've found to work with. It's like a little tribe. Like it used to be with me and Ben but bigger and better and—now I have to admit—more honest.

"You think we're going to pull this off?" I ask Todd. I don't even look up to see his face; I'm staring at the tiny cracks in the floor. The concrete is the one detail that surprises me about the office. Travino went for the big bucks on all the furniture and the art, but he didn't pay for the hand-distressed wood planks that all the other "cool" offices have. Maybe that give-and-take is why he's such a damn good businessman—knowing when to go for the gold and when to pull back. If we can just get him alone before the pitch, there's no way he'll miss the gold in our idea. He has to understand how big it could be for Kola.

"It's a helluva plan," Todd answers. "If we pull it off, it could be the stuff ad legends are made of. And *damn*, I have always wanted to be legend!"

I laugh. Gotta love Todd—he's the leader and marching band in his own parade.

"But my honest opinion, Kay," he goes on, and now he's not joking at all, "we'll get the pieces together; this is a good team. But the big wins, the big ideas—they always require a little touch of magic."

I hear what he's saying and the truth of it shakes in every cell of my body. I reach for my jacket, slide my arms through, and grab my purse.

"Lemme guess. Nut run?" Todd is starting to know me too well.

"Not this time. There's someone I need to see."

If magic is what I need, then it's time to find the closest thing I've got to a fairy godmother.

The walk to Bloomingdale's is long thanks to the midday throng of tourists itching to take selfies in Soho, but I need the fresh air and a little exercise. The only things that have been getting a workout lately are my fingers on the keyboard.

As soon as I hit the street, I whip my phone out of my purse and give Kell a call. It will be the first time in forever that I've seen her face without cracks jetting through her French pucker. This Kola operation is making me feel like more of a grown-up than I ever have—but I still need my childhood best friend to cheer me on. That would probably make some girls feel stupid, but I'm glad some things never change.

"Bonsoirrrrrrr," Kell answers the phone. She's in her night-shirt with her computer open on the bed. "I'm getting ready to pull an all-nighter."

"What are you working on?" The smell of cashews reaches me from a vendor on the street, and I make a mental note to indulge at some point this afternoon.

"Well, I am about to write a paper on modern art. But before *je commence* I was just doing a few checks on vidéos célèbres. Kay, Copygirl stats *keep getting bigger.*"

"Kell, I was in the Apple Store yesterday and a guy told me his cousin in Japan watches them."

"Oh je sais. I totally know that, Japan's been onto you from *le début.* But the cool thing is, you're starting to spread across

America now. Manhattan was like *la seule* place in the states that was paying attention *initalement*, but now you are growing *de plus en popularité*. You're in the heartland, *bébé*."

My heart jumps. This is excellent news but I've got to keep my eye on the bigger prize.

"Hey, Kell, so did you send the screenprint design to that e-mail address I mailed you earlier? They're going to start running more shirts on the presses this afternoon."

"Done!"

"You're the best, Kellkell!" She smiles but now that my screen's in one piece, I can see something lurking behind her eyes that I need to finally address.

"Listen . . . I'm sorry I was off for a few weeks there. The Ben thing threw me for a loop."

"I'll say, Kay. But you are forgiven. Have you talked to him?"

I look away from the screen for a moment at all the strangers on the street who would make eye contact with me a gazillion times faster than Ben would right now.

"He's still avoiding me. We haven't talked since he stole my idea."

"Since you *kissed* and he stole your idea," she corrects me.

"I'm not interested in the kissing part of that sentence anymore."

Kell smiles a real smile into the camera. "Good. It's so *blah blah* to change for a guy, you know? You seem much more yourself right now."

"Fingers crossed for the pitch." I'll take all the good vibes I can get.

Kell holds up her overlapped middle and index finger. "Fingers crossed from France. I know you're going to be busy, so I'll just send you a ShoutOut if anything crazy happens with stats on the Copygirl site, all right?"

"Perfect." I blow her a kiss and then we hang up.

The wheels are turning. Or as Kell would say: *Les roues tourne.* I decide I need to see Renee sooner rather than later, and I notice a cab letting out passengers right next to a cashew vendor. Obviously today is my lucky day.

What is it with the air in this Bloomies? It always smells more expensive than regular air. Maybe it's all the fragrance sprayers. Or the leather from the purse section. I give my contraband bag a jiggle on my arm. She may not be from here, but she fits right in.

I head to the auction where Bouffa and I did our damage, and ding a small little silver bell next to the cash register. The floor is so empty I immediately regret making such a racket. I reach to silence the bell but somehow knock it off the table and onto the floor. I'm scurrying on my hands and knees across the carpet to pick up it up when I hear a British accent above me, "May I *help* you, Miss?"

Bell in hand, I stand up and try to straighten my jacket. This is typical Kay—rumpled and crawling on the floor while a well-heeled Brit looks down her perfectly pugged nose in my direction. What's *not* typical Kay—instead of my insides crumpling up into a ball of self-loathing, I have to silence a giggle in my belly. *Wouldn't Suit laugh if he could see me now.*

Wait—what, Suit? Why on earth would he come to mind right now?

But there's no time for introspection.

"You *can* help me," I tell the woman. "I'm looking for Renee, the seamstress who did alterations for me a few weeks ago."

"Was there a problem with your garments?" The woman peers over her cat-eye glasses with extreme concern.

"Oh no—no problem. I just want to—um—say hi to her."

"Well I'm afraid you'll have to wait a week. Renee is on vacation, but if it is a question about the alterations we have someone else who can assist you.

A week? We definitely do not have a week. I thank the woman and head for the escalator. All the way out of the store I'm trying to think of another solution. It's New York—there's definitely a way to get the shirts sewn, but getting it done on next to no money is going to be an issue. The problem with planning a secret campaign as a coup is that you don't get access to the big ad budget. It kills me that money we could use to get these T-shirts done right is currently being leveraged to hire a Jizz Whizz look-alike for the presentation.

I reach in my pocket for the cashew bag I dropped in there earlier. I ate most of them but I expect at least a few kernels to still be rolling around in the greasy paper. It's easy to lose track of time when you are sitting on a step, munching nut bits and thinking about massive problems that could derail your entire career as well as your self-esteem. When I see the shadows moving onto the cement in front of my feet I realize it must be later than I thought so I look up to see where the sun is, and find myself staring into the face of another radiant force—Renee!

I'm so happy I hug her, totally forgetting that I don't even really know her. But I have been wearing clothes she bought me every day . . . That has to make a hug at least semi-appropriate.

"I take it you got my gift," she chuckles. Always prim and proper, she reaches a hand to her perfectly poufed gray hair to make sure my embrace has not dislodged her do.

"I take it you didn't get my thank-you note," I answer. "I sent it to you via Bloomingdale's."

"Ha!" Renee laughs brighter. "I don't even know if I have a mailbox there. I am not what they call a standard employee. Kind of come and go as I please."

"I was actually just looking for you—a woman on the fourth floor said you were on vacation, but here you are, right now."

"I take vacations frequently. Sometimes to loosen my arthritis. Sometimes to loosen my spirits. That's the luxury of being an old woman—you can do what you want; people let you have your way."

"Well, I was coming to see you with a sewing request," I say. "But if you're taking a break then I don't want to bug you."

"No, no, dear. This was a break for the spirit. And I have a feeling maybe you can help me with that. Young people always make me feel alive. That's actually why I was heading to the store. I just wanted to lose myself in the perfumes . . . Don't they take you away? They just remind me of the girl I was and the men I knew."

I take Renee's hand and invite her to sit back on the step where I was earlier. Now that she's not in front of me, the sun is bright above our heads—shining yellow warmth through the buildings to shoo away what's left of winter.

Everything comes out—more than I expected to tell—about my job and my videos. How right now I am trying to win the

Kola business and keep the doors of the agency open. How all these amazing people I've met at work are helping me and how she's already helped me out with my new life in New York but now I need her help one more time. And then when I deliver my most heartfelt request for her to help me make the shirts, she takes one look at me—as though I've just asked her whether she's planning on having dinner that night—and says, "Of course, dear."

"Where are the shirts?" She looks like she's ready to start sewing at once.

I tell her that I will be sending Bouffa to her in the morning—if she doesn't mind giving me her address. And like that Rene signs over the address and name of a building in the West 80s. I don't know the building but I'm sure Bouffa will.

"I'm glad I ran into you." She smiles at me with her eyes. "I feel my spirits are lighter already."

"Thank you, Renee. I knew I needed magic to get this all done, and it's happening."

"Oh, it's not magic, dear." Renee speaks with the wisdom of a Buddha, wrapped in the body of a grandma. "Never underestimate being in the right place at the right time. It's the most important skill a person can master.

"And one last thing," she adds. It's as if she can see through my eyes, into my psyche. "My late husband used to say that not every problem can be solved. Some are okay simply to avoid. Go around them, go under them, whatever it takes to reach your higher goal. Sometimes you have to fail your way to success."

I thank Renee and I truly mean every word of appreciation I give her. Now the sun is setting and I have to head back across town for the shoot. I help her stand, then she waves me toward the subway. "I will run into you again soon."

"Right place, right time." I wink.

She winks back. "Exactly, my dear."

If Todd weren't so squeamish about kissing girls, I would plant a big fat smacker on his face right now. He was such a pro with the camera Peyton borrowed that the shoot went off without a hitch. The scenes of New York City at night are pure magic, and as I watch it all now on the big monitor in the editing room, I get goose bumps. The footage, as Todd says, is a-may-zing.

We're holed up here after hours, putting the finishing touches on the plan. Peyton is using her whizbang CGI skills to add special effects that bring my idea to life. Everyone else is busy working the phones and e-mails, and the place looks more like a crisis center than a state-of-the art production suite. There are still quite a few loose ends to wrap up, like the tiny matter of finding people to wear the shirts—preferably the uber-gorgeous model type so the Kola client notices them. And there's the much bigger matter of figuring out how exactly to get our work seen. I can tell by Todd's expression that he's not having any luck on the model front.

"Gael, can't you just promise them free blowouts or something? Goddamn divas! Fashion Week has 'em all thinking they're God's gift," he sneers into his phone before ending the call.

"Any volunteers?" Even though I know better, I'm still clinging to a sliver of hope.

"Not even one." He pouts. "The models Gael knows want

two hundred dollars each plus cab fare or there's no way they'll haul their cookies to Chinatown that early without a guaranteed part in a Kola commercial."

I look down at my iPhone. Still no response from Suit. I've already texted him three times asking for Cheyenne's number. She's *got* to know girls at her new modeling agency, and I bet she would help me out if she could. I dial Suit's mobile phone instead and am immediately sent to voice mail. If I had any doubts earlier, I'm sure now: Suit is definitely avoiding me. But why? If he's so against what we're plotting to do, why did he give me all those insights from the client on strategy and target audience? Maybe he's distancing himself from the whole operation in case it backfires, so we don't take him down with us. Funny, but I never pegged him as a coward. Not that I've proven to be the best judge of character.

Plan B. Time to call Naomi. It's late, so I dial her at the apartment she shares with my brother. Brian picks up.

"K-9! I was *just* thinking about you, little sis." He sounds happy to hear from me, or slightly buzzed, or both.

"Were you, Bri? Were you thinking about me or were you kicked back on your sofa sipping a bit of scotch?"

He laughs and I'm glad, because I'm teasing; I actually love it when my brother loosens up—I can talk to him without feeling like I need to hurry up and finish. But tonight, unfortunately, I don't have time to chat.

"I'm actually calling for Naomi, Bri," I say, shifting gears. "I need Cheyenne's number for a work thing."

"Sure, no prob. She just walked in from the gym. Before I pass off the phone—how *is* work going? Mom told me you're slammed."

"Yeah, I've been busy." Immediately, everything at stake with this pitch flashes into my mind. My stomach ties tighter than a sailor knot—what if this is my last week of being busy? How could I ever explain being such a loser to my family?

"That's good. At first I wasn't sure about you and advertising, you know? I wanted you to do something more intense. And Ben's nice enough—but he's kind of passive, not much fire in his eyes."

"Fire in his eyes?" I repeat.

"Yeah, no hunger in there. You're the one that works with him so you know better than me, but that's my read."

I have to admit, it's an interesting "read." Before I can even digest this, Brian is marching on.

"Ben came on the scene when advertising did and so I wasn't sure how it was going to go. I wanted to see you FIGHT, Kay. You know what I mean? Really get in there and FIGHT for something."

Every time he says *fight* I have to hold the phone out from my ear a little. This is intense Bri—the Bri who quarterbacked a state finalist football team, the Bri who brokers the big-dollar deals. And he's just getting started. I'd cut him off, but I miss these little fireside chats—they were common in my high school and college years, especially after Bri had a few brewskis. And right about now I could use some brotherly love.

"Learning to FIGHT for your ideas and your worth—that's what this is about, you know? They tell you it's the 401(k)s and health insurance and yearly pay bumps that matter—and I gotta admit I do love the pay bumps—but you get out of bed because you want that rush of throwing your hat in the ring . . . when you roll up your sleeves . . . and you . . ."

He trails off and suddenly I realize he's waiting for me to finish his sentence.

"Fight?"

"Kay . . ." I can hear the ice cubes tinkling in the glass. I can picture him on his black leather sofa—unless Naomi has already made him eliminate that last remnant of the bachelor pad he kept before they moved in together. "No sister of mine whispers that word. Tell me what you do at your job."

"I fight." This time, I'm slightly more emphatic.

"Kay, Mom told me you've been killin' it at work lately. Don't tell me our mother is wrong about something."

His tongue is in his cheek, but my stomach unties just a little bit . . . Mom does make a point to be right about everything, maybe I am killin' it at work, maybe I am close to giving her something more than an imaginary Super Bowl ad to be proud of.

"I *fight*." Now I can feel myself believing it a little more.

"Don't make me come over there and give you the biggest wedgie in the history of siblings."

"FIGHT!" I finally scream. And in the silence that follows I can hear that word with my voice echoing in my ears. It sounds right.

Then I hear Naomi in the background. "Wait a minute. Thought you were a football player, not a cheerleader."

"Ha-ha," Brian tells her. I am swelling with love for him at this moment and also for my future sister-in-law, who isn't afraid to put some of her own intensity to keeping Brian with both feet on the ground. Maybe for her I can stomach the pastel taffeta.

"Naomi's taking the phone." Brian's voice gets more distant. Before Naomi speaks I hear him roar one last time, so loudly

I'm sure he'll be getting a letter from his co-op in the morning, "Fiiiiiggghhhhtttt!"

"I think scotch is going to become a Saturday-night-only drink," Naomi says by way of hello. And I have to laugh. I'm intoxicated from my talk with Bri even though I haven't had a drink since I was at their party with Suit. Not *with* Suit but next to Suit. And now he won't get next to me to save his life! Not *next to me, next to me*, like in bed. That's definitely not what I mean to think. Is it?

Even thinking about Suit is crashing my high, so I launch into the subject at hand. I explain to Naomi why I want Cheyenne's number and she gives it to me in a heartbeat. She also tells me to call her if I need her. I phone Cheyenne and leave a message with the important details of what's been happening and how she can help. One hurdle down. A few more to go but I'm pretty sure I can take on the world right now.

When I walk back in the editing room, Peyton is at the mixing board, adding sound effects to her cut. She's in charge of putting the whole film together, and when I see her working intensely I can't help but think back to Brian's words. Her, Todd, Bouffa, me—every person helping on this team is hungry for the win. None of them has backed down an inch from the fight. This could work—no, no, it *has* to work.

Peyton looks back at me. "Listen to this song Suit found. It's perfect! We're going to rerecord it. Actually, Kay, *you're* going to rerecord it."

"Suit's still helping us out?" His involvement surprises me. Even though I know he's way into music. And his job. Guess the one thing he's not into is me.

Peyton clicks play on the mixing board, and the song—Suit's song—blares through the editing room's surround sound. It's a punk rock version of one of my favorite children's songs, and I can't help but smile. I'm not much of a singer, but as I listen to the lyrics she wants me to record, I realize that doesn't matter. The words couldn't be more right if I'd written them myself. *How did he know?*

"It's perfect," I agree. "Okay. I'll do it."

kolacoo!

The scene inside the Starbucks on Canal Street looks like a casting call for *America's Next Top Model*. Each girl is leggier than the next. Cheyenne came through in a huge way for our stunt. Now if only the other 5,243,001 details will go off without a hitch. I can't—I won't—let myself think about everything that *could* go wrong; today's the day to make it all happen.

"This T-shirt is super cute!" one of the models exclaims when I hand it to her. Another model emerges from the restroom with her shirt on, and I pause to admire Renee's handiwork. The seams have been cut and resewn with colorful ribbon, and she blinged out the "Don't Be a Copygirl" graphic with rhinestones. I would never have guessed that a woman who spent her life on the Upper West Side would know her way around a Bedazzler, but I guess that's what you get for making sweeping generalizations about people you meet in McDonald's.

"The girls look great, don't they, G?" I turn her way and almost fall off my chair—Gina's mid-sip into a can of Kola, nodding. Sure, she's got a grocery bag full of the canned soft drink, enough for Cheyenne and all fifteen of her friends, but I did not expect to see her drinking one herself. I raise an eyebrow.

"What?!" She's all defensive. "Ya know, Kola actually has less of an aftertaste than Diet Coke? And everyone I know drinks Diet Coke. Finally, I was like, why? We date the same guys. We wear the same designers. Do we really have to all drink the same soda?"

"Wow, Gina."

It sounds to me like someone's been drinking the koolaid in addition to her Kola. But that's cool. If Gina buys into our idea, other people will, too.

"Plus, Kola's, like, gonna be our client. So I'd better support them." Now she actually sounds rational.

"Atta girl, I like your confidence." I check my watch and turn to Cheyenne. "It's almost go time. I can't thank you and your friends enough—you always think supermodels have to be bad people, you know? Like no one gets to be gorgeous and nice? But here you all are, proving that theory wrong."

"Thanks. I think." When Cheyenne laughs there is the lightest shadow jetting out from her right eye. I zero in to examine— could she be one of us mere mortals with crow's feet? Nope, it's just a mascara smudge.

"You know what to do?"

"Yes. We'll walk up and down Grand Street, some of us alone, some in groups of two or three, sipping Kola, acting like we belong there," Cheyenne says, repeating my instructions for the stunt.

"Right. You're all so tall, you'll totally stand out in China-town! Our receptionist, Veronique, said the town car is coming from uptown and will be heading south on Grand, so spread out a few blocks north of the agency, too, so they can see some of you from the car."

"Will do," Cheyenne assures me. "And if we see any business-men or women pacing the block, we'll make sure they're not lost."

"You remember where the green door is?" I double-check.

"Of course, Kay, I've been to the office plenty. Don't worry."

Right. Suit and Cheyenne. Were a thing. But they're not any-more. Right?

"Have you spoken to him lately?" I spit it out before I can chicken out. Now's not the time, but for some reason, I can't help myself. "He's been really distant, like he doesn't approve of any of this."

Cheyenne wrinkles her perfect little nose, hesitating. Then she leans in close, almost whispering. "*This*, he totally approves of, Kay. He doesn't approve of you hooking up with your ex-partner . . . It kind of crushed him."

"What are you talking about?!" I'm flummoxed. "Ben and I didn't hook up. We never hooked up. There was just one kiss and it was a mistake!"

My brain is spinning in circles, trying to grasp what she said. And didn't say. My heart does a tiny backflip. "Why would he care, anyway?"

Cheyenne just looks at me, really looks at me, and suddenly, finally, I understand.

"Oh," I say.

"Yup." Cheyenne nods. "You really need to have this con-versation with *him*."

I don't even have time to fully process this all because suddenly

Gina is in my face, grabbing my arm. "Veronique just texted! Travino is in the office! Come on, Kay, it's time."

And like that, Operation Kola Coup is underway.

"Kola Coop? Kola Coo? Kolacoo! Kay, say it five times fast!" Gina fills the air with nervous chatter, but I'm trying to stay calm, mostly by ignoring her.

Phase 1 is about to start down on the street, but we're almost one floor above that, riding the elevator up to STD. Phase 2 begins the minute we get off.

The plan is pretty straightforward. I am going to walk right into Travino's office and say, "Fred, got a minute?" Gina will be there with me so he can't say no. I mean, he's her dad's goombah—they go to the gun club together, for heaven's sake—so not hearing us out would be totally rude. Not to mention reckless endangerment of his own safety. Then Veronique will interrupt, saying there's an urgent interoffice ShoutOut we all need to see. She'll patch the video through, the work will speak for itself, and voilà—Travino will agree to let me show it at the pitch meeting.

I know. It almost sounds too easy. The direct approach was Todd's idea. He's worked with Fred long enough to know crazy theatrics don't impress him nearly as much as honesty does. And without Schmidt or Elliott in the room, the big man will have an easier time going with his gut.

Kay, stay calm. You've got this. Inhale. Exhale. Stay calm. I am a picture of poise and serenity when the elevator doors open to reveal . . . *all hell breaking loose.* The lobby is cluttered with half a dozen humongous floral arrangements, each made up of shriveled black roses, with banners that say things like, *Deepest Sympathy, Our Condolences,* and *Rest in Peace.* Veronique is screaming at the floral delivery guy: "Sugar, I am NOT signing for these! Get these dead flowers on out of here this instant or it's goin' to be *your* funeral."

Adding to the commotion is a man rapping freestyle in the waiting area. It takes me a moment, but then I realize it's the fake DJ Jizz Whizz, who apparently comes complete with a fake entourage that hoots, hollers, and fist pumps.

Gina furrows her pierced eyebrow and whispers, "Geez, like, who died?"

I pluck a card off one of the funeral bouquets and read it aloud. *"Our thoughts are with you at this difficult time. —Your friends at Blood Pudding . . .* What jackholes!"

Now Gina is even more confused. "Whaddya mean, Kay? That's so nice of them!"

"G, don't you get it? No one died. Blood Pudding is just fucking with us on Pitch Day."

"Ain't nobody fucking with no STD ON MY WATCH!" Veronique glares as she shoves the deliveryman and all the flowers into the elevator we just stepped out of. "Gina, help me take these down to the curb quick before the big man sees."

I'm so thrown off by all the confusion, it takes me a full second to remember what I'm supposed to be doing.

The big man. "Veronique, is he in his office?"

"Yeah, he's in there, but I wouldn't—"

The elevator doors close before she can finish, and Veronique is gone, taking my wingman with her.

Shoot. Now I have to go in there alone. I look at the clock and see there's no time to waste. *Stay calm, Kay. Inhale. Exhale.*

I steel myself and march past the fake Jizz Whiz and his crew, pushing through the glass door to Travino's office. The last thing I hear is Jizz Whiz yelling into his cell phone, probably to his agent: "I don't care if the gig is canceled, homey! I still expect to be PAID!"

The minute I'm through Travino's doorway, I realize my mistake. He's in there, all right, but he's not alone, and he's definitely not happy. He's erupting at Elliott while Josh, Ben, and Schmidt stare at their shoes: "Arrested? For being a *PIMP*?! Are you *FUCKING* kidding me? There's no goddamn way we can present that work now!"

Travino is so hopping mad I don't even think he realizes I'm in the room. I glance over at Josh and he mouths the words *Jizz Whizz* then *jail*, bringing me up to speed. In spite of this obvious nightmare, Elliott is calm and slick as ever. "Fred, he was only *indicted*, not convicted. Rappers get accused of stuff all the time. Helps with their street cred. But it doesn't mean he's guilty."

The sheer stupidity of this statement makes Travino's eyes pop clear out of his head. "This epic lack of judgment won't help with *our* street cred! Elliott, you may be a fucking idiot, but we don't need Kola to know it! Your campaign is dead. Go tell the studio to pull it from the leave-behinds."

Elliott slinks out obediently, walking past me like I'm invisible, with Josh trailing on his heels. Even though E's been a total prick to me lately, I feel a tiny smidge of sympathy. I know how much it sucks to have your work die a premature death when you want so badly for it to see the light of day.

Before I can get a word in, Travino continues on with his expletive-laced rampage, addressing Schmidt while Ben squirms next to him. "This fucking pitch is turning into a fucking pig fuck. If we fucking win, it'll be a fucking miracle."

"Yo, ve still got 'More Bubbly,'" Schmidt reminds him. Unlike Travino, he seems happy that his is the last campaign standing.

"We'd better sell the hell out of it, boys. Fuck! I'd feel better if we had a backup."

And here it is. My big chance. I can't believe the universe is just going to hand me this one so easily. With nothing left to lose, I open my mouth. "Fred . . . sorry to interrupt but there's something I need to show you . . ."

Travino looks surprised to see me, even though I've been in the room for the last five minutes. "Kay, *NOT* NOW. Can't you see we're at DEFCON five?"

Where the hell is Veronique with the interoffice ShoutOut? She's supposed to patch my video through so Travino has to watch it . . .

I forge ahead anyway. "I know. But I have more work . . . for Kola. Something Todd and I put together that can help—"

The door flings open before I can finish my sentence and Elliott is back. "Kola's here! Veronique's bringing them back to the conference room."

"They're way fucking early!" Travino rises from his chair.

Elliott shrugs. "Richard said they allowed extra time so they could find the office, but some Kola-drinking Gisele Bündchen look-alike showed them the way."

"What? Whatever! We can't leave them waiting. On with the death march." Travino signals for the guys to follow him out of his office and I'm left standing there, forgotten. Now what? My phone pings. It's a text from Todd:

I'm on way to conference room. We good to go?

Shoot! We are most certainly not good to go. I have to stop Todd before he goes in there thinking we're clear to present our work. I barrel out the door and nearly collide with a delivery-man who's wheeling a vending machine through the lobby. Veronique isn't at her perch, so the man turns to me, handing me a shipping form. "Drop-off for Schmidt Travino Drew. Which way is the conference room?"

Without even thinking, I motion for him to follow me toward the frosted glass wall at the end of the hall. No sign of Todd. All I can do is pray he's behind me.

I am three steps away from the door to the conference room, when I notice my reflection in the glass, or, more accurately, I notice the reflection of what's behind me. The HUGE RED reflection behind me. *Mother of God. What have I done?* I look back and confirm my worst nightmare. What's on the hand truck isn't just any old soda machine. It's a Coke machine. As in Kola's former parent company before the contentious split and subsequent archrivalry. As in, banned from this office until further notice. And, thanks to me, this Coke machine is being wheeled toward the conference room where the Kola client and my bosses are about to start the most important meeting in this agency's history.

I stop dead in my tracks. "Wait! You can't bring that in there!"

"Those are my instructions, honey."

I scan the shipping form. The sender is N. Davies . . . *N. Davies, N. Davies*—why is that familiar? *Nigel!* From Blood Pudding! Another prank. No way can I let those jackholes sabotage this pitch.

"Stop! There's been a mistake." I hurl myself in front of the vending machine.

"Move it, toots. I got orders to follow or I don't get paid." He pushes the hand truck forward and it bumps my foot. Even though my motorcycle boots have steel toes, it still hurts like a mother. "Owww!"

The conference door opens, and there's Suit in the doorway, watching me hop on one foot. "Are you okay?" he whispers, actual concern in his eyes. What was the last thing Renee told me? *Fail your way to success.* Yeah, I'm nailing the failure part . . .

"Kay?" Travino is behind him and his face says I have about five seconds to explain what the fuck is happening here. He's staring at me and the machine, which the delivery guy is rolling off the hand truck. In fact, everyone in the conference room is staring. Schmidt. Ben. Elliott. A seriously confused Todd. And a whole bunch of business people I don't recognize. Except for one . . . that well-tailored guy from Atlanta who needed help finding the office way back when. Richard something . . . That guy was so nice I figured he had to be one of the minions. *Why is he sitting at the head of the table?*

Richard recognizes me, too. "My tour guide! I was wondering if you'd be joining the meeting—my fishing buddies think I'm crazy but I always tell them it *is* possible to have too much testosterone on the boat."

All the other Kola clients around the table chortle at Richard's remark, which confirms my suspicion. He must be more important than I thought. Suddenly it hits me: He's Richard *Snow*, CEO of Kola Worldwide. And he's smiling, speaking to me as if I actually belong in this room, instead of in a padded cell.

"And this entrance of yours—very memorable," Richard continues, nodding toward the Coke dispenser.

The delivery guy snatches the shipment receipt out of my hand, taking his pink copy and handing me back the yellow one. "Here ya go, Miss." Great. Now it definitely looks like I'm responsible for this whole Coke machine fiasco.

I'm sure Travino is going to lose it, but the anger in his eyes shifts to a calm, calculated expression, like he's decided something. He breaks into a warm smile that matches Richard's. "Yes, Richard. Of course Kay is joining the meeting! One of our best writers. In fact, she's an associate creative director."

I am? Since when? It takes me a second to realize Travino is faking it to make it—Richard Snow wants to chick up the room, and Travino is smart enough to oblige him in the biggest way possible. Having a female junior writer in attendance is not nearly as impressive as having a female ACD. Travino turns back to me and the stupid Coke machine. "Kay, I see you've brought our little prop . . . Now that you've got our attention, care to kick things off?"

Huh? What?! Kick things off? How??? Here Travino is giving me the "go" I've been praying for, but how on earth am I going to pass off this huge "prop" behind me? All this time I doubted I could become an ad legend so early in my career. And now it's at my fingertips: the junior writer who brought a Coca-Cola vending machine to a Kola pitch meeting and didn't live to tell about it. That fizzy noise isn't a Diet Kola being opened—it's the last gasps of air slowly seeping out of my career.

I clear my throat and search for an answer. Travino's eyes are bearing down on mine expectantly. Ben is in the room, but he's no longer my life jacket. I need someone who believes in me, someone I can count on to lift me up. I shift my head ever so slightly and raise my gaze, and there he is—Suit, positioned at the side of the table. His stare is clear and strong and he gives me an ever-so-slight nod of the head. Brian's boozy battle cry echoes through my ears. *Fight!*

This Coke machine might be a huge failure, but it's not going to stop me. I'm going to sidestep this red elephant in the room and get to what I believe in with every last breath of my body: Copygirl.

"Fred is exactly right," I begin. I feel tentative, but one more quick glance at Suit bolsters me. I raise my voice. I'm not screaming, but I'm loud—like Bri would want me to be.

"This prop is here for a very important reason. You might be wondering—why would we have a Coke machine at a Kola meeting? Why would we do something so crazy? Well . . . you think Coke is your enemy, but it's not. Look at it. You see these red and white machines *everywhere*. They're a dime a dozen. Like cockroaches in New York City. You can't avoid them."

No one is smiling now—they're all just staring again. But Suit is still encouraging me with his calm and steady eyes. So I go for the gold with my main sell line.

"These machines aren't your enemy. Lack of originality is your enemy. Ubiquity. The status quo. People who aren't inspired to go their own way." A small smile curls up Suit's lips and I can tell he gets where I'm going with this.

I make eye contact with Todd, who's been sitting nearby the whole time, watching me fend for myself. He takes this as his cue to join in, standing up beside me like he'd rehearsed. "Kay is exactly right. Coke is ubiquitous. It's not special or original or different. And ubiquitous is your enemy. You broke away from the tyranny of Coke control when your division split away. You went your own way. And we applaud those who go their own way. That's what your brand must stand for . . ."

Todd walks over to the presentation monitor and starts fiddling with the controls. *This is it. He's going to show our work. It's do or die.*

I can't look at Fred or Suit or anyone. Now that Todd's got the video started there is no turning back. I stare at the screen, wondering if I should have gone into boring finance like my mother wanted.

> The film opens on the Williamsburg Bridge at night, shot in moody black and white. My wax Kay doll walks toward the camera wearing the miniature leather motorcycle jacket and high-heeled boots that Veronique made.
>
> We hear a dramatic marching boom of drums, and a familiar children's song begins to play over the action—only it's been rerecorded by me, singing in my Copygirl voice:
>
> *"BOOM BOOM BOOM BOOM. The ants go marching one by one, hurrah, hurrah!"*
>
> The camera pulls out a little and we see that the Kay doll is being followed by another doll who could

be her twin, wearing the exact same motorcycle jacket and boots. She's also singing.

"The ants go marching one by one, hurrah, hurrah!"

We pull out further to a wide shot, revealing there are dozens and dozens of identical dolls, all singing and marching in tune to the music as they cross the bridge into Manhattan.

The scene cuts to Soho, where the dolls march past the boutiques on Spring Street. Next, the dolls all ride the subway together, then march up Fifth Avenue, an eerie army of copycat wax Kays taking the city by storm.

Finally, the dolls file out onto the observation deck of the Empire State Building. One by one, they slip through the safety railing . . .

"The ants go marching one by one . . ."

. . . and each copycat Kay jumps off the ledge.

The last doll pauses, takes off her high-heeled leather boots, and throws them off the building instead, singing the last verse of the song:

". . . the last one stopped to have some fun.

And they all go marching down . . .

. . . to the ground."

She unzips her motorcycle jacket and tosses that, too. We pan down to the sidewalk. There's a heap of identical dolls and boots piled six feet high, all flattened like pancakes.

Back up on top of the Empire State Building, we see that our lone Kay doll is wearing a tiny DON'T BE

A COPYGIRL T-shirt, sipping a can of Kola as she rel-
ishes the view. She throws her hands up in the air,
triumphantly raising up her Kola, and handwritten
type scrawls across the screen:

MARCH TO YOUR OWN BEAT.

The film fades to black, and ends on the Kola logo
and our proposed tagline: Drink Different.

I unbutton the flannel I'm wearing and take it off, revealing
my own unique DON'T BE A COPYGIRL T-shirt underneath. I'd
planned this to be a Superman moment, like I'm the advertising
hero who has swooped in to save the day. But the whole room is
so quiet I can hear Elliott grinding his teeth. That can't be good,
can it? I smile anyway because I *do believe* in this work, even if
no one else knows what to make of it. Right now I wish I really
were a wax doll so I could wear this smile forever—then nothing
any of these people say could ever wipe it off my face.

My eyes sweep the room. Travino is cool like a poker
player—if he likes the hand I just dealt him, you'd never know
it. Richard Snow is staring through me as his underlings wait
for him to tell them what to think of it all. Finally, he breaks the
silence. "Your T-shirt? 'Don't Be a Copygirl.' We saw people on
the street wearing it."

Todd is a bundle of excited energy. "Copygirl is the star of
an extraordinarily popular video blog created by our very own
Kay. It has a huge following, over a million unique views since
its inception last month," he explains. "The film we just showed
you was only uploaded yesterday, and it's already gone completely viral."

Richard leans forward in his seat. "How viral are we talking?"

Now Suit stands up. He hits a button on his laptop, and suddenly a series of pie charts appear on the projection screen. *When on earth did he make these?*

"In just twelve hours, its gotten six hundred thousand hits," Suit says. "Based on the number of Copygirl return users versus new users and the arcs of past videos and how that viewership has multiplied from one to the next—we project this video will reach over three million people within the week. And of those, eighty-three percent are your core target audience."

Holy guacamole. Even without a translator decoding the stats Suit is spewing, I know those numbers—my numbers—are freaking impressive.

Now it's time for the part *I* actually rehearsed. "We know you asked us strictly for a TV campaign, but again, TV is what everyone does. It's where these guys are—" I stop talking and jack my thumb over my shoulder in the direction of the almost-forgotten machine.

"The Internet will spread the message of Kola far and wide—breaking from the mold, stepping away from the pack. And we feel, by sponsoring the right content, like the Copygirl website and other unique media, you'll gain the popularity you seek, without coming across like a cheesy sellout, or worse, another me-too brand chasing Coke."

Todd holds up a series of boards, showing our ideas for print work and other videos. As we describe the concepts, I keep my eyes focused on Richard, who seems to be listening intently. I don't dare look at Travino yet. The fact that he hasn't yanked us offstage with a cane is all the blessing I could hope for.

When Todd is done speaking, Travino purses his lower lip and nods. "Thanks, guys." I've only seen him make that face a handful of times since I've been at STD, but I know what it means—we have his approval. I exhale for what feels like the first time in more than an hour.

Now that we are officially done, Schmidt comes from the back room with Ben following at his side, to present their Kola work. As Travino signals for Ben to dim the lights, Todd and I find a place on the side of the conference room. The big man gives More Bubbly a grand introduction, backed by the flashing visuals Peyton and I threw together. It's a train wreck I can't bring myself to watch, so I glance over at Ben. I don't want to stare, but I can't help myself. He doesn't look anything like the guy I met in Atlanta, even the one I was inseparable from months ago. That was the Ben who used to be up for anything—especially a laugh. But now, as he holds boards of More Bubbly TV commercials for Schmidt to read through, an honest-to-goodness smile is the last thing I expect to pop up on his face. With the vibrant red machine behind him, his pale skin looks lifeless.

Todd leans over and whispers in my ear, "Darling, *that* was fabulous." And I know he is right. But he doesn't know the half of it—he still thinks I cleared our work with Travino before this meeting. When he learns we just went rogue, I'm not sure if he's going to kill me or kiss me. I guess it depends if the client picks us. Of course Kola could choose More Bubbly or they could go with another agency altogether. There are still two other shops in the running. Obviously—as Blood Pudding showed today—this is more than a pitch, it's war, and they're ready to fire with everything they've got. And that's okay, because today I gave it every last bit I had, too.

I still can't believe Suit was secretly crunching all those numbers for Copygirl. I take my eyes off Ben to look over at him—
hoping to flash him a quick smile or mouth a totally inadequate
thank-you. But I don't have to work very hard to get his attention
because he's already watching me. And I can tell by his expression that he has seen me staring at Ben for longer than a few
seconds.

I attempt the smile, but his eyes shrink to slits and he quickly
looks away, back toward Schmidt, who sounds like he might
talk all day if no one interrupts him.

Nice job, Kay. If what Cheyenne said is true, and now Suit
thinks I'm staring at Ben, then he will have the totally wrong
impression. Suddenly the most important thing in the world is to
set the score straight with Suit. He's got to know I'm not some
silly girl who gets attached to a guy who's all wrong for her. He's
got to know I wouldn't have drunken sex with someone who
doesn't give a shit about me. He's got to know I wouldn't celebrate my biggest career victory yet by staring in adoration at the
person who tried to derail it.

That's what other girls do—and I am not a Copygirl.

For some reason, my heart is racing. I'm worried Todd will
hear it thumping out of my chest and call me out on it. He always
does seem to figure things out first . . .

special delivery

"Celebration party at the Hole!" Bouffa bounces into the room wearing her "Don't Be a Copygirl" shirt—sleeves ripped out with the words spray painted on at a side angle. I'm not completely sure where she came from, but I've been disoriented since the pitch let out.

When Schmidt finally ran out of things to say and Travino flipped on the lights, it was like the end of a concert—where you've been in this intense world and suddenly you're thrust out into the bright glare of reality.

I blinked my eyes a few times and then focused on the main man in the room: Richard Snow. My heart sank when I saw he was typing on his phone—how long had he been absorbed in e-mail?

Travino asked if anyone had questions, and I calmed the flutter in my stomach that warned me maybe I'd have to be in front of the room again.

But Snow put a quick stop to those concerns.

"We've got no questions," he said, stuffing his phone in his pocket. "But I do have a hankering for some lunch." Then he looked up and smiled at Travino. I mentally calculated if the smile outweighed the bored typing on his phone. Did it mean he liked us or hated us? Would we win the pitch or lose it? I needed to talk to Suit—he was the only one I could trust to have the right answer.

"Let's eat," Travino boomed. "I prefer to answer questions with a full stomach, anyway." And like that, all the clients and Travino, Schmidt, and Suit got up to leave the conference room. They had to maneuver around the Coke machine to get out the door but no one seemed troubled by that. I was the only troubled person in the room—if Suit was going to lunch with them, I'd have to wait forever to get him in private so we could talk. I wanted to rehash the pitch, I wanted to explain about Ben, I kind of wanted to know his favorite Thai food and whether or not he played Little League when he was a kid. I could think of—off the top of my head—two hundred thousand topics I would spend the day discussing with Suit.

"Earth to Kay." Todd leaned over. "Are you reliving the glory of our presentation?"

"He was typing on his phone!" I pointed out. "Can't be good."

"Good, schmood, maybe you misunderstood." Todd dismissed me with a wave of his hand. "He was ignoring More Bubbly, doesn't matter at all."

"But this isn't just about beating More Bubbly," I had to remind him. "It's about beating those other agencies, and what if we didn't pull it off?"

"Rule one of pitches, when the work is done you must have fun!" Todd walked over to his messenger bag, which was stowed under the conference room table, and pulled out a bottle of Crown Royal whisky.

"Crown and Kola anyone?" Everyone in the room cheered, and now Bouffa's joined the party, along with others from the office who weren't directly involved with the pitch but have probably been feeling tremors from it for the last month. Peyton comes in now, too. I desperately want to pull her aside and tell her every little detail, but I feel like Dorothy waking up in an alternate universe after being whipped around by a tornado—I need to sit down.

"Looks like you need to take a load off!" Veronique mind reads, breezing in with plastic cups and ice. She wheels one of the conference room Aeron chairs in my direction as she passes the party favors around to Josh and Jay. Even Elliott smiles as she hands him a cup of ice, making a snarky remark I can't quite hear. I don't believe it, but when Todd comes along right behind her pouring two parts Crown and one part Kola over Elliott's ice—*those two* even shares some kind of joke. Is a pitch like a really nasty, horrible, muddy, violent football game? Where you put all your energy into beating up the other guys but once the final whistle blows you all go back to being humans who shake hands and say "excuse me" when you bump into one another?

Is that what it means to fight like a grown-up? You just have to know when to spit fireballs and when to blow smoke?

"This seat taken?" I hear a voice above me. Instantly I know who it is, and even though I don't mind, it isn't the one voice I really want to hear.

"Good job today," I tell Ben as he sits down.

"What," he snorts, "good job holding the boards?" I look up but he doesn't have that wounded look on his face he's been wearing around me lately. Instead he's actually kind of laughing.

"I couldn't believe you up there. I can't believe Copygirl is yours. I mean, Kay, that's huge. I remember when I was in your apartment, and those dolls showed up. I never would have thought to do something so cool with them." He's shaking his head in disbelief and I can feel my cheeks starting to get red.

"It's not that big of a deal, Ben." I stare down into my still-full cup like I'm searching for hidden meaning in the ice. "You have like twenty amazing creative ideas every day. I know that for a fact."

"Because we used to talk every day."

"We used to work together every day, we used to live together for a while there. You know, it wasn't *so* long ago."

Thinking about all this makes the Crown and Kola look oddly appetizing even though I didn't even want a sip of it a minute ago.

"Where's your celebratory cocktail?" I change the subject. I don't want to talk about what he and I were, before he threw me under the bus and ran with my idea.

"I'm taking a break from that." He nods to the drink. "The more I party, the more screwed up things get. These guys are great, the agency's great, but I don't really like who I am in this place. I think I'm going to move home for a while."

I catch my breath. This is not what I expected.

"Or maybe forever," he continues.

I start to shake my head no. Because, yeah, I've got new friends, and yeah, Ben did some lousy things—I mean, hey, he stole my idea—but still, I don't want him to leave. He was my starting point in this city, and I can't imagine a New York without him in it. I wouldn't even be here if it weren't for him. Plus, who will make fun of bad subway ads with me?

"I also want to apologize, Kay. I can't leave with everything bad between us. The idea was yours. I stole it. I know. And that kiss . . . I never should have done that, it was so wrong to force that on you."

"Well, you weren't forcing anything on me," I protest. "But you did steal the line. I can't believe you did that."

"I don't think I ever would have been able to forgive myself if it weren't for what I saw today. Kay, you guys killed it—you didn't need that line. Any decent writer can come up with a good line, but your ideas are always great—and original. You're on your own track for success."

"Are you on a track for success?" I am quite serious as I look into the eyes I used to stare at so longingly.

"I think so." Ben meets my gaze. "I just feel like Wisconsin is where I'm supposed to be. Like, there, I can really be myself. If I stay here, I think I'll just be trying to keep up with everyone else for the rest of my life. That's no way to live."

I blink back the tears that are creeping into my eyes. This really is good-bye. For a while, at least.

"You don't want to be a Copyboy," I say.

Ben shakes his head no. "The last thing I want to be is a Copyboy."

"No one-on-one huddles allowed!" Peyton swoops in to interrupt like she's saving me, taking a seat between us right on the conference table. "I've heard a few opinions on how the Kola show went but you two are the ones I trust."

"Do you know he's leaving us?" I can barely conceal my shock.

"Oh please, it was my idea." Peyton flips her hair triumphantly and I remember Elliott's in the audience. "He's going to rock Wisco, aren't you, Wildman?" She squeezes his shoulder playfully and I'd think she's flirting if I didn't know better.

"Ben, you fill Peyton in on all the juicy details of the presentation." I rise to my feet. "I promised Kell I would call her the minute it ended."

"Well, hurry." Peyton swigs her cocktail. "Everyone is going to the Hole in five. If Cheyenne and her crew linger on the sidewalk down there any longer I think business in Chinatown will shut down permanently. None of the men can work. Cars are stopping in the middle of the road so the drivers can stare. It's freaking ridiculous." She turns to Ben.

"What is it with you guys? Can't you think with something besides this?" She points at his crotch and does the most flamboyant flip of her hair I've seen yet—like a tidal wave of shiny locks.

I don't have to look to know she's spotted Elliott staring and is making the most of it. No one could ever replace Kell, but I do really love Peyton. Can't believe just two weeks ago I would have poked her eyes out with one of Bouffa's shellacked nails.

"Okay, I'll hurry," I promise. "When do you guys think we'll know something about the pitch?"

"Don't hold your breath," Peyton warns. "I called a friend of a friend who said Blood Pudding is the last agency to present. He said it's scheduled for tomorrow, so probably nothing till then *at least*."

I don't feel like I can wait that long, but I guess I have to.

I leave the conference room and make a beeline for the windows along the back wall of the office. I whip my phone out of my pocket and am dialing Kell's number as I walk. This action is so automatic it's practically programmed into my fingers. I sit up on the ledge and wait while the phone rings, just hoping she'll pick up.

I'm not sure where to start. The pitch? Ben leaving New York? The fact that the only person I want to celebrate with right now (besides her, of course) is the one person who probably wants nothing to do with me? And who happens to be out to lunch with the one person who holds the future of my career—and the agency—in his hands: Richard Snow.

She doesn't answer—damn time zones!

I press end with my thumb and slap the phone down on the ledge.

"Whoa there, didn't you just get that thing fixed?" I hear from a voice behind me. Before my brain registers who it is my heart does a leap, and I know: Suit.

I turn around. "What are you doing here?"

"Well, hello to you, too." He's wearing his lopsided grin, the one I haven't seen in a while.

"I thought you went to lunch with Travino and Richard and all the Kola clients."

"Nope. Travino invited some senior account people to go with them instead—guess he wanted to show Kola what a deep bench we've got. And it's just as well. I wasn't really up for bull-shitting this afternoon."

"I thought you were a Southern gentleman," I tease. "Isn't that's what you boys do best—drink whiskey and bullshit?"

Suit's face twists up and I could kick myself in the shin with my steel-toe boot. Why am I making a joke at his expense? What's with the cool-girl façade? Why can't I just get to the heart of the matter and tell him what my heart has been up to lately—flipping out when he is in the room.

Could it be that I'm way more of a phony than I ever thought?

"There is another thing Southern gentlemen do well." He takes a step toward me.

"What's that?"

Kiss is what I'm thinking. I'm thinking Southern gentlemen kiss really well. I can't stop staring at his lips while he talks. I can't stop thinking about him under that tree in Central Park. Why didn't I know then how badly I would want him now?

"We always have a nice handkerchief on us." He reaches in his pocket and produces a perfectly pressed and folded square of fabric.

That's definitely not what I had in mind.

"Look . . ." I am so nervous I can hardly hear myself think. But I know I have to speak now or I never will. "I know you think Ben and I have a thing—but we don't."

"I don't think you and Ben have a thing." He shakes out his handkerchief. Is he nervous, too?

"You don't?"

"I don't. I asked him two nights ago when I was helping them with More Bubbly, and he told me the two of you do not have a thing. In fact, he said, he would be lucky if you ever spoke to him again. Then he told me about taking your line."

"You're kidding." I can hardly believe this. An apology to me was one thing, but why was Ben trying to explain to Suit that I was at the root of his campaign?

"I'm not kidding." He stuffs the hankie back in his pocket. "I don't kid about things I care about."

"Things you care about?" I repeat, but he doesn't answer, he just looks directly at me.

"Thank you for your help on Copygirl." I want to squeeze his shoulder, touch his hand, something that would better convey my feelings, but I'm not like Peyton—a girl who always has the right moves. All *I* have are words. "Those numbers you put together were out of this world."

"You should thank your friend Kellie." His eyes motion toward the window, to a world outside this office.

"You know my Kellie?"

"I e-mailed the webmaster of your site to get help with analytics. I had a hunch you wouldn't have the first clue how to help me get the information I needed, and you and Peyton were locked up editing the video. Kellie e-mailed back right away, I explained who I was, and she was happy to help."

"She didn't mention a word to me!" I look at my phone as though if I shake it Kell's face will appear with an explanation.

"I told her you were stressed with the pitch and that we should leave you out of it. She agreed."

Now it's my turn to look out the window. Suit talked to Ben? And Kellie? I thought I was the one pulling all these strings— but he was working behind the scenes, too. He was on my team all along.

"Have you seen what's going on down there?" Suit points down the block.

"Honestly, I've been watching that lady put laundry on her clothesline," I tell him.

"When you're done staring at a stranger's underwear, check this out."

At the opposite end of the street I see Jizz Whizz rapping on a street corner with his entourage looking on and Cheyenne and crew moving to the beat.

"Are they serious?" I ask.

"You can't tell people to be originals and then criticize them for dancing to a faux pimp rapping in the streets of Chinatown."

"You've got a point," I agree, laughing.

"I have something to show you, then we can get the party at the Hole started."

He reaches out his hand and I take it, ready to go anywhere he leads.

"Where are you taking me?" I ask, even though I don't care.

"When I came in from putting Travino and the clients in town cars I saw a delivery guy coming up the street. Snow rolled down his window and I swear to God, the guy winked at me. I thought surely not, but then I looked at the delivery guy and I thought, 'Well, maybe.' The delivery is for you and I want you to see it first. It's waiting in reception."

When we get to the doors that open to the lobby, he pauses.

"I think you might need this." He pulls the handkerchief back out of his pocket and presses it into my hand.

I examine the checkered cloth for clues, but am at a loss. "It's wrinkled," is all I can think to say. "That's not very gentlemanly of you."

"In a minute, it will be more than wrinkled." He pushes the doors open to reveal the most beautiful, shiniest, biggest Kola machine I have ever seen, standing smack in the middle of the lobby of Schmidt Travino Drew.

"Is—is—is this another joke from Blood Pudding?"

Suit shakes his head no. "Check out the note." He points to a piece of paper taped to the center of the machine.

I walk over and unfold the paper, hands trembling. It reads, *To Copygirl. From Richard Snow. Cheers to the next chapter for Kola—Drink Different.*

"Does this mean what I think it means?" I can barely speak.

"Yes." Suit's gorgeous, full-faced smile—seldom seen around here—says all there is to say.

"But Blood Pudding hasn't even presented work yet," I stammer.

"Guess in the end, the joke's on them."

The news sinks in, and it's like my birthday, Christmas morning, and the Fourth of July all rolled into one moment I can't control.

Rivulets of tears begin to pool on my lashes, threatening to remove my mascara and my dignity. I can't hold them back, try as I might. "I'm sorry, this is a strict no-cry zone for me. I don't know what's happening."

Then I remember his hankie, the one I'm still holding. *He knew I'd cry!* I dab it at the corners of my eyes. Now Suit walks over and puts his hand on the note. He's so close to me I can smell his soap. He's so close to me I am picturing his shower. As different as I will always try to be—I guess there are some parts of a girl that are always the same. The smell of soap on a man you like equals thinking of that man's shower equals wanting to be in that man's shower. And I'm just about to tell Suit that I like whatever soap he uses—which would probably be a massive embarrassment and the totally wrong thing to say—when he leans forward and without saying a word, kisses me on the lips.

It's not a congratulations kiss. It's definitely not a kiss from my brother. It's a kiss from Suit—who at this moment, feels like the furthest thing from a Suit than I could ever imagine.

"What! What's happening in my lobby!" I suddenly hear behind me. I pull away from Suit and turn around to find Veronique standing there with her hands on her bright green muumuu.

Assuming she's mad about my public display of affection with Suit, I start to explain but she cuts me off.

"Don't you tell me they dropped off another one of those machines. I done sent those Blood Pudding boys one delivery of duck carcasses from the Chinese market on the corner, and they best know not to mess with Veronique or I will be sending something much more serious."

Suit laughs so hard I can see every one of his perfect, white teeth. "Whoa, Veronique, hold back on the voodoo, girl. This is a good delivery. This means we won."

Veronique leans forward with her hands on her knees. "We won? We won! Then she runs over and gives us the hugest Mama Bear hug. "You two get back to your kissing and I'm off to tell everyone! Not about the kissing but *about the winning*! I didn't see no kissing. We're winners!"

Then she freezes for a second and looks at me. "Copygirl won, right?"

A huge, freeing smile breaks out across my face. I can't believe this is happening. "Yes!" My tears are just crusted corners in eyes that are now crinkled in happiness. "Copygirl won."

Veronique lets out a shriek they probably hear all the way in Brooklyn, then takes off in the direction of the conference room.

For just one more minute Suit and I have total peace in the

lobby, staring at what is currently the most coveted advertising trophy in agencies across Manhattan. It feels like it's almost too good to be true. Kola. Suit. All of it.

"Was that, um, was that thing with us that happened just now . . ." It's Murphy's Law—*now* I can't find any of the right words.

"That kiss?" Suit half smiles. He's so sexy when he does that.

"Is it what you meant to do?" It felt deliberate to me. Hell, it felt meant to be. But I need to make sure the feeling is mutual. I know people can get caught up in a moment . . . and after all, Suit is used to dating girls like Cheyenne and—

"Kay. It's what I've been meaning to do for a while now." He grabs my hand again and gives it a meaningful squeeze. I squeeze back.

"Does it need to be a secret?"

"Aren't secret office romances what *everybody* does?" He's got me there.

And of course, he's right. I absolutely can't wait to go to the Hole and sit next to him and drink beer. It sounds heavenly. Maybe that's what a good relationship is—something that makes you feel like you might be in heaven even when you're in a hole.

"You go on ahead without me," I tell him. I have one thing to do before I go there, but I'll be there before they've finished their first round.

He squeezes my hand and I might as well be leaning against my locker with visions of proms dancing in my head, because I'm giddy as a schoolgirl.

After the shoot, I stashed a bag of dolls under my desk. I grab it now and bring them to the window ledge where Suit found me earlier. The doll I used for the pitch is still wearing her "Don't Be a Copygirl" T-shirt, and as I lift her up out of the bag, I think about where I want this to go, what I really want to say to . . . well, *geez*, to people all over the world.

The last hour may have been a whirlwind, but my head isn't spinning. All of this feels right. As Todd would say, it feels like "that moment you slide into the back booth that's reserved for you, and without asking, the waiter brings you a fresh margarita with a shot of Patrón and you know you have *arrived*."

I don't hear any noise in the office, so I know everyone has cleared out for the Hole. It's been a long time since I was here alone. The last time was the night I saw Ben kissing Peyton on ShoutOut. So much has happened since then. But now, even though I'm alone, I'm not lonely at all.

I start running through the office, picking up props that will make for the epic vid.

I want Billy Idol "Rebel Yell" with Kell and my side pony-tails swinging in the air.

I want "Eye of the Tiger" with Brian fist pumping in the back-ground.

I want Gloria Gaynor for my mom.

I want anyone who takes a minute out of the day to tune into Copygirl to want to sing, because that's how I feel right now.

Veronique is gone. Do I dare swipe her voodoo doll pincush-ion? It's got such a mysterious vibe. Lifting it up, I wonder if it's a he or a she. Does it matter? Suddenly, inspiration hits: What this office needs is a cleansing ritual. And the voodoo doll is totally perfect.

I'm going to need the basket of backup tampons in the ladies' room, too.

Joshjohnjay have all kinds of random junk littering their desks—they're like the hipster version of *Sanford and Son*. I'm sure they won't mind if I borrow a prop or two.

After my supermarket spree, I create a throne of female thingamabobbers, tampons and hair ties, a purple convertible Matchbox car, a bar of fine chocolate I swiped from Todd's secret stash in his desk, plus a sculpted kitten I nabbed from the boys' club that one of them made out of foil burrito wrappers. Maybe the success of Copygirl has inspired them to start their own blog animating inanimate objects—I *could* see foil animalia being big with the hipster set.

A woman has never had the spotlight in this agency before, but tonight I'm going to change all that and put one on center stage. What was it that my mom used to chant to me and Kell before our peewee soccer games? *We are women, hear us roar, in numbers too great to ignore!* Or something like that.

I put Veronique's voodoo doll in front of the girlie shrine and stand my favorite female wax dolls around it: It Girl, Manhattanite, Bridge and Tunnel Girl, Queen Copygirl, plus my latest Kay.

I remove the straight pins from the pincushion and press one in each doll's right hand, bending their arms up so it looks like they are holding microphones. My phone's in my back pocket so I pull it out, press record, and as soon as the red light starts flashing I know with all certainty I'm not just speaking to my fans. I'm speaking to my mom. And Kellie. And Peyton . . . Bouffa . . . Renee . . . Naomi. Veronique. Cheyenne. All the chicks who've always been on my team, even when I was too daft to know it.

"Welcome to the girls' club! If you have breasts—any breasts—even the breasts that jerks in junior high called 'ant bites'—you belong.

"And for the record, your ant bites are fabulous.

"If you've ever been told 'you can't,' 'that's not for you,' 'you're too delicate—too pretty—too weak to try that,' and instead of listening you just went ahead and did it anyway—you belong.

"If you've ever been judged by your clothes, your hair, or your smile, instead of your wit, your loyalty, and your heart . . .

"If you've ever wondered what guy wrote all those fairy tales, locking us up in murderous corsets and ivory towers, waiting for our princes to come . . . and then you thought, 'Screw that. I'll rescue myself . . .'

"Welcome. This is where you belong."

I pause the camera to scroll through the music on my phone. I find Pat Benatar's "We Belong," another one of the chick anthems my mom hammered into me and Kell—why has it been so long since I remembered any of her lessons? Now I play it as loud as I can, continuing the recording.

I sing along, taking turns using each of the different wax dolls' voices, while making them sway to the music. I'm getting really into it, dragging out every note like Kell and I used to back when hairbrushes were microphones and encores were as easy as pressing rewind on the tape deck.

Suddenly I'm startled to hear a high-pitched voice behind me, belting out the chorus:

"WEEEEEE BELONG, WE BELONG, WE BELONG TO-GETTTTTHER"

I turn to see Peyton singing into a manila folder she's rolled up into a microphone. I give her a thumbs-up, still recording, and we continue our duet as she hops up on the ledge where the dolls are "performing." All I can see of her in the camera frame are her three-inch red heels strutting around the shrine, but it looks pretty cool.

Right before Peyton hits the big high note of the song, she digs the heel of her stiletto into a wrapped tampon, spearing it. Then she goes around spearing all the rest of the supplies while we finish the chorus. Suddenly, Peyton's foot slips out of the frame, and she starts to teeter off the ledge. I drop my phone and lunge forward to catch her but I'm a second too late so she falls on top of me. We wind up sprawled out on the office's ugly pile carpeting, erupting in a fit of junior high giggles.

"I guess that's a wrap," Peyton quips, making me laugh even harder. She lifts up one of her bony butt cheeks and pulls something out from under it: it's my iPhone, which she must have landed on. She flips it over and goddamn if the screen isn't shattered *again*. Seeing this sends us into a fit of hysterics so bad I am simultaneously laughing, crying, and getting a better ab workout than I've had in years.

"Girlfriend, I'm gonna have to buy you a Marc Jacobs wristlet for that phone once and for all!" Peyton wipes smeared mascara from under her eyes—I make a mental note to tell her later she'd be better off slumming with my drugstore Maybelline variety; it never runs.

"Why? You don't think I can afford one on my junior copywriter salary?" I'm sarcastic, but in a playful way.

"Ben told me Travino promoted you this morning. Maybe the new gig will come with a company phone!" Peyton actually sounds serious.

"I wish! He was just pretending for the meeting, so Kola wouldn't think this place was such a misogynistic boys' club."

"Well, if we win the pitch he'll *have* to make good on his lie."

"*If?* Peyton, you mean you don't know? That's not why you came back here?" I'd just assumed she'd heard, assumed that's why she was in such a good mood.

"I came back to make sure you weren't doing anything crazy, like skipping all the fun so you can catch up on Little Kitty scripts."

I look over at the pile of wax dolls and my Girls' Club shrine, then say with a totally straight face, "Nope, not doing anything crazy at all."

"So I saw. Also, there *was* one other thing . . . I was walking to the Hole and I was behind Elliott"—here she rolls her eyes, which is a good sign—"and I was kind of eavesdropping"—not as much of a good sign—"and I kinda sorta heard him say to Travino on his cell phone that he sent you a ShoutOut with 'the news.'" Now she bites her lip. "And I was just so curious what the news was—I couldn't wait."

I can't keep it from her another second. "It's probably that we won Kola." I say it low, all nonchalant, just to torture her more.

Peyton shrieks so loud I expect the plaster to peel. "Check his message, check his message—what if he has more details!"

I tell her I will check it as long as she promises to stay far away from Elliott even if she has ten vodka tonics.

"I promise I don't want him." She pinkie swears. "I just want to know we really, really, hands-down, no questions asked, no lingering 'maybes,' kicked total ass and won."

I scroll to my ShoutOuts and sure enough, there's one waiting for me to view.

I tap the button and Elliott's face immediately pops into view behind the spiderweb cracks on my screen. He's walking down the street, rambling, stream-of-consciousness style.

"Special K, hey, just got off the phone with Travino. First thing tomorrow morning, have the studio order you up some new business cards. You're our first female associate creative director so *please* don't blow it. Kola's the big time. If you fall from this height, you will get hurt . . . But seriously, nice job. You're smart . . . though I'm even smarter for hiring you . . . and I still need you to finish that Little Kitty script ASAP, so go easy on the Crown and Kola. You know what the reward for hard work is? *More work.* No fucking excuses."

And like that, it's over. First I think, *What an E-hole.* Then I dissect what he just said as Peyton lets loose her second high-pitched shriek of the day and I realize this is for real. Not only did we win Kola but *I* won, too.

They're making it official! I'll be the first chick at STD to be an associate creative director. Ohmigod. Maybe my dreams will come true—or maybe they have come true. Now I can actually hold my head high in a family conversation about careers. My mom might even end up with a Super Bowl ad by me saved on her phone so she can show all her friends and her clients and the grocery checkout cashier and the plumber and the . . .

But before I can even think about telling my family or even calling Kell, I realize there is someone else I want to share the news with first. And not through a text, FaceTime, ShoutOut, or some other stupid Internet messaging service. I want to be up close and personal.

I stuff my phone in my pocket and start to trot to my desk, where I grab my bag. "Let's get out of here," I shout back to Peyton over my shoulder.

"Don't you wanna post your video first?" She's holding her mini–alter ego, "It Girl." "You know, I never noticed how cool these boots are on this doll . . ." she says. Which makes sense, since she owns a pair just like them.

"No more video stuff today. And maybe not for a while. I want to spend some time in the real world, with non-wax people and conversations that happen without screens."

I'll always believe in girl power and I will always fight to be on top. But there are some guys who want to help me win just as much as my girls do . . . and right about now there *is* a certain guy I wouldn't mind doing a victory dance with.

I head for the stairs because I know the elevator isn't going to move fast enough for me. I needed to be at the Hole five minutes ago.

This kitty *does* cuddle, and I can't wait for Suit to hear me purr.

acknowledgments

Thank you, Jackie Cantor, Susan Golomb, Scott Cohen, Anne (You Probably Think This Book Is About You) Bortz, Sara (Bitter's Good, Bitter's Funny) Woster, Patsy Wornick, Dave Mitchael, Mike Mitchael, Michelle (If the Voodoo Doll Fails Us the Plan Is Martinis) Sassa, Karen (Let's Start by Throwing Away the Green Poncho) Manganillo, Phyliss Mitchael, and, always, Andrew Snyder.

—AM

Beyond thanks, Mom and Dad, the twisted tree this apple didn't fall far from.

Also Jackie Cantor, Susan Golomb, Krista Ingebretson, and Soumeya Bendimerad for making me feel legit.

Much love and gratitude to: my SIL Carrie for being my first and most enthusiastic reader; BFF's Rissy-T and Meli-B for Pat Benatar and endless pilferable memories; Ad-taq, Pfaffy and Murphy for all the inside jokes and advertising laughs; Lamphearless for "finding it in us"; all the friends and family who always believed more for me than I did for myself. To Anna the rattlesnake hunter for making me Just Do It, then pushing me to do it better. To Luke, Jack, and Nina for giving me a reason to prove the power of dreams. And to Den, my Coach Kersee, for encouraging me to fail my way to success. *Everlong.*

—Michelle